Mozart's
LAST ARIA

Mozart's
LAST ARIA

A Novel

MATT REES

HARPER ⬤ PERENNIAL

NEW YORK • LONDON • TORONTO • SYDNEY • NEW DELHI • AUCKLAND

HARPER ● PERENNIAL

Originally published in slightly different form in 2011 in Great Britain by Corvus.

Map on pp. xii–xiii copyright © 2011 by Jeff Edwards.

P.S.™ is a trademark of HarperCollins Publishers.

Designed by Betty Lew

ISBN-13: 978-1-61793-383-7

To Devorah,

who is all the music I need.

With thanks to: Dr. Orit Wolf, for showing how great musicians work; Louise and Dieter Hecht, for taking me high above the Karlskirche and demonstrating how scary old Vienna can be; and Maestro Zubin Mehta, who told me that he, too, would find it hard to live without Mozart.

In October 1791 Wolfgang Amadeus Mozart, the greatest musical genius the world has ever seen, told his wife he had been poisoned. Six weeks later, at the age of thirty-five, he was dead.

The truth, the truth, even if it be a crime!

The Magic Flute, Act I, scene 18

Vienna, 1791

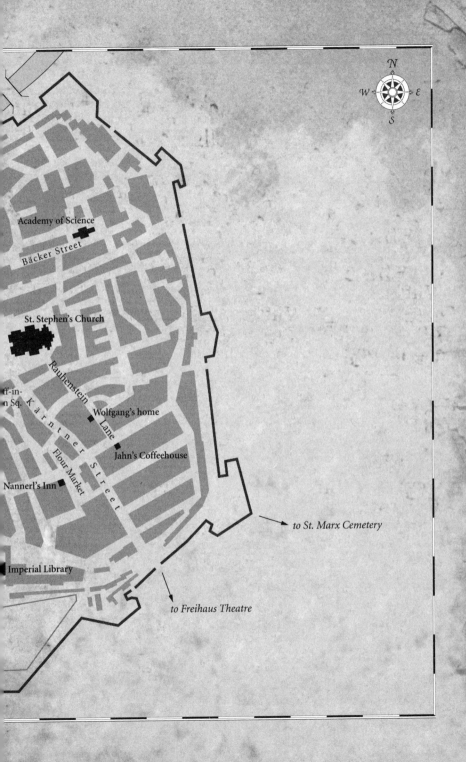

MAIN CHARACTERS

Maria Anna "Nannerl" Mozart, *sister of the composer*

Johann Berchtold, *Nannerl's husband*

Karl Gieseke, *an actor*

Magdalena Hofdemel, *Wolfgang's piano pupil*

Baron Konstant von Jacobi, *Prussian ambassador to Austria*

Leopold II, *Emperor of Austria*

Prince Karl Lichnowsky, *a patron of Wolfgang*

Constanze Mozart, *Wolfgang's wife*

Franz Xaver Wolfgang Mozart, *Wolfgang's youngest son*

Maria Theresia von Paradies, *blind piano virtuoso*

Count Johann Pergen, *Minister of Police*

Emanuel Schikaneder, *theatrical impresario, actor*

Anton Stadler, *musician and friend of Wolfgang*

Baron Gottfried van Swieten, *head of the Imperial Library and chief of government censorship*

PROLOGUE.

*W*hen she sang, it was hard to imagine death was so near.

Her maid let me in at my usual time in the mid-afternoon. A soprano voice of considerable purity came from the front of the apartment.

"Someone's visiting her, Franziska?" I asked.

The maid shook her head. "She's alone, sir."

I passed through the sitting room. She was singing Zerlina's aria from *Don Giovanni*, in which the peasant coquette describes the desire beating in her chest. Her voice quieted for the last line, an invitation to the girl's suitor: "Touch me here." A raw tone infiltrated as she repeated those words to a crescendo. The concluding note weakened and quavered.

I heard a dry cough as I went through the door to Aunt Nannerl's bedroom. Her thin hand conducted an imaginary orchestra through the coda.

She laid her fingers on the bedspread and dropped her chin

to her chest. Was she hearing the applause of an audience? Perhaps the effort of singing exhausted her.

The lids of her blind, old eyes flickered. I pondered the life she had led and all that she had seen, gone now forever. As a musician, I understood the secrets a composer hides in the pages of his score, locked away from those unable to comprehend the fullness of his creation. I was hardly aware of it, but I had been less perceptive as a nephew.

My visits to her home near Salzburg's cathedral had been so frequent, I would have been tempted to conclude that I knew everything there was of her to be learned. Her renown as a child prodigy on the keyboard, her adolescent performances with my father in Europe's great cities. Marriage to a provincial functionary and elevation to the minor nobility, so that she had borne the title Baroness of the Empire since 1792. Then after her husband's passing, her return to Salzburg, where she taught piano until her eyesight failed.

This presumption to summarize her seventy-eight years was, in fact, the thoughtless dismissal of an enfeebled old woman by a younger man. I say this with certainty, because today she revealed to me a life more fantastic even than her famous history would suggest.

Her singing done, my aunt lay silent and still in the narrow bed. She wore a lace nightshirt and a simple shawl around her shoulders. I kissed her dry cheek, drew up a chair, and recounted the gossip of the town. She didn't register my presence.

When I grew silent, she reached out, moving with a swiftness that surprised me, and pressed hard on my hand. Her fingers retained the power of a lifetime in which she sat at the piano three hours or more each day, exercising the skills that once entertained kings and princes and counts. "Play for me," she said.

Her pianoforte was a fine old grand by Stein of Augsburg. I gave her the Sonata in A by my father. I wished for her in her frailty to feel roused by the dance rhythm of its Turkish rondo. As I played, she fingered a gold cross inlaid with amber which she wore around her neck. Her blank, sightless eyes were wide. When I finished, she croaked out my name: "Wolfgang."

"Yes, dearest aunt," I replied.

She turned to me as though she had expected someone else to respond.

When I first came to play for her, she told me that I reminded her of my father. In truth my hair and eyes are dark like my mother's and my talent at the keyboard is of a kind that he would no doubt have described as mechanical. I have nothing of his genius. But I *am* named Wolfgang, and perhaps for Aunt Nannerl that much resemblance sufficed. Until that moment. I sensed that she spoke directly to the man thirty-eight years dead who had been her little brother. The man famed throughout Europe and even in America as an unmatched composer.

Wolfgang Amadeus Mozart.

"On that shelf. In a box inlaid with mother-of-pearl." Her hand lifted from the quilt with an unaccustomed grace that made me wonder if she were already dead and I was gazing upon her spirit, rising free of her fragile bones and decaying skin. I opened the casket and, beneath some old painted ribbons, I found a volume in nicked brown leather. I placed it in her grasp.

"I'll be dead soon enough," she murmured.

"May the Lord forbid it, dearest Auntie. Don't speak of such things."

She flipped back the book's cover and ran her fingers over the dry, yellowed pages within. A quill pen such as few have used for years now had filled the book with lines slanting upward from left to right. I recognized the hand as her own, for she had often written to me as I toured the concert halls of Poland and Prussia. She turned a few pages and spread her bony fingers across the text. On the first line, I read a place and a date: *Vienna, December 21, 1791.*

She shut the book with a clap that was like a cannon shot through the silence of her apartment. In the instant that it took me to blink in fright, the leather-bound volume swung toward me and dropped into my fumbling grasp.

"Don't show it to your mother," she said.

"Why not?" I smiled. "What secrets do you keep, Aunt Nannerl?"

Her faint eyebrows lifted and I felt that a much younger woman fixed me with those melancholy brown eyes.

"Upon my death I shall leave to my son Leopold all that I have," she said. "He'll inherit my money, my few valuable pieces of jewelry. Also my papers, my diaries, my daily books. Mostly dull chronicles of the simple routines of Salzburg and the village where I passed my married life." She sucked for breath. Her head lapsed against the pillows.

I lifted the volume in my hand. "But this—?"

"Something different. Only for you."

"Is it about my father?" I could ill disguise my eagerness, for I was just a few months old when he was taken from us.

He has been with me always at the piano, though only as the mythic gods of Olympus could be said to have been with the Greeks when they ground wheat for flour.

My aunt swallowed hard and coughed. I thought perhaps I had been mistaken. After all, when I used to ask her about my father's last years in Vienna, she always pleaded that she hadn't seen him after 1788, when my grandfather's will was settled in her favor and a coolness arose between the siblings. She had remained with her husband in the village of St. Gilgen. My father had continued his career in the opera houses and aristocratic salons of Vienna, until he was cut down three summers later in his thirty-sixth year.

Her lips pursed, she gathered herself. "That book records the truth about events that have shaped your life—and all musical history."

"It *is* him," I said, striking the notched surface of the leather binding in excitement.

"It's his death."

"The fever? Yes, Auntie, I know."

She shook her head. The hair, which her maid had dressed high and old-fashioned even though she lay in bed, rustled across the pillow as if it were hushing me, commanding my silence.

"His murder," she said.

I heard a sound like the final exhalation of a dying soul. I couldn't tell if it emanated from my aunt or from me, or perhaps it was the grieving spirit of my poor father. I would've spoken, but my breath chilled, my ribs seemed to close in on my lungs, and my cravat was suddenly tight around my high collar.

Flicking her wrist in dismissal, Aunt Nannerl subsided onto her pillows.

I hastened to my room in my dear mother's house on Nonnberg Lane, almost at a run up the steep steps beneath the cliffs. The leather of my aunt's diary darkened with the sweat of my palm, though the day was cold enough that the first snowfall threatened.

At home, I wiped the perspiration from the cover onto the leg of my breeches, closed my eyes to whisper a Hail Mary for my father's soul, and opened the book.

FRANZ XAVER WOLFGANG MOZART
Salzburg, October 9, 1829

1.

December 1791
ST. GILGEN, NEAR SALZBURG

s I returned from early Mass at St. Aegidius, snow screened the summit of the Zwölferhorn and layered the village in white silence. Approaching my door through the garden by the lakeside, I heard little Leopold picking out one of my brother's minuets on the piano. I smiled that this should be the only sound on the shores of the Abersee that morning. The snowfall smothered all but the essential music that joined me to dear Wolfgang. I wondered if he was watching the same gentle drift cover the streets of Vienna at that moment.

In the hall, Lenerl took my fur and handed me a letter delivered by the village bailiff, who had returned from Salzburg late the previous night. I ordered a hot chocolate and pulled my chair close to the fire in the sitting room. I watched the snow gather in the window mullions, grinning each time the boy struck a false note in the drawing room.

The discordant tune was hardly little Leopold's fault. The piano sounded ill enough when I played it. By the mountain lakes of the Salzkammergut, cold and damp had warped the instrument's wood, made the keys stick, and moldered the hammer casings, so that a true note was rare enough. Even so the boy spent an hour each day at the piano, because he hoped to gratify me.

To tell the truth, it pleased me that my son played only as well as a six-year-old ought. My brother, of course, composed his first dance at six, and it had been my departed father's desire to re-create that prodigy in my firstborn. But that was never my intention. I had come to resent the fact that true happiness was mine only when seated at the piano. Even when playing cards with friends or shooting a pistol at target practice, I moved the fingers of my free hand through an imaginary arpeggio, for if I didn't I became distracted and irritable. The curse of the artist is to have the best part of one's faculties occupied only with one's craft. Friends and family skim your existence like a fisherman on the Abersee, while your real self is as inaccessible to them as the depths of the lake. But I had long since ceased to live the life of an artist, and I sometimes felt this preoccupation rather as a cripple might his useless foot.

I beat a rhythm on the letter lying in my lap. Perhaps it carried news of my brother. In the winter, it was hard to keep up with events beyond the snowbound village. The latest news sheet to reach us reported that Wolfgang had another original opera in production. Acquaintances returning from Vienna told me that his health wasn't of the best. He was frequently sick, so I earnestly wished for tidings of his recovery in this letter. I felt sure I recognized the handwriting.

For Madame's personal attention
Madame Maria Anna Berchtold von Sonnenburg
Living at the Prefect's House
St. Gilgen
Near Salzburg

I read my name as if it belonged to a stranger. A collection of surnames, earned by marriage to the man working alone on his accounts in the study across the hall. These things, which ought to have distinguished me, served only to make me anonymous. Before Berchtold had brought me to this remote village—thus adding a geographical anonymity, too—I had a name that everyone knew and which I admit I still applied to myself in the privacy of these moments seated before the fire.

Mozart.

The memory of that name sounded in my head like a dream. The soft Z and disappearing T with which the French had pronounced it when we entered the salon of Louis XV at Versailles. The long English A I had noted from the mouth of King George's chamberlain announcing us at Buckingham House.

Lenerl laid my hot chocolate on the table and curtsied. "Will there be anything else, madame?"

I lifted my chin to dismiss her.

It was deluded to muse on my family's long-ago travels to Europe's capitals. If I no longer bore the name, I had to acknowledge that even then I had been merely *a* Mozart. Only he had ever been "Mozart." One might have addressed a letter in Milan or Berlin with that single word and it would have found my brother in Vienna. I had inherited the miniature watches and golden snuffboxes, gifts from delighted aristocrats in the time of our joint fame as touring child musicians. But my brother had retained *the name*.

To the people of this village I wasn't a Mozart. Few of them had ventured farther than Salzburg, six hours' journey away through the mountains. What could they know of the palaces of Nymphenburg and Schönbrunn where I had displayed my mastery of the keyboard, wandered the gardens, chattered with the king, worn clothes made for the empress's children? The villagers' lives didn't extend beyond the church, the bath-house where the surgeon pulled their teeth, and the stall by the lake where the sexton sold rosaries and devotional candles.

No one even called me Nannerl anymore, now that Mamma and Papa were gone. No one, except he who had been silent for three years. Though it had been unsaid in our last letters, I feared that the unpleasantness of our father's testament, in which all the fruits of our early fame were bequeathed to me, had broken the bond with my brother, my dear Jack Pudding, my Franz of the Nosebleed.

These years without communication were, I assumed, harder for me to bear than for him. Were he to consider the painful task of writing to his sister in her simple marital home, there would be the distraction of a salon at which to perform, a ball to attend, a concerto to be scored.

I enjoyed no such diversions. Still, I delighted in the re-views of his operas in the Salzburg news sheets and subscribed to each piano transcription of his works, playing through them with wonder at his compositional development. Even my poor, restrained husband had failed to hide his tears when I sang "For pity's sake, my darling, forgive the error of a loving soul," from Wolfgang's *Così fan tutte*. Throughout these years of silence, I comforted myself that one day he might visit our village and we'd play together once more.

I sang that aria as I slipped my finger behind the seal and unfolded the letter. It was from my sister-in-law, Constanze.

My song caught at a high G and transformed to a sob.

Your beloved brother passed away in the night of December 5, she wrote. *The greatest of composers and the most devoted of husbands lies in a simple grave in the field of St. Marx. My fondest, most desperate wish is to join him there.*

Constanze gave the dreadful details. Wolfgang had succumbed to "acute heated miliary fever," which she explained meant that he had been afflicted with a rash resembling tiny white millet grains.

My chin quivered as I read her description of his last days, the swelling of his body, the vomiting and chills, the final coma before his death at one hour past midnight. He had been gone a week.

I crossed myself and mouthed a prayer that he should be delivered to the company of Christ. I pressed the letter to my breast and wept. "Wolfgang," I whispered.

On the piano, my son stumbled through a French nursery rhyme, *Ah, vous dirai-je, Maman*. I had taught it to him one morning after I played Wolfgang's marvelous set of variations on its theme. The simple melody stabbed at me. I bent over, pain sharp in my abdomen.

The piano went silent. Leopold's small feet skipped across the hall. He entered the salon with his green jacket buttoned to his chubby chin and blew a kiss at the portrait of Salzburg's prince archbishop on the wall because he knew it made me laugh. When he hugged me I pressed his face to my neck, for in that moment I couldn't look upon features so like my brother's had been in his infancy. I stroked his blond hair behind his ears.

"Would you play for me, Mamma?" he said. "My fingers are tired."

"Tired? And it's not yet eight in the morning. Will you have no energy to make mischief during the day?" I grabbed his cold little hands and blew on them.

He giggled. "*I'm* not tired. Just my fingers."

"I'll play for you in a little while, my darling. First, Mamma has a letter to read."

"Who wrote it?"

"Your aunt Constanze in Vienna."

Never having met my sister-in-law, the boy shrugged.

"Go and see if Jeannette is still sleeping," I said. "It's time Lenerl gave her breakfast."

He grinned at the mention of his two-year-old sister and hopped up the stairs.

I closed my eyes. In my mind, I heard *Ah, vous dirai-je* through the dozen complex variations Wolfgang had composed, changes of tempo, legato to staccato, the running scales in the left hand ascending and descending the keyboard. I could feel my own touch light on the keys, see the manuscript, his delicate fingers scribbling the notes across the stave with his characteristic slight backward slant.

Upstairs, Jeanette protested her awakening, until Leopold tickled her into laughter, as he did each day.

I read on through Constanze's letter. I skimmed the lengthy

account of her sister's desperate errands to priests and doctors, none of whom appeared to have helped my brother. It was far from clear that he had even received the final sacrament.

The letter wound back in time through the premiere of my brother's new opera *The Magic Flute*, until I found myself with Constanze and Wolfgang in the public gardens of the Prater on a fine fall day in October. On that occasion, I read, Wolfgang had told his wife that he knew he would "not last much longer. I'm sure I've been poisoned."

The cup shook in my grip. Chocolate slopped onto the rug. I laid the cup on the table so hastily that it caught against the saucer and overturned. My fingers smudged cocoa across the letter.

Constanze had been unable to shake Wolfgang from the dire perception that his death was preordained, she wrote. From time to time, he had recovered himself enough to describe his suspicions as temporary fancies. Yet he soon returned to the certainty that his end was coming—at the hands of a poisoner. It grieved Constanze deeply that her last months with Wolfgang should've been marred by this melancholia.

The letter gave a brief account of Wolfgang's funeral at St. Stephen's Cathedral, organized by his friend, the noted musical connoisseur Baron van Swieten. Constanze closed with a few sentences of condolence, though I sensed that she wished more to impress upon me her extreme suffering and assumed that I'd mourn little for the loss of my estranged brother.

I would've put the letter aside, but I noticed another page folded behind the others. A postscript on a smaller sheet of paper:

*It may be that gossip shall reach you asserting
your brother's infidelity to me. I beseech you
to place no faith in such slanders. On the day
of Wolfgang's funeral, his dear friend and
Masonic brother Hofdemel slashed with a razor
at the face of his wife, Magdalena, who used to
receive lessons from your brother at their house
behind Jews' Square. Poor Hofdemel then took
his own life. It has been spoken among some
whose shame should be eternal that Hofdemel
lost his mind in a fury of jealousy because of a
romance between Wolfgang and Magdalena.
Some have even asserted that the enraged
Hofdemel murdered my beloved Wolfgang by
poison. I urge you to reject all such scurrilous
conjecture and to know that to his final breath
your brother remained a most true and devoted
husband and father.*

A strange heat flared in my face and darkness crossed my
sight. My agitation drove me from my chair. As I came to my
feet, the fire crackled in the drafts from my skirt.

I looked into the gilt-framed mirror above the mantel. I
saw only death in my pale skin. Wrinkles marked my eyes like
the rings of a tree trunk, though signifying the onset of another winter rather than a new spring. Then there he was, clear
in my face, rising out of the image of this woman in the last of
her younger days—the wry lips of my brother, his prominent
nose, and his quiet eyes. He watched me stagger away from

the mirror, upsetting the table, smashing the cup of chocolate to the floor.

From his study, I heard my husband clear his throat in annoyance at the noise. I imagined the doctors indulging in the same gesture of impatience when my brother told them that he had been poisoned. He was, after all, someone who always made a fuss about minor injuries and ailments.

Surely Wolfgang had known something they had not. The symptoms may have suggested a "miliary fever," but only to one who didn't suspect foul play. Could this Hofdemel have been a killer? I forced myself to consider the reprehensible possibility that my brother's selfishness, cultivated by the indulgence of the many who lauded his genius, may have overridden his moral scruples and led him into the sin of adultery.

As soon as I allowed any credence to the possibility of poison, I was struck by the number of other murderous suspects who occurred to me. Wolfgang never learned to deliver a politic opinion and was often frank and disparaging, so his killer might be a singer he scorned. Or a rival composer robbed of a commission by the greater artist. Then there was his uncouth little wife and her conniving Weber family, which had blackmailed my brother into marriage. I found it hard to imagine them as murderers, yet why was Constanze so determined that I should dismiss Wolfgang's suspicion of poisoning as the delusion of a melancholic spirit?

Everything about Wolfgang's life was extraordinary. Now I was asked to accept that his death had been so commonplace it could be explained by a doctor's examination of a rash on his skin. I wouldn't believe it.

Another glance in the mirror. I couldn't look away. My eyes, like his, large and brown, a clear hazel. My cheeks, a little marked by pox, though less than Wolfgang's had been. Were our faces entirely alike? What was solely mine of all these features? Not the mouth, with its thin lower lip and gentle, sardonic upward turn at the corners. That, too, resembled my brother.

As I stared into the glass, I discovered one thing new in this face, something I didn't recognize as my own characteristic: I found it to be strong. Perhaps it was the same strength that had allowed Wolfgang to defy our father, leaving Salzburg to make his way as an independent composer in Vienna. I had never dared even to imagine that power and certainly hadn't imitated it. Wolfgang's defiance had pained me, because I was left alone in our dull provincial town, charged with the care of our father. Yet now I perceived that same boldness in my own gaze.

I crossed the hall, knocked upon the study door, and entered.

My husband turned his thin face toward me and lifted the fur collar of his dressing gown. I read annoyance in his eyes, then he disguised it with the aloofness that greeted petitioners seeking his approval for some official document.

"My brother has died, may God give him rest." I held Constanze's letter toward him.

"Surely he was dead to you already." He glanced at the chocolate smudge on the paper and raised a single eyebrow. He saw the reproach on my face and cleared his throat. "May the good Lord protect his soul, my dear." His voice was as thin as his body under the gray velvet of his gown.

"My sister-in-law writes that he died of a fever last week."

"I shall pray for him, of course." He waved away the letter and made to return to his papers.

From obedient habit, I stepped backward to the door. The face I had beheld in the mirror stopped me.

I looked my husband over. He had married me so that there would be someone to oversee his household and his five troublesome children. When we wed, my father made it clear that this was my last chance to avoid the lonely life of the old maid. In seven years, I had given Berchtold three more children, though one girl had been lost that spring after only five months. I knew his remoteness to be the reserve of a man never warm who found himself frightened to love me for fear that I should be taken from him like his first two wives. At fifty-five, he was fifteen years my senior, though he saw the marriage as an act of charity on his part toward a spinster from a lower rank of society. Love had been no part of the bargain Papa had struck with Berchtold. Even my virginity had been accorded a monetary value. My dowry was augmented by five hundred florins after the wedding night, when Berchtold had ascertained that he had possessed me intact.

He looked up and took in a loud breath through his nose, exasperated to find me still there. He tapped his hand on the documents before him to signal that he wished to focus on them—perhaps a customs record of iron transported from the mines across the Abersee to Salzburg, or an order for a fornicator to be taken to the torture room in his assistant's house next door.

I stepped forward.

He righted his periwig and I glimpsed the blue baldness of his scalp beneath.

"Wolfgang believed he had been poisoned," I said.

"Surely not. Ridiculous man. Oversensitive."

"There could've been intrigues against him. It's Vienna, after all."

"Madame, what do you know of such things?"

"I haven't lived all my days in this village, sir. I know the ways of court life and of the cities." As my husband, born in the village and educated no farther away than Salzburg, did not.

He caught my insinuation and his lips tightened. "Let a Mass be said for him and be done with it."

"I would visit his grave."

He tapped his bony fingers against his writing desk. "I have no time for such a journey. My work here is pressing."

I knew this for a falsehood. He shut himself into his study not for the perusal of administrative papers, but with the intention of escaping the demands of social life and the expenses incurred by it.

"I'll travel alone," I said.

"Alone?" Surprise disturbed the officious stillness of his face. He was unaccustomed to my determination. In seven years of marriage, I had never pretended to be anything but deferential and far from self-sufficient—behavior promoted to deep habit by my duties during the widower years of my papa.

"I'll take Lenerl to attend to my needs," I said.

"It's a journey of five days, and expensive." He seemed muddled, thwarted and a little desperate, so that I dared wonder if, faced with my departure, he considered that he might miss me.

"I'll bear the cost from the bequest of my father. I shan't burden you."

"You never have done so," he stammered. His eyes dropped to the floor and his fingers fretted the fur of his collar.

I halted at the door with the handle in my grasp, moved by his emotion. Did all death recall for him his own losses, his wives and infant children? It was cold in the room and I saw that the grate was empty to spare the cost of a fire, though Berchtold had already saved ample funds to provision his children in a lifetime of comfort. "Johann," I said.

"I shall wait upon your swift return, madame." He shuffled the papers on his desk and straightened. "This departure inconveniences me and leaves my children unattended."

"I shall make haste to come back to you."

"And when you do, we shall hear no more of this brother of yours or of fanciful plots against his life."

To Berchtold, all professional musicians were alike, disreputable and irresponsible. No doubt he assumed Wolfgang to have died dissolute and alone in a basement tavern. If my brother had been poisoned, surely it would've been to avenge some immorality. Whatever I wished not to countenance, my husband would willingly have suspected.

"You shall hear no more of such things." I shut the door.

In the hall, I called for Lenerl, ordered her to pack my trunks and to send for my husband's carriage.

When my mother passed away, I fell into a fit of weeping so violent that I vomited and took to my bed for days. My father's end caused me to drop into a strange darkness from which I didn't emerge for months. But I was a mother now, a mother who had experienced the loss of one of her own infants and had continued with her life for the sake of the children who remained. I was no longer so feeble before extreme emotions.

When I faced Death, I was able to deliberate on which cheek I would strike him. That was how I resolved to go to Vienna.

Seating myself in the drawing room before my piano, a wedding gift from my father, I warmed my fingers under my arms. I looked toward the wall and its simple papering, thin green vertical stripes on white. Beyond it, my husband shivered in the cold and scowled at the documents on his desk. *You shall hear* this *of him*, I thought. I played the Sonata in A Minor Wolfgang wrote after our dear mother's death in Paris.

Its opening theme, dark and disturbing, sounded true even on my half-ruined keyboard. The D-sharp in the right hand was discordant over the relentless basso ostinato of the left hand, built around the A minor chord. I hammered at the frenetic Allegro maestoso as if I wished my brother's soul to hear it, wherever he was.

"I'm coming, Wolfgang," I whispered.

2.

VIENNA

The goddess Providence watched me leave my inn after breakfast and cross the empty Flour Market in the cold wind. In her bronze hands the two-faced head of Janus frowned back upon the past as a bearded old man, while youthful and open he peered the other way into his future. Wishing I might know what lay ahead of me, I shivered. Even the mythic embodiment of foresight could find herself abandoned in a frozen fountain at the center of a blustery square. I prayed that I shouldn't be so isolated.

Beyond the statue was the gray, shuttered Flour Pit Hall, where Wolfgang often gave concerts, and the terra-cotta façade of the Capuchin Church, crypt of the Habsburgs. I kicked at the muck and snowy slush with my high boots, and headed in the direction of the younger Janus's gaze.

The innkeeper had directed me toward a narrow street of five-story houses, their ground floors in heavy, broad granite and their gables stuccoed orange or yellow or white. The buildings were bright, despite the dull, flat light filtering through the clouds. When I came to the foot of a church spire on my left, I turned into Rauhenstein Lane and looked for my brother's home.

A gentleman in a broad-brimmed English hat was kind enough to guide me into a modest courtyard. Horse feed and wet hay ripened on the cold air.

"You'll find the apartment of the late composer at the first landing, madame," he said. "You won't be the only one to pay your respects to his widow today, though you may be the earliest. Our little street has been crowded with distraught music lovers this entire week."

"I'm sure it has." I made for the entry to the staircase.

"I knew him only by sight," the gentleman called after me. "One would never have thought— Such a small, unassuming man, and yet his work— Masterpieces, genius. But to look at him—well, one hardly *would* look at him, really. Did you know him, madame?"

"As if he were my brother," I said.

The gentleman's mournful smile faded into confusion. He raised his hand like someone trying to place the face of a remote acquaintance.

The wind rushed into the courtyard. I stepped past the open door of the building's toilet, and onto the dark staircase.

One flight up, I pulled back the hood of my cloak and spread it over my shoulders. I heard a high voice within the apartment calling someone's name and I knew it was my sister-in-law. I felt a twinge of anger toward the woman who had stolen my brother away from my family. I kicked my knuckle against the door and was answered by the high-pitched bark of a lapdog.

A short, thick girl with red cheeks and black hair raked under a white Bohemian bonnet opened the door and curtsied.

"*Grüss Gott*. May you greet God," she said.

"*Grüss Gott*. Please tell Frau Mozart her sister is here," I said.

The girl led me through the kitchen, past the stove and a pair of metal bedsteads for the servants. We came into a living room with a half-dozen chairs upholstered in canvas and arranged around a sofa. She took my cloak and proceeded to the next room.

A gilt-framed mirror hung on the wall. I looked into it, massaging my cheeks to bring some blood to my skin after the cold walk.

My sister-in-law appeared in the glass. She stood in the doorway in a black woolen shawl and a loose black dress that gathered beneath her breasts. Her mouth gaped, and her bright teeth made her look ravenous and despairing. In her hands she held a short jacket she had been unraveling so that the wool might be reused.

I came to her, laid aside the wool, and held her hands. Her black eyes were reddened with the despair of these last days.

"Dearest Constanze." I pressed my lips to her cheek and found it cold. I touched my palm to the black curls dropping over her pale forehead. She was still only twenty-nine and even shorter than me, with a figure whose boyish slimness had been undiminished by her many pregnancies.

A white spaniel brushed against my skirts, barking with excitement. Constanze bent to lift the dog. "Gaukerl," she whispered. She seemed to draw warmth and life from it. Smiling at me, she caught my hand. "Come, sister."

We entered the sitting room. Two plain lacquered cabinets stood against the walls. Behind a pair of divans, lemon-striped wallpaper decorated three large panels.

In the corner a newborn baby wriggled in its crib. A boy of about seven hid behind his mother's skirt. "Karl, greet your aunt Nannerl," Constanze said. "She's Papa's sister."

The boy scuffed his foot against the floorboards and retreated to the next room, slamming the door. I thought of my Leopold, at home with my unruly stepchildren, and felt a flash of guilt for leaving him.

Constanze smiled awkwardly at the boy's behavior. She leaned over the cradle, rocking it with her foot.

"This is little Wolfgang," she said. "He's not yet five months old. But of course you didn't know—" She covered her mouth with the back of her wrist. A small gold watch dangled about her thin forearm. I recognized it as the present Wolfgang had given her on their wedding day.

"That's true. I didn't hear about little Wolfgang's birth," I said. "Is he healthy?"

"He's had a touch of the flour dog."

The infection that nearly killed my Leopold at two months. A white rash on his tongue and between his legs. Coughing, whining, never sleeping. I still carried the rosary I had bought to pray for his health—a string of dried nuts from the Holy Land which had imbibed Christ's healing power as they grew from the soil near His tomb.

I glanced at the baby. Constanze seemed to sense my anxiety.

"The little thing's all right now, as far as I can tell," she said. "Still, I've had four babies pass away within a few months of birth, God bless them every one. Each seemed sound to me and I did everything I could for them. But——"

Another memory: Babette, the cramps and spasms that took her from me only half a year ago, while she was still a newborn. I squeezed at the rosary in my pocket. "I, too——"

Constanze didn't notice that I had spoken. "I fed all the babies on water gruel to be sure that they didn't contract the milk fever from my breast, and I followed the instructions of the doctors. But medicine was as much help to them as it was to my husband." She let the dog scramble to the floor. "Why did he leave us like this?"

I came close to her. "Where did my brother die?"

She leaned back against the door to open it and extended her arm into the next room.

To save space, the chamber was used for entertaining guests and for sleeping. Two beds were pushed together against the wall. An iron stove with its pipe running toward the ceiling clicked and rattled in the corner. My sister-in-law braced herself against the billiard table at the center of the floor and shuddered, despite the heat.

"These four walls where we now stand—it's as though they sucked the life of the entire world away. Everything good that ever was, died in this room," she said. "For more than two weeks he lay here, until——"

I approached the beds. My mouth was dry. Perspiration stood out on my scalp. For a moment I thought he still lay under the lumpy covers. I opened my mouth to excuse myself, to beg his absolution for the hurt I had caused him.

But I halted. The bed was empty. If I was to find forgiveness, it would be elsewhere.

"Before his illness," Constanze said, "this was a room of great happiness for him. He'd play billiards with other musicians and smoke a pipe. They'd joke about the pompous aristocrats they were required to entertain. And then, of course, this was where he and I passed our nights."

I thought it crude to refer to marital relations at such a time. Constanze registered the disapproval on my face. She put her hands to her stomach and wept.

I wished I could've been alone with my imaginings of my brother's final moments, to have listened to the traces of the last notes he might've played in this place. Instead I went to her and touched her cheek. "Let's go to his study."

Constanze led me to the last room in the apartment. The gloom of the enclosed bedroom lifted. Winter light crossed white through two windows set in a double aspect. It flickered over Wolfgang's piano as though ghostly hands played on its ivory keys.

The instrument drew me toward it. Its polished chestnut wood was luscious, inscribed with the name of Anton Walter, the Viennese master keyboard maker. I sat at the stool.

I played a soft chord and closed my eyes. Something frozen seemed to breathe over my neck. My fingers trembled. I pressed them into my lap.

Constanze leaned against a high desk. It was designed for a man to stand as he wrote. She picked up a cut-glass scent bottle from the inkwell shelf, pulled out the stopper, and held it beneath her nose. A hint of jasmine suffused the cold air.

"Wolfgang's eau de cologne," she said. "This room used to

be like a busy workshop. At that table, his copyists would transcribe his scores. He'd pace between them and his composing desk and his piano, leaving traces of this perfume behind him. I used to cut the quill pens for the copyists. Sometimes I'd help copy Wolfgang's pages for the orchestra. There was such energy here. When he completed *The Magic Flute*, we were all industrious and happy. We knew it was a masterpiece."

Constanze's speech was fast, overwrought, in a high, plaintive register. She had been like this on the only previous occasion we had met, when she had been anxious for the approval of my father. The loss of her husband had added a demented note to her ingratiating tone. I worried for her and for Wolfgang's two boys.

"The new opera has been a success?" I asked.

"*The Magic Flute*? It's more acclaimed than any other of his works. Not only for the music, astonishing though that is."

"For what else?"

"For its philosophy. That everyone should exist in peace and brotherhood. Wolfgang wrote it with his friend Schikaneder, the impresario of the Freihaus Theater. Well, really you should go and talk to Schikaneder about it, but it's clear to me that *The Magic Flute* encapsulated Wolfgang's belief in equality and brotherly love."

"How so?"

"I don't really understand these things, you know. But the opera's about a princess who undergoes a series of ordeals for the sake of her love for a prince. The priests say a woman won't be able to endure the trials. Yet she succeeds. Ah, you should simply see the opera and make up your own mind."

"Schikaneder still gives performances?"

"To packed houses."

A copy of Bach's *The Well-Tempered Clavier* lay on top of the piano. I brushed the dust from its cover. "In your letter," I said, "you wrote of Wolfgang's . . . presentiments."

Constanze frowned, but her puzzlement seemed feigned.

"His fear that his own death was imminent," I went on. "That he had been poisoned."

"Let's not talk of this. I wrote that letter in a very emotional state. I wasn't in my right mind."

At first I thought to tell her that I hadn't come all the way to Vienna in the snow just to console her. Instead, I reached for her wrist. "I have to know, Constanze. I'm his sister. Tell me."

She stared at my hand for a long time, distant and engrossed. It was as though she reviewed the weeks in which her husband had been dying, reliving their pain and seeking different paths she might have taken to help him. I released her arm.

"In his quiet moments," she said, "he was more and more consumed—not by music, but by black thoughts. He told me, 'Stanzerl, I can't shake them.' He claimed he had been poisoned with *acqua toffana*."

"What's that?"

"Some mixture of different venoms." Constanze sobbed. "I can't believe he was poisoned. So many other things might have been responsible for his melancholy mood. He was overworked. He owed a great deal of money—much of it on my account."

"How so? Surely his compositions paid well?"

"My last pregnancy caused some trouble with my feet. Bad circulation. He sent me to Baden to take the waters. I was away from him for some weeks. The hotel at the spa was expensive."

"Could he have been so embarrassed by his debts that he became depressed? Enough to convince himself that someone wished him dead?"

"It can't be. The only men who even knew of his troubles were Prince Lichnowsky and poor Hofdemel. Both of them were brothers of Wolfgang in the lodge."

"You mean, they were Freemasons?"

Constanze settled in an old damask chair. "Wolfgang often said that among the Masons there was no inequality. Merchants, nobility, tradesmen, and musicians all attended meetings of the lodge wearing the spurs and dress sword of a gentleman."

I understood the attraction to Wolfgang of such an egalitarian brotherhood. He had always hated rank. In the service of the prince archbishop of Salzburg, he had been treated as a lackey, dining with the valets and writing only the music his master considered suitable. It was to escape this servile position that my brother ran off to Vienna.

"The high regard in which the Masonic brothers held him was of the utmost importance to Wolfgang." Constanze clasped her hands at her chest. "He had a great need to be loved."

I recognized the truth in this. It was a craving born in his childhood, when he received the adulation of the most important people in Europe. No matter how he matured, he required admiration and acclaim.

"He didn't always get the love he needed from——" She halted.

"His family." I turned fully toward Constanze. "Sister, Wolfgang used to refer to me in his letters and conversation as a prudish, affected girl. I can't deny that I was too concerned with ribbons and hairstyles and the latest fashion in hats. Marriage and motherhood have matured me. He'd find me a different person now, and so shall you."

Constanze's smile, a wavering turn of the lips, was at odds with the tension in her eyes. "He spoke of you often," she said. "At the end. You were much on his mind."

I pondered that. "Was I? Yet I had neglected my relationship with him."

"For three years at least."

"At least." I wondered at the anger hiding beneath her fragile features. "I beg your forgiveness for that, just as I pray to his spirit that he'll absolve me of the guilt I feel. I always thought we'd be together again. But now that it'll never happen, I wish to know how he lived his life during our separation. Did he leave no record of his thoughts in that time?"

"Only his music."

"No writings? No diary?"

"No, but I—" Constanze sucked at her lip. She went to a roll-top bureau beneath the window and folded back the lid. "I was organizing his papers this week. I thought of putting together a biography of Wolfgang for publication. To earn some money while—"

"While there's still interest in his life?"

She rocked her head side to side. "His debts have to be paid. For the future of the boys."

"I understand. Of course."

She drew a single page from one of the cubbyholes in the bureau. "I found this in his desk."

I took the sheet and read it. "It's an idea for a new Masonic body."

"Written in Wolfgang's hand."

"He writes that he wished to set up a lodge named the Grotto. What a strange name."

"Isn't it? There are just those few paragraphs about his intentions. Then he leaves the page incomplete. He must've been writing it when he was taken ill."

"He suggests that his lodge would 'break new ground.' How so, I wonder?" My brother had always liked secret languages known only to him and a few friends, inventing imaginary countries of which he might be the king. Evidently he had wished to rule at least a branch of the secret society of Freemasons. "He never mentioned it to you?"

"He kept the Masons to himself. If only he had shared his idea with me—" Constanze shrugged.

"You might ask one of his brothers in the Masons if Wolfgang explained this Grotto to them," I said. "They could complete his outline, describe the purpose of the lodge."

"What use would that be?"

"Perhaps when you come to compile your biography—"

Her eyes became shrewd and conspiratorial.

The maid came to the door.

"Yes, Sabine," Constanze said.

The girl curtsied. "Herr Stadler is here."

3.

*A*nton Stadler greeted Constanze with a kiss on the hand and the fragile joviality of a nervous mourner. When she introduced me, his thin lips tensed into a flat smile.

"My brother wrote to me about your friendship and talent, Herr Stadler," I said. "He valued both greatly."

His eyes were pained and wistful, as though I had leveled an accusation that he couldn't deny. Wolfgang had often enthused in his letters that Stadler was able to re-create human speech in the tones of his clarinet. The virtuoso's own voice deserted him before me, however.

He lifted my hand and bowed.

Constanze led him to the couch. "Nannerl arrived today, Anton," she said, perching beside him on the edge of the seat.

"I very much wish to attend *The Magic Flute*. I came just for that." I didn't want to talk poisons with Stadler. Not yet. "I wanted a last opportunity to see my brother's work on the stage."

"Last opportunity?" He spoke with an unwarranted aggression that I found curious. "Madame, do you have such little faith in the future popularity of his work? It'll survive longer even than this city of ours."

"You're right, of course. But I travel very little. I doubt there'll be a performance in my remote village, no matter how long Wolfgang's fame persists."

Stadler folded his arms. "Constanze, I came to discuss the concert for tomorrow night. I've booked the hall at the Academy of Science."

"Perfect. It's so good of you to organize the benefit for my children, Anton. I'll sing an aria, and so shall my sister Josefa."

"I have an orchestra of no less than thirty-six musicians for the performance," he said. "We'll give Wolfgang's last symphony. Maestro Salieri agrees to conduct. We'd also like to do one of Wolfgang's piano concertos. As the soloist, I had thought of Fräulein von Paradies."

Constanze grabbed his hand. "Paradies is exceptional, of course. But you're forgetting what talent has fallen into our laps today."

I flushed, nervous and excited. I hadn't performed in years.

Stadler pushed a knuckle against his teeth, and frowned at me. "Do you think you can——?"

It had been a long time. But thirty-six musicians? There would be such a contrast between the great, stately volume when the orchestra played and the delicacy of the piano in its solos. In a single moment I experienced an urgent fear of failure and a rush of exhilaration at the thought that I might be allowed to exhibit my skills in Vienna. "I'd be honored, sir."

He hesitated. Perhaps Stadler doubted my musical capabilities after my long seclusion in the mountains. So did I. But he didn't wish to disappoint Constanze. "His Concerto in C, then."

"In C?" I said. "There are four. Which one?"

Stadler hummed the theme of the concerto's second movement, gliding his hand through the air as though he were conducting the music. "The most beautiful one, of course."

"The most beautiful, yes," I said. I heard the Andante in my head and moved my fingers along my leg as though picking out its lilting melody. It was so lovely I felt tears in my eyes. I raised my hand to disguise them.

"Shall we rehearse tomorrow morning? At my house. Jews' Square, number three."

"I'll be ready."

Constanze clapped. "How perfect. Wolfgang's joy would've been complete."

"I'm content to see *you* so happy, Constanze." Stadler's face was grim. He seemed to resent the ascription of happiness to his friend, as though Wolfgang's death had been so tragic it had forever erased all the pleasures of his life.

"Then perhaps you'll complete something else of Wolfgang's," my sister-in-law said. She beckoned for the page Wolfgang had written about his Grotto. I handed it to her and she passed it to Stadler. "What can you tell me about this?"

Stadler read.

"Anton, you were the closest of Wolfgang's Masonic brothers," Constanze said. "He shared everything with you. You must know what he intended. Perhaps I'll need it when I come to prepare his biography. Tell me what it's about?"

Stadler leaned his elbows on his knees, his head low over the sheet of paper. "You want to put this in his biography?"

"I want people to read the story of his life. Those who love his music should know about the good man who wrote it."

"Indeed." Stadler's voice was a whisper.

"A biography from his birth to his last days. Nannerl will be the one to recall for me stories of Wolfgang's early life, I hope."

I inclined my head in assent.

"So you must help me, dear Anton, with his years in Vienna and his final illness." She gestured toward the sheet in Stadler's hand. "This, after all, was what he was working on at the end."

"Was it?" Stadler still didn't raise his eyes from the page, though there were only a few sentences on it.

"Well, for one thing it's not finished. Also, I went through his papers only a few weeks ago looking for the letter that commissioned him to write his Requiem, and this page wasn't there then," Constanze said. "So, yes, I'm sure it's very recent."

"It's nothing, Constanze," Stadler said. "Just some of his musings. Nothing serious."

He folded the sheet until it was small enough that his hand hid it. Constanze pouted and would've tried to persuade him further, but her baby cried out in the next room. With an apologetic smile, she went to soothe the child.

Stadler moved his hand toward the pocket of his jacket, watching Constanze through the door as she bent over the baby's crib. I glimpsed the paper between his fingers.

"May I see that once more?" I said.

Stadler jerked upright in his seat, as though he had thought himself alone.

"My brother's note?" I held out my hand.

His lips opened to speak, but he hesitated. It seemed he might deny that the page existed, palming it up his sleeve like a conjurer at a Saturday market. Then he stiffened his jaw and held the small square of paper toward me with a gallant flourish of his wrist.

I unfolded the page and pointed to the line that interested me most. "What 'new ground' would this lodge have broken?" I asked. "What did Wolfgang mean by that?"

Stadler pursed his lips, working them as though they gripped the reed of his instrument. They were supple and muscular from constant exercise with the clarinet, but they were firmly shut to me.

"Surely you have some idea," I said. "You were one of Wolfgang's closest friends. Why don't you complete his essay, as Constanze asked? He must've explained to you his vision for this Grotto. No doubt he would've canvassed you to become a founding member."

"His vision?" Stadler looked at me with the eyes of a tradesman caught cheating on a bill, fearful and brazen.

"You're mounting a concert in his memory tomorrow. What better way to memorialize him than to found this new lodge in his name?"

Stadler rose and stepped to the window. He grasped the frame, laying his forehead against the cold glass.

"I can't do what you ask." His breath misted on the window. "You don't know how dangerous it is."

"Dangerous?" I saw that he had expected this word to shock me into silence. Yet I already suspected something more wicked than a fever had taken my brother's life. I gave a quiet laugh tinged with mockery. "Surely you're exaggerating, Herr Stadler?"

He shook his head. "If you love him—loved him, I advise you not to get involved, Madame de Mozart."

Five days freezing in an uncomfortable coach. Three years with barely a word from my dead brother. I was already involved.

I held out the page with Wolfgang's handwriting. "Tell me what this letter means, my dear Herr Stadler. It can be our secret."

He grabbed the sheet, screwed it between his fists, and threw it into the open lid of the piano.

"For God's sake, woman, do you want us all to end up like Wolfgang?" he shouted.

The paper played a soft, metallic scale as it rolled across the wires inside the piano.

Stadler circled the center of the room with his hands over his eyes.

I was fearful of his sudden rage. Yet I was also content. I had been right to come to Vienna. Something was wrong here.

Stadler took a heavy breath, made a swift bow, and left. In the doorway, Constanze reached for him, but he brushed past her and the baby on her shoulder. He wrenched his hat from the maid's hand, slammed the door, and descended the stairs fast.

I leaned into the piano and took out the ball of paper. I smoothed it against the cover of *The Well-Tempered Clavier*. When I held it up, it shook in my agitated hand. I put it in the pocket of my dress.

4.

$\mathcal{O}$utside the Freihaus, I paid the coachman fifteen kreuzers for the ride to the suburbs. It was almost noon. The ruts in the road were iced hard. I tottered over the frozen mud to the gate, where a spray of straw made walking easier.

I entered a wide courtyard. It was laid out with flower beds, sparse now, but in summer no doubt quite lovely. The thorns of the bare rosebushes glinted dull gray like the tarnished silver of old knives. Faded brown patches of grass showed through the snow. Beyond the lawn stood a tall stone building with a red-tiled roof: the theater. The lime-green double doors were shut. A printed sign advertised performances of *The Magic Flute*.

At the center of the courtyard was a small pavilion with a deck across the front. Its wood was dark as tobacco. Smoke rose from the chimney and a circle melted around it in the snow. I had come to Vienna to probe Wolfgang's death, but Constanze's praise for *The Magic Flute* awakened a desire to learn more about his life, and he truly lived in his music. It was with this in mind that I approached the wooden hut to ask for Herr Schikaneder.

An irritable voice answered my knock. When I entered, a pasty face squinted at me with suspicion.

The man wore a black worsted frock coat with silver buttons. The coat was stained at its lower hem with something that might have been thick cream. His white shirt was open at the neck and a cravat dangled untied. A film of sweat glimmered on his pale chest in the light of the lantern on the table. He rubbed his sandy hair, which was thin though he appeared to be no more than thirty years old. "Yeah?" he said.

The air smelled of warm brandy punch. There was a yeasty undertone of spilled beer. I assumed this must be the room where the actors and singers celebrated their performances late into the night. I stepped into the circle of the lantern.

The man started upright, lifted the light, and stared at me with a wary curiosity.

"I'm looking for Herr Schikaneder," I said.

"Does he owe you money?"

"No."

"Has he dishonored you?"

I leaned toward the man, unused to such effrontery. It had been a long time since I was around theatrical types. "How dare you!"

He smirked. "I suppose you're a bit old, even for him. Perhaps he's been after your daughter?"

I opened my eyes wide.

"Just checking. You'll find him over there." The man wiped his nose with the back of his index finger and extended it toward the darkest corner of the room.

A tall, broad-chested man came toward me with his arms extended. "Forgive my friend Gieseke and his poor jokes," he said. "There are so many charlatans in this city, one must guard against them."

"In order to protect one's reputation as the greatest charlatan of them all," the man in the black coat muttered.

The tall man laughed, deep and resonant. "Emanuel Schikaneder, at your service, madame. Actor, singer, theatrical producer, and admirer of well-bred ladies who don't allow themselves to be perturbed by ill-mannered lackeys." Glancing at the other man, he bowed and caught my hand to kiss it. As he straightened, he paused, looking down at me with his head angled to the right. He raised his finger and smiled. "Ahh, Madame Berchtold, if I'm not mistaken."

"You're correct, sir."

"Or as I prefer to remember you from my journeys through Salzburg: Nannerl. Little Nanna Mozart." He took both my hands. "Gieseke, this is Wolfgang's sister. Give her some punch."

Gieseke slouched to a counter along the back wall and poured a glass from a ceramic pitcher. He watched me steadily. I would've been unnerved, had I not found Schikaneder's warmth so welcome after my strange meeting with Stadler. I grinned along with him as he recounted his visit to our family home.

"I spent five months in Salzburg in '80, if I remember right," he told Gieseke. "I had my whole troupe with me then and we performed our entire repertoire to great acclaim. Singspiels, ballets, a daring play by Monsieur Beaumarchais. I gave my Hamlet, of course. Yet the highlights of my stay were my evenings with the Mozart family at their home. Young Wolfgang and this talented sister of his improvised at the piano with flair and delicacy. I gave the family free passes to all my performances, you know."

"An act of unaccustomed generosity," Gieseke said.

He handed me a glass that was sticky in my grasp, either from lack of washing or from his palm. The warm punch thawed me after the cab ride, and I accepted Schikaneder's invitation to eat a light lunch with them. I sat at the table as he went to the porch to bellow for his maid.

Gieseke leaned against the wall, his body hidden by shadow. "Your face," he said.

I peered into his unlit corner.

"No, don't move," he said. "As you were. When you raise your chin, the lantern casts strange shadows."

I regarded my hands on the rough pine tabletop.

"You look so much like Wolfgang, it's actually rather disturbing," Gieseke whispered. "It's almost as though you're his ghost."

My smile had little humor. "You saw Herr Schikaneder clasp my hands. I'm rather too substantial for a ghost, don't you think?"

"In Vienna, even the ghosts need to be proficient dissemblers. Perhaps you're just a clever phantom."

I sipped the punch. The rum predominated. It bit as I swallowed, and I coughed.

"You taste the rum? There's port, brandy, and arrack in there, too. Don't be confused by the sweetness," Gieseke said. "Just because Schikaneder fills his punch with sugar doesn't mean it won't put you under the table if you overdo it."

I coughed again.

Schikaneder returned. "Ah, the punch. *Zum Wohl!* Your health. Yes, yes, it's strong stuff. Wolfgang could've told you that. Right, Gieseke?"

"I never saw him partake of too much alcohol except under your expert tutelage," Gieseke said.

"True. A most temperate little fellow he was." Schikaneder's lips quivered and his brow descended like a man experiencing the utmost pleasure. He widened his eyes and seemed to search the shadows in the corners of the room. "His spirit follows me everywhere."

Gieseke laughed. "Then he must be damned."

Schikaneder shot a finger out toward the younger man, and the laughter halted.

"Damned he could never be," Schikaneder said. "I'm five years older than he was. Imagine what he would've accomplished had his life been spared only that much longer."

I coughed through another sip of punch. Its heat tingled in the roots of my hair. "Did Wolfgang seem content, before he passed away?"

"He wasn't given to displays of emotion, as I'm sure you know," Schikaneder said. "Except when absorbed by music. Then he would indulge in a burst of joy which might carry him away from his instrument as if borne on the air itself."

"He seemed pretty miserable when you'd poured enough punch down his throat," Gieseke said.

Schikaneder dropped into the chair at the end of the table. "That I will concede," he said.

"Miserable?" I asked.

"Our new opera premiered not long before Wolfgang's

passing," said the impresario. "It's a tremendous success. We celebrated late into the night in this pavilion. Wolfgang drank more than his accustomed glass or two. He became quite morose."

"Did he mention death?"

Gieseke's heel struck the floorboards, but when I glanced toward him he was still.

"Death?" Schikaneder said. "No, he only said that when he was young he had been feted in the palaces of Europe, the toast of kings and princes. Whereas now he struggled to make ends meet."

"Did he say nothing more?"

"After that, no matter how we teased him and joked with him, he merely mumbled and sank into the kind of somberness that overcomes many of us when we've taken too much drink."

Gieseke paced along the wall in the darkness. I made out his pale hands clasping and unclasping behind his back.

"It was in this pavilion that your brother wrote much of *The Magic Flute*." Schikaneder spread his hand around the room as though he were showing me a wide hall. "It's true that this is no palace. But he produced a work which shall resonate through the centuries and be applauded by millions, when all our monarchs and aristocrats are nothing more than faded portraits hung in the most remote corridors of their castles."

"I look forward very much to attending a performance this week," I said.

Schikaneder bowed his head and smiled a welcome.

"What's the subject of the opera? I read a little in one of the Salzburg news sheets, but it hardly made any sense," I said.

"Its plot is open to misinterpretation, that much is true," he said. "To be frank, Wolfgang wished very much to compose an opera that would, if you will, be an advertisement for a certain secret brotherhood."

Gieseke's tread grew heavier, faster.

Freemasons again, I thought. Wolfgang's note in my pocket burned against my hip. How important can his membership have been to him? What might he have risked for it? "My sister-in-law said the opera is about a young prince and a princess who find love."

"That as well, of course. My company is famous for popular romances. For special effects, too. There's a battle with an enormous dragon in act one. People find it most impressive. But when I wrote the text for Wolfgang to set to music, he was quite determined that our opera should counter the unnatural suspicion the emperor has developed for the Brotherhood."

"What does the emperor suspect?"

Schikaneder rolled his shoulders and took a long breath. "Our beloved emperor appears to consider that the Masons harbor malign intentions toward the monarchy."

"But why?"

"There has been revolution in France, madame. Our emperor's sister, Queen Marie Antoinette as the French call her, has been under arrest these past six months. The philosophy of the revolutionaries—liberty, equality, brotherhood—is rather similar to that espoused by the Masons."

"The emperor believes the Masons wish for a revolution here?"

"Perhaps. Any secret is cause for suspicion these days."

"Secrets? What secrets do the Masons keep?"

He ran his tongue around his lips and leered. "Nothing of

such great interest, you might think. But they enforce their secrecy with measures ranging from the harmless to the—theatrically bloodcurdling."

"With violence?"

"With the *promise* of violence." He waved a hand in dismissal. "Usually it's just a matter of coded symbols they use to recognize a brother. They draw little triangles, or they write to each other in English. Things like that."

"Wolfgang's English was poor."

"He had studied it much of late. Maestro Haydn has been on a lucrative concert tour to London. Wolfgang intended to follow him there next year."

"But why do the Masons employ English?"

"The Masonic order was first created in Scotland. The use of English acknowledges those early traditions."

"That seems harmless."

"To the emperor even such innocent fun might look like the Masons are trying to hide secret knowledge. English is a language spoken by few people in Vienna."

"Does the emperor act on his suspicions?"

"He has gone so far as to order that no more Masonic lodges be formed."

No new lodges. I understood a little of Stadler's fury about the Grotto. "Then why did Wolfgang create an opera about Masonry?"

Schikaneder shook his head. "People sometimes think Wolfgang was less than serious. Because his laughter was a touch manic and he used to hop and skip when he was overexcited. But he had his intellectual side. He was a great admirer of the new Enlightenment philosophers—for their belief that reason, equality, and the human spirit are greater than the authority of the church and of kings. As a measure of this, Wolfgang rejected hierarchies. He judged everyone by their talents and their character alone, rich or poor, man or woman. He injected these ideals of his into *The Magic Flute*. He wished to show the true, beautiful face of Masonic Brotherhood, regardless of—of the potential for misinterpretation."

It was I who felt naïve amid this talk of suspicion and revolution. I was disturbed that my brother had risked offending our emperor. "Yet you collaborated on the opera with him."

"Wolfgang was determined," Schikaneder said. "God knows, I owe the order of Freemasons nothing. My lodge was Charles of the Three Keys in Regensburg. But I was expelled."

"Why?"

"For immorality," Gieseke snapped. "With two actresses in his company."

Schikaneder's laugh was wistful, as though he recalled some long-ago pleasure. "Quite so."

"How then does this opera, as you put it, advertise Masonry's best elements?" I said.

He fluttered his hand. "Symbols," he said. "Some symbols, that's all."

Gieseke clicked his tongue.

Schikaneder cast a dark look into the shadows where the younger man paced.

I wondered at their silence. It was heavy with things they would surely have spoken to each other had I not been present. *Do you want us all to end up like Wolfgang?* Stadler had said. Perhaps "us" referred to the men who might have joined his new Masonic lodge. "Can my brother's love for Masonry have endangered him?"

Schikaneder let his mouth and eyes open in surprise, as though my meaning dawned upon him slowly. "Madame, you can't possibly mean— But your brother died of a—a what's it called—some kind of a fever. Military?"

"Miliary."

"Quite. Well, no, no, don't ever think I would've allowed such a precious man to place himself in danger for the sake of an opera, no matter how immortal its music."

The lantern's flame appeared to die, then it rose again. Schikaneder glanced at it with momentary horror. "No," he said, louder than necessary. "There's nothing sinister about any of this."

Gieseke stepped forward and slammed his palms onto the table. He leaned over Schikaneder, sweat gleaming on his face. "The Rosy Cross," he shouted.

Schikaneder reached for the man's hand.

"Don't touch me." Gieseke pulled up a chair, close to me. He smelled of unwashed clothing and his breath reeked like a dog's panting. "The Sovereign Rosy Cross is the secret symbol of some Masonic lodges. It's represented by the number eighteen."

"Karl, Karl." Schikaneder's voice was low and powerful, a baritone stage whisper. It rumbled in my bones.

"Shut up," Gieseke said to him. He gripped my wrist. "In *The Magic Flute*, the name of the high priest is spoken eighteen times and sung eighteen times. He speaks eighteen sentences and sings one hundred and eighty bars of music. When he comes onstage, the chorus that accompanies him is eighteen bars long."

"What does this mean?" I asked.

Schikaneder puffed out his cheeks. "Our friend here is an actor, but also a would-be scientist. Myself, I have no patience for accounting."

"Listen, woman." Gieseke pressed my wrist so that the skin twisted. "Wolfgang died eighteen days after the first performance of *The Magic Flute*. That's true. One need not be a scientist to count a couple of weeks. And he died in his thirty-sixth year, which is two times eighteen, in the year of 1791, whose digits add up to eighteen."

"Now you're just being ridiculous," Schikaneder said with good humor. He went to the corner to pour himself another punch.

"My dear lady," Gieseke said, "this has been driving me mad."

"You don't say?" Schikaneder smiled.

"I wrote the text for your brother's final Masonic music. The last thing he ever wrote for them."

"Them? Don't deny that you're one of them." Schikaneder drank.

"That's right. I was a brother Mason in Wolfgang's lodge."

"What was the piece you wrote with him?" I said.

"A Masonic cantata for performance at one of our lodge meetings," Gieseke said. "The score is eighteen pages long. *Eighteen* pages."

He rose from his seat, his arms wide, appealing.

The door opened and a thickset maid brought a tray to the table.

Schikaneder lifted the lid of a pot. "Look, Karl, eighteen slices of potato, served by Johanna, who is eighteen years of age, and cooked in a kitchen eighteen paces from here. And she earns three and a half kreuzers a day, which makes twenty-four and a half a week, which— Oh, but that doesn't help your theory, does it."

The maid looked puzzled. Schikaneder waved for her to leave.

When the door shut, Gieseke hammered the edge of his fist onto the table. "Wolfgang's music was filled with the secrets of the Masons, for anyone to recognize. Even those who weren't initiated into the Brotherhood. He was poisoned because he betrayed these things."

"The number eighteen?" I said.

Schikaneder spooned out some sauerkraut. "If such trivia is kept secret, it's only because to reveal it makes one look ludicrous and quite possibly insane."

"Wolfgang's body didn't become stiff and cold after death. You told me so yourself," Gieseke said to him. "Just like the famous case of the last pope, who *was* poisoned. There should be an investigation."

Schikaneder played with the hair around his ears, studying the actor. He made his voice quiet and penetrating. "If there were an investigation, who do you think they'd come to first?"

"What do you mean?"

"You were a member of Wolfgang's lodge, Karl. You're quite certain he died by foul means. You worked with him on the cantata which, as you point out, was a magical eighteen pages long. You might have some explaining to do."

"I have nothing to hide."

Schikaneder ladled a thick brown sauce onto two pale dumplings. "Yes, nothing. And also *nowhere* to hide. Not from them."

He laid the spoon in the gravy dish. The two men stared at each other, silent and tense.

"Them?" I said. "Who do you mean?"

They held their stare. Schikaneder shoved the plate toward Gieseke. "You need to eat, to keep up your strength, Karl. You aren't yourself," he said. "Remember, you have performances this week."

Gieseke swept the dumplings onto the floor. "Starvation would be a better, quicker death than this," he yelled.

He rushed out into the cold.

The door swung in the wind. Schikaneder closed it, turned the latch, and leaned against it a moment. He returned to the table and made up a plate for me.

"A quicker death?" I said.

"Pay no attention to Gieseke. Wolfgang's tragic passing has affected us all in different ways," he said. "You understand?"

I inclined my head.

Schikaneder put the plate before me. "*Mahlzeit. Bon appétit.* Liver dumplings and sauerkraut," he said. "Wolfgang's favorite."

5.

A dizzying throng of people and animals weaved along Kärntner Street as my cab returned from Schikaneder's theater. Coachmen rattled their vehicles over the snowy, half-frozen mud, yelling at pedestrians who stumbled on the rutted dirt. So different from the quiet of my village.

We reached St. Stephen's Square. The cosmopolitan lower echelons of the imperial capital hurried about, slowing the carriages to a walking pace. People from every part of the Empire passed the window of my cab. Serbs twisting their mustaches. Greeks with the bowls of their long pipes glowing in the twilight. A pair of Jews, black-bearded and with long side curls, their dark coats limp over meager shoulders, speaking something that sounded like Polish. I heard Hungarian from the mouth of a man in a greasy sheepskin coat, and the language of Bohemia from a blond-haired youth shoving a knife into the top of his tall leather boots.

It was a long time since I had witnessed a scene so bustling and alien, and the first time I had ever experienced a city alone. I was cautious and thrilled, like an adventurer entering the heart of a forbidden civilization in some far continent.

The cab continued beyond the wide Graben. Amid all the strangeness, I noticed a place I recognized. I called to my driver, climbed down to the street, and dismissed him. Beside the great church in the square of Am Hof, the Collalto Palace glowed by the light of the lamps at its entrance. I had made my debut in the imperial capital here as an eleven-year-old. My brother had been the star that night. Though only six, he had played accurately even with the keyboard obscured beneath a cloth. Count von Collalto wrote a poem for Wolfgang which said that though he was "small in stature, like the greatest he plays." It had been an audition of a kind, and we had succeeded. An invitation soon came to perform before the empress at Schönbrunn.

I stood on the corner by the palace, gazing up at the relief columns of the otherwise plain façade. I had passed through these heavy chestnut doors thirty years ago with so many dreams. I had been accompanied by my father, my mother, and my brother. They were gone from me, as surely as my aspirations for fame as a musician. The count's verse had fretted that Wolfgang was so frail he would "too soon outwear" his body. My family had overlooked that foreboding reference. We reread only the poem's laudatory lines, delighted by the entrée Collalto gave us into Viennese society.

At home, where I was content to be with my children, I might've said that the desire for acclaim had been my father's ambition alone, grafted onto me until I thought it had been my own, then slowly stripped away by bitter years of attending to him in Salzburg. But as I stood before the majestic Collalto Palace and speculated which of the windows gave onto the room where I had performed, Vienna entered my veins once more. The fantasies were revived of the little girl who had curtsied and blushed at the praise of the aristocratic connoisseurs, even as her father gathered the trinkets offered in payment.

I wondered if I would cope differently with such praise now. In the glow of the palace's lamps, I understood that for much of my life my reactions to people and places had been hollow, like a musician manufacturing sensations with a flawless technique. Perhaps it had been the inevitable result of my childhood performances. I had played music filled with the delicacy of romance and the rage of passion, before I was old enough to have experienced either. When I faced such emotions in reality, I merely faked my responses, as I had done at the keyboard.

I lived with this emptiness until I became a mother. Then I had no more need to pretend. Every smile or tear or retch from my babies awoke in me a tremor that burst through the counterfeit emotions I had known so long. I was no longer a faker. I knew myself. Before this palace, which I had entered as a provincial girl and departed as a celebrated prodigy, I felt exhilarated, like someone meeting an exciting stranger whom she was eager to know.

A footman scampered through the gates of the palace and waved to a coach in front of the Am Hof Church. The coachman walked his team up to the gates. Two men emerged from Collalto's mansion and paused beside the carriage.

The first was Stadler. He held his hat in his hands, turning it in agitation.

The other man squeezed Stadler's arm as if to reassure him.

He was tall and broad. His frock coat was a lively green with delicate piping.

The Collalto footman unclipped the steps of the carriage. I couldn't identify the crest on the door he held open, but I understood that the tall man was of some importance. He gave a comforting tap to Stadler's shoulder.

Wolfgang's friend grinned, pleased with the familiarity shown to him by this nobleman, whatever else was worrying him. His smile disappeared when he noticed me.

His companion followed Stadler's gaze. His dark eyes found me. They widened just enough to reveal surprise. His lips parted as though he were about to call, but he frowned and was silent. He lifted his hat in greeting.

I curtsied.

When I raised my eyes he was on the steps of the carriage. He spoke a brief sentence to Stadler, who responded with a hesitant nod.

As his carriage pulled away, the nobleman watched me with a face that seemed marked by pain and loss. For a moment his expression softened and we looked at each other as though it were not our first meeting.

His coachman looped around the square and went toward the Hofburg, where the imperial family lived.

A freezing gust rushed past the palace and lifted the fur hood of my cloak almost off my head. I looked toward the gate of the Collalto Palace. Stadler was gone. I shivered and decided that I ought to linger no longer in the open air.

I considered calling upon the many Viennese who stayed a night or two with my family in Salzburg since that long-ago concert for Count Collalto. Traveling musicians and writers, noblemen and impresarios, all had broken their journeys to enjoy the convivial music making my father encouraged and to observe the young prodigies at home. But I found my steps drawing me through the lamplight to the door of someone who had never partaken of our provincial hospitality.

6.

A maid hauling a heavy basket of herbs and poultry against her hip pointed out the house of Magdalena Hofdemel on a narrow, dark street behind Jews' Square. The façade was a washed-out blue, like an old woman's irises. A statue of the Virgin nestled in a niche above the windows of the second floor. In the gateway, the cobbles were small rectangles of wood to damp the noise of carriage wheels and horseshoes.

I mounted a wide staircase to the Hofdemel apartment two flights up. It would've been the most expensive dwelling in the building, above the dinginess of the street and not so demanding a climb as the garrets farther up the stone steps. When she had told me where Magdalena lived, Constanze had mentioned that the deceased husband had been a chancery clerk. Strange that a mere functionary in the courthouse should earn a salary sufficient to pay for such a well-situated apartment.

A peephole slid back in the door. A maid stood on tiptoe to reach the opening, blinking at me in the dark stairwell.

When she guided me into the sitting room, my surprise

at the sumptuousness of the Hofdemel apartment increased. The furnishing was rich, even given the simple designs then in vogue. I touched my fingertips to a gilt-chair covered in satin of great softness, but I didn't sit. I was drawn to the piano. It was quite newly made, by Stein of Augsburg, the craftsman my brother had always loved for the delicacy of his pedal effects.

I laid my right hand across the keys. It was on a pair of Steins that I had performed with Wolfgang for the last time a decade ago. My fingers tripped through a delicate melody. The second movement of the concerto I was to perform the following night. I struck some of the notes late by a fraction of a beat. My father had once written to tell me Wolfgang played it that way.

The door opened, pulled back with great force. A woman of about twenty-five years entered. Her eyes signaled anger. She glared at my hand until I withdrew it from the piano, then she turned her ferocious gaze on my face.

I gasped, and the woman seemed to forget her fury. Her eyes receded into her head and she lifted a fan to cover her nose, her mouth and jaw. Though I had exclaimed only in surprise at her sudden entry, I believe she thought it a reaction to the injuries evident on her face. It was gashed all across with lurid strips of scabbed blood, the skin between each slash bruised yellow and green.

I gathered myself and approached her. "Madame Hofdemel?" I said. "I am—"

"I know who you are. It's obvious, to look at you. When he cut my face, my husband didn't take my eyes." Her voice was curt and bitter.

A suicide, her husband must surely have been damned forever. She winced, as though her speech had split the scab over one of her wounds, and I thought that it was she who had been condemned. I dropped my chin. Her stance softened and she reached a hand to my cheek, lifting my face.

"Excuse my ill manners." Her expression became strained and melancholy. "The pain of my wounds takes over and I forget myself."

She led me to a green linen sofa. She sat at its edge, very upright as though at a piano, and I remembered that she had been Wolfgang's student.

"The Stein. It's a beautiful instrument," I said.

"When I started my lessons with Wolfgang, he commented to my husband on the quality of Stein's pianos. My Franz insisted on purchasing one, though I told him it was too great an expense. It cost him three hundred gulden. That's how he was, my Franz. Generous, loving. He was the best of husbands before—all this."

Magdalena drew a lace handkerchief from her sleeve and touched it to her eyes. As she did so, she lowered the fan from her face and I noticed that she had been pretty, even beautiful, before her suicidal husband attacked her. Her brow was a little high, but her hair rolled away from it in brown ringlets. Her eyes were hazel and soft. She held her full, lower lip between teeth of such whiteness that I imagined they must be enchanting when exposed in a smile.

"Franz would sit where we are now and listen all night as I played the piano," she said. "I had some hopes of a concert career. But that's all at an end now."

I twitched a smile, as though someone had pinched the

back of my hand. I had come to her because I wished to know the part her husband might have played in my brother's death. Now that I sat beside her, I could think of no way to approach the subject that wouldn't be like another cut to the skin of her damaged face.

I cleared my throat and looked for another way to approach her. "Did Wolfgang intend to perform with you?"

"With most of his pupils he did. He wasn't concerned with teaching young ladies to amuse their husbands' dinner guests. He wanted to bring us out before the public."

"So he was training you for that?"

"It's in my blood, after all. My father was the music master at St. Peter's Church in Brünn." She touched the back of her thumbnail to her lip. "But Franz wasn't interested in me performing."

"Yet he wanted you to have a fine piano, to take lessons with a great composer."

"Only so that I could play at soirees here in our home. Franz didn't pick Wolfgang for the social cachet of a famous teacher. He arranged for me to study with your brother because they already had a—a connection."

The Masons again, I thought. "Of what nature?"

The fan rose above her chin again and her eyes were wary. "They had business ties. Franz lent money to Wolfgang."

I recalled Constanze's talk of my brother's financial problems. "A loan? For what?"

"A trip Wolfgang made to Berlin. About two years ago. There was a position for him at the court of the Prussian king, but he returned disappointed."

Disappointed and indebted, I thought. "My sister-in-law

reorganized Wolfgang's finances this last summer, I gather. Did he repay Franz then?"

"I believe not." Magdalena dropped her eyes behind the fan and sobbed. Her chest trembled, lifting and stretching her scars. "It's so dreadful, madame."

I blushed to consider it, but I imagined Wolfgang alone in Vienna with this sweet woman while his pregnant wife hobbled into the hot springs at Baden on her bad foot. It seemed quite possible that the teacher could've fallen into sin with his pupil and that, in turn, the wronged husband had taken his revenge.

"Why did—?"

The door opened. Magdalena's maid brought us each a cup of hot red wine. I inhaled the scent of cinnamon and cloves, listening to the maid shuffle back to the kitchen. I sipped the *glühwein* before I spoke again, but I still found it hard to ask my question.

"Why did your husband— What reason had he to hurt you?"

"Must a man have a reason to hurt his wife?" Bitterness took over Magdalena's eyes.

"What spurred him?"

She closed her fan with a snap. The marks about her eyes and brow were little more than scratches compared to the parallel gashes I saw now across her neck. They were so deep they had been sewn. She ran her finger above the stiff, black stitches.

I flinched.

"He didn't try to *hurt* me. He aimed to kill me." Her tears made the scars on her face damp and bright, as though they bled once more. "Franz believed he had slit my throat and that I would die. Only then did he do the same for himself. I watched him pull open his collar to ready himself. Hate in his eyes, where I had been used to such love. As though he detested me above all creatures in the world. Then he pulled his razor across his throat and I saw that it was himself that he hated most, and only then me."

Despite myself, I returned to the notion of Franz Hofdemel as a betrayed husband. What other reason could he have had for such butchery?

"I pleaded with Franz, begged for the sake of his soul," she said. "I told him that he'd go to Hell. Not, you understand, because I wished to chastise him. It was only that I feared for the immortal spirit of the man I loved."

"Even as he tried to murder you?"

"Even then."

"Didn't he fear Hell?"

"He said Hell was full of the foolishness he had committed before he gained wisdom, and neither I nor Satan could force him to live that way again." Magdalena slouched forward.

I touched her wrist. It was hard, like bone, as though she had willed her skin to such a thickness that it might never again be cut.

"I feel so guilty, Madame de Mozart. So very guilty." She sniffled into her handkerchief. "Don't think badly of my Franz. Though I never would've intended it, I'm sure I drove him to this."

"Did you? Did you really?"

She swallowed hard and tried to make her expression bright. "Wolfgang often spoke of your skill at the piano. He used to tell me that if I worked very hard I might be almost as good as you. Would you play for me? Something by your brother."

"He spoke of me?"

"Do play. It soothes me to listen to a fine pianist."

Until I played the opening triad, I hadn't known that I would give her Wolfgang's Adagio in B Minor. The piece ran through my fingers without any thought. Instantly I parted from the company of the woman with the scarred face. Instead, I was with Wolfgang. I became calm, savoring the symmetry of the music, even as I sensed the tension my brother had injected with its unexpected key transitions.

More tears lay on Magdalena's face. But they seemed now to be drawn from some happy recollection. She smiled at me.

As I reached the coda and the piece turned to B major, the door opened. A woman several years younger than me stood there in a thick fur, her hand supported by a squat, swarthy maid. Her eyes rolled in their sockets, the pupils swinging up into her skull, so that only the whites were visible.

I hesitated, and the blind woman sensed it. She rotated her hand, gesturing for me to continue. When she removed her fur hat and thrust it at the maid, I recognized her as Maria Theresia von Paradies, a virtuoso of the piano who had visited our family in Salzburg while on her way to perform in London and Paris.

Paradies listened to the silence after the final notes. Her nose lifted as though savoring the scent of the music. She shrugged her coat off her shoulders for Magdalena's house girl to catch. She turned her body toward the sofa, and the dark maid pulled her to Magdalena.

"My dear." Paradies leaned close to Magdalena and glided her fingers over the scars on the woman's neck. "Better?"

"Much better."

The maid stomped to the other side of the room and leaned against the window frame, staring into the evening darkness.

Magdalena took Paradies's arm and guided her onto the sofa beside her. "How did you know it was I who sat here on the sofa?" she said.

"Little one, there were two people breathing in this room when I entered. The one playing the piano was—I'm sorry to tell you—evidently not you." Paradies rubbed Magdalena's forearm. "Who's our performer?"

"It's Wolfgang's sister."

Paradies held out her hand until I grasped it. "It's been a long time," she said.

"Eight years," I replied.

"I've played hundreds of concerts since then and written a few operas. What've you been doing?"

I would've withdrawn my hand, but I knew better than to struggle against the powerful fingers of another pianist. "I married a district prefect. I live some way from Salzburg."

"It's clear that you continue to practice hard. You haven't lost your talent."

"You're too kind."

"But a concerto is no easy thing."

Her tone was sharp. I saw that Paradies was offended Stadler hadn't chosen her as the soloist for the benefit concert at the Academy. So here, I thought, was one person who'd be willing me to fail when I played Wolfgang's concerto.

"Quite. No easy thing," I said.

"Still, it's easier than sitting down to write a simple letter to one's younger brother, apparently. One's only living relative."

Magdalena pulled at Paradies's skirt. "Theresia," she whispered.

Wolfgang, it seemed, had known these women with enough intimacy to have complained to them about me. After our father's death, there had been financial disputes. But more than that had come between us. Perhaps both of us had been cut adrift when Papa went, the commanding polestar of our lives was eclipsed. Certainly my emotions had spun in all directions. For some time I had thought only of my own loss. I had been unaware of the feelings of others.

"You're quite correct, Fräulein von Paradies," I said. "A concerto is difficult, but not impossible."

She let go of my hand. I sat in an upright chair beside the sofa.

"I've learned sixty concertos by heart," Paradies said, "but I'd forget them all before I would neglect one of Wolfgang's."

I was silent.

"What do you say to that?" She raised her voice.

"I agree," I said. "I'd consider it a dreadful burden to have neglected anything of Wolfgang's."

Paradies's eyeballs twitched. "I shall be content to play one of his sonatas tomorrow night at the Academy." She lifted her hand to her powdered hair. It stood high, combed loosely back to her neck. "I remember telling your father he ought to send you to Vienna."

"Did you?"

"You played during my visit to Salzburg. I was struck by your technique."

I recalled that time well. My thirty-second birthday. Wolfgang had bought me ices in the afternoon after target shooting near the Mirabell Gate and served me punch in the evening. But he had been visiting with his new bride, while I was losing hope that I'd ever be wed. I had resented his cheeriness and pretended to choke on the ices. I didn't remember that I had played so well for Paradies, but I bowed in acknowledgment. "Thank you for this compliment."

"Your *father* didn't thank me. He said his daughter had no interest in travel or performance."

I pressed my thumbs against each other. My father had decided everything for me, just as he had attempted to do for Wolfgang. But he was long gone.

"Well, now you're here in Vienna, after all," Paradies said. "And with a major performance tomorrow."

I spoke softly. "Here I am."

7

On Jews' Square, lawyers and petitioners headed for the massive Court Chancellery, where Magdalena Hofdemel's husband had worked. Its pink stone glistened in the morning rain like that poor woman's wounded skin. I crossed the square toward the private houses on its southern side.

A clarinet played somewhere before me. An aria of Wolfgang's composition. My brother had written the piece to showcase the virtuosity of his friend Stadler on the bass clarinet. As I listened, the melody dropped below the E at the bottom of the range of most clarinets, down to a low C.

The tone of the instrument was like the song of an enormous, magical bird. I followed the clarinet to a narrow house and up the stairs.

Stadler answered my knock himself. He wore a brown waistcoat and a rough blanket across his shoulders. He held his bass clarinet in one hand. His finger was still depressed on the key of the last note he had played.

He edged backward, hesitating to invite me inside but unable to turn me away.

"*Guten Morgen*, Herr Stadler." I passed him, unlacing the neck of my cloak.

"You'd better keep it on," he mumbled.

I tipped my head. "Do you mean for me to leave, sir?"

"You're welcome, of course. I didn't intend to sound ungracious," he said. "It's a bit cold in here, I mean. The maid was too sick to come the last few days. I've had no fire and—"

"Never mind. We have work to do."

He shut the door, leaning against it and pushing home the bolt, as though he was afraid someone might burst into his rooms behind me.

"Did you forget our rehearsal? For my performance for tonight," I said. "The concerto?"

"No, of course not. The C major."

I smiled. "Where shall we—?"

"I keep a clavichord in the studio. Please."

He led me to a high-ceilinged room overlooking the Court Chancellery. The walls were painted to resemble white marble.

I played a few simple triads on the clavichord. Its metal tangents struck the iron strings with a sound that was sharper, spikier than the hammers of the pianoforte I had grown accustomed to playing. The white sharps and flats stood out like strips of ice against the black keys. Still, it was well-tuned.

I warmed my fingers with a brief scale, and played a minuet by Emanuel Bach.

As I played, Stadler moved closer to the clavichord. He sat

on the edge of an embroidered stool, fingering the keys of his clarinet, eager to join in the music.

When I had finished, he laid his hand on the body of the clavichord with reverence. "If you dressed in the red suit Wolfgang wore for all his concerts, we'd be able to have him back. You look just like him. You play just as he did, too."

In Stadler's deep brown eyes I glimpsed his enjoyment of my performance. The pain returned to them quickly, as though he had remembered that the red suit wasn't mine to wear, after all.

"Let's get to the concerto." He worked his lips on the reed of his instrument. "I'll play the orchestral line, so that you may refresh your memory of the piece."

We played through the opening movement. At first I watched Stadler for signs of his approval. But soon I was absorbed with the music, its joyful piano part, and the melancholy of the woodwinds as Stadler figured them on his clarinet.

We finished that movement. Stadler wiped his lips with his forefinger. "Good. Just the right tempo. Many people play it too fast. Now for the Andante."

"You know, when my father first sent me the score of this movement, I thought it had been copied wrongly."

"The unusual counterpoint?"

"Exactly."

"When I think how Wolfgang could manipulate an orchestra, tease us and make us examine new horizons without our quite knowing it—well, that's when I see the difference between my kind of talent and his genius."

"This movement makes me think of a dream." I played the

melody of the piece as I spoke. "It's andante, walking speed. As though you were sleepwalking through the dream. There's a little dissonance. But it always returns to a tone of serenity."

Stadler brandished his clarinet with enthusiasm. "That's it. If you were dreaming in your bed you'd be safe. Sleepwalking, though, you're never sure where you are."

"Wolfgang gives us these dissonant moments, as though the security of a warm bed were slipping away from us."

"But he brings us back to the resolving key."

"To sleep. Calm and restful."

Stadler's smile was wide. "You have it, you really do."

He lifted his instrument to his lips and went into the orchestral theme that introduced the movement. I closed my eyes for the piano solo. I imagined it wasn't I who played. I was listening to Wolfgang.

When we finished, Stadler rocked on his stool. "I remember when he debuted this piece. That must be six years ago now."

Six years in which I hadn't seen my brother, years when he had surpassed all other composers. The last three of them, years in which we hadn't communicated. Stadler averted his eyes. The warmth of our musical collaboration was gone.

"I didn't forget him, Herr Stadler."

"Naturally."

"I had his music, even if I didn't have him."

He tapped at the keys of his clarinet.

We played through the concerto again in full. He was distracted this time. When the music was over, he stared at my hands on the keyboard with such agitation that I hid them behind my back.

To escape Stadler's glare, I turned to the window. The

hood of a woman crossing the square lifted in the wind. I was reminded of the gust that had caught my own cloak outside the Collalto Palace.

"Who was the gentleman I saw you with yesterday?" I asked.

Stadler laid his clarinet across his knees. "What?"

"A tall gentleman. A nobleman, in fact, by the crest on his coach," I said. "You spoke with him as he departed. I think he went toward the Hofburg."

Stadler coughed. His reluctance was evident. He whispered, "The Baron van Swieten."

Swieten had been my brother's greatest patron at the palace since Wolfgang's arrival in Vienna a decade before. He had often written to me of him. "Tell me about the baron?"

"What's there to tell? He was born in Holland. He came here as a boy, when his father was ordered into the service of the late empress as her physician. He's close to the emperor."

"Shall I meet him tonight? At the concert?"

Stadler rapped his knuckles on the clavichord. I sensed he wished he had chosen a different soloist after all. "It'll be hard to miss him. He commands—"

"Attention?"

He shrugged.

"Love?" I asked.

Stadler looked at me curiously. "Respect. He commands respect."

I remembered the way the baron's gaze had fallen upon me in the square, the moment when I had thought he would speak to me.

"Did he recognize me?" My voice had an unseemly eagerness. Stadler rubbed his nose. Perhaps he had heard it.

"The baron asked me if the person he saw could be Wolfgang's sister. I told him it was."

He stood. "Perhaps you'd like something to drink, madame? The air is cold, but your exertion at the keyboard shall have put you in need of sustenance." He tried for joviality and kindness. But the discomfort in his voice was like an ill-tuned string, the sound that would be heard above all others.

"Very kind, thank you."

He excused himself with relief and went through the apartment to the pantry.

I wandered across the room to Stadler's desk. Sheets of music in my brother's hand spread over its slanting surface. A concerto for clarinet and orchestra in A major. Wolfgang had signed and dated the manuscript only a few months ago. It would've been one of the last pieces he wrote.

I took up the sheets, reading across the orchestral and solo parts of the first movement. Wolfgang must've written it for Stadler, because it required the low tones of his friend's bass clarinet.

Stadler called from the kitchen. "I can find only brandy, madame."

So absorbed was I by Wolfgang's beautiful composition that the loud voice startled me. I went to the door. "Very good, Herr Stadler. Brandy will do just fine."

As I returned to the desk, I noticed that the score had lain on top of a souvenir book, Stadler's record of friends and visitors to his home. It was open to a page marked with a few lines of script and a signature. The same signature as the one on the music I held.

The text was in English. I recalled what Schikaneder had said about the Masons, writing to each other in the language of England in token of their Brotherhood's origins.

> *To my dear Stadler, whose clarinet is a magic*
> *flute to free mankind and promote higher*
> *feelings. Never forget the brother (you know*
> *what I mean) who loves you from his heart.*
> *Wolfgang Amadeus Mozart.*

The signature was followed by two triangles drawn one beside the other.

The brother. Indeed I did know what that meant. Stadler had admitted that he was Wolfgang's Masonic brother. Schikaneder had told me about the triangles Masons drew as signs between each other.

I traced my fingers across my brother's handwriting. *You know what I mean.* His suggestive, winking voice. I flipped the pages, looking for another message from Wolfgang.

Two more triangles caught my eye. They concluded a note by a different writer, though in the same language. It was on the most recent page of the book to have been used, dated only a day before.

> *Be industrious. Flee idleness. Your sincere*
> *friend and brother, the Baron Konstant von*
> *Jacobi.*

On the facing page, another note in English. Signed by the Prince Karl Lichnowsky, followed by two triangles. Constanze had named Lichnowsky among Wolfgang's Masonic brethren. Here was the proof in the prince's own hand.

I would've examined the book further, but I heard Stadler returning. I laid the concerto over it and pretended to read through the score.

"Some brandy to revive us both, madame." Stadler came in with two tumblers.

I realized that I hadn't turned the pages of the souvenir book back to the one signed by Wolfgang. I hoped Stadler wouldn't notice.

My pulse picked up. The strange signs in the souvenir book. The fear that my intrusion would be discovered. I took the cup of brandy and drank.

"It brings some color to your cheeks, anyway." Stadler laughed.

I flushed and laid my hand on the desk. "I was enjoying this concerto for clarinet, Herr Stadler. It's wonderful."

"I premiered it in Prague less than two months ago. A great success. I couldn't have imagined then—" Stadler picked up the score. He hesitated.

His glanced hovered on the souvenir book. I was sure he had noticed that its pages had been turned. He hummed the opening theme of the concerto. "Couldn't have imagined then what a disaster was to come with Wolfgang's passing."

He put the manuscript on the desk. "Enough of such things. No more disasters await us. After all, I've heard you play now. Tonight's concert shall be a triumph. Don't you think?"

"I'm sure of it, sir."

As I crossed Jews' Square I glanced from under the hood of my cloak. Stadler stood in his window. He rubbed his eyes with the heels of his hands. When he saw me, he bowed and retreated from the light.

8.

*A*s the afternoon light faded on Rauhenstein Lane, I halted my exercises at Wolfgang's piano and listened to my sister-in-law singing in the next room. An aria of my brother's composition, about the pain of love. He wrote it during their courtship, for a character in his opera who bore his future wife's name. Now she practiced it for the concert at the Academy, to raise funds for the family that had lost him.

"Sorrow dwells in my breast," she sang. Her ascending trills made me grasp at the shawl covering my chest. Her technique was exceptional, but it had been more than fine breath control that inspired Wolfgang to write such music for her.

On the sole occasion when Wolfgang had brought Constanze to Salzburg, I had been cold to her. I might've blamed the influence of my father, who had thought her a poor match for his only son. But in truth I had been jealous of their love and companionship—things which had been denied to me. I saw now that I had overlooked her talent as a singer. Perhaps this wasn't all I had neglected to notice in her.

She came to the door, with little Karl behind her skirts again. Her smile bore a touch of apprehension that reminded me how soon we were to perform. "The carriage will be ready shortly," she said.

We negotiated the narrowness of Bäcker Street toward the University Square, our carriage rocking over the cobbles. Constanze's thin shoulder bumped against mine.

"Tell me about life in St. Gilgen, sister?" She watched the passing houses as though searching for something in the courtyards beyond their arched entranceways. "Is it peaceful, out there in the mountains?"

I wondered if there was something about Vienna she wished to escape. Maybe only the painful memory of her husband's death.

"There are seven children in the house. My five step-children are quite unruly," I said. "The boys are little liars whom my husband refuses to discipline. In her studies, the eldest girl has no application. My home is no more peaceful than the Graben during the hour when all the rich Viennese promenade."

"But it must be delightful to have so many children around?"

"My husband's children from his first wives lack concentration. I tried to teach piano to the twelve-year-old, but she couldn't focus. She won't brush her teeth or eat when she should. She runs about the house, screeching. It's all so irregular. My husband is a good man, but he's unconcerned with the education of his children—something I consider to be paramount and, of course, to be handled competently only by the parents."

She mumbled something into her hand, but it was inaudible over the horses' hooves on the cobbles.

"What was that?" I said.

Constanze's black eyes rested on me with a frankness that was blank and terrible. "I said, you sound like your father." She returned her gaze to the window.

I loved my father and believed him to have been a warm parent, but I hoped I was a more forgiving educator. I saw that Constanze had been hurt by his rejection of her marriage. I decided not to reason with her about Papa's true character. Better to concentrate on my performance. Inside my fur ruff, I let my fingers trip through the Allegro which begins the Concerto in C.

Our driver turned into the square beneath the austere towers of the Jesuit Church, where my father once conducted Wolfgang's Dominicus Mass. We drew up before the classical façade of the Academy of Science.

The tall windows on the upper floor illuminated the Corinthian columns to a rich cream. Where the lights were brightest, there would be the hall. It ran across several of the windows and would surely hold a large crowd. My breath was quick, but not with nerves. I was expectant, excited to play before such an audience once more.

Stiff from the drafty carriage, Constanze stamped her feet. She inclined her head toward the entrance and took my arm.

Inside, we halted at the bare stone and whitewashed walls of the stairs. Constanze stared up the steps, as though they would be too far for her to climb.

"I've never sung his music when he wasn't there to applaud," she whispered.

Her tiny hand clawed my upper arm. "It was surely not for his applause alone that you sang," I said.

In the mellow flickering of the stairwell lamps, her black eyes swam with tears. We went up.

As we reached the first landing, I noticed Stadler at the top of the stairs. He circled a man of aristocratic bearing who lifted his chin so high he seemed almost to be examining Stadler's cropped hair, though he otherwise ignored him. Both men looked dour and sullen. I supposed that ought not to have been a surprise. It was a concert in support of a dead man's impoverished family, after all.

Rushing skirts gained on us. "Stanzerl, wait, my darling."

A small woman with a rounded face and cheeks red from the cold came to our side, her chest and neck wrapped in fur. From the resemblance in the wide black eyes I saw that this was one of Constanze's sisters, and by the easy resonance of her voice I judged her to be Josefa, who had appeared as a soprano in the Vienna premiere of Wolfgang's *Don Giovanni*. She kissed Constanze, then laid her cheek against mine. She touched my shoulder and gave a mournful look.

"My dear, my poor, poor dear," she said. "We must bear up. We simply must." She shook her head and led us up the stairs with a dramatic gasp.

Constanze raised an eyebrow.

Her sister approached the gentlemen at the top of the steps, extending her hand for a kiss, exuding the emotional exhaustion of the demonstratively bereaved.

Stadler bowed to Constanze and took her hand. When he kissed it, her skin was pale against his flushed features. He gave an edgy, apologetic glance to the man beside him, before reaching out a hand to introduce me. "The Prince Lichnowsky," he said, with another bow.

One of the men who drew triangles in Stadler's souvenir book. Lichnowsky lowered the lids of his eyes in acknowledgment of Stadler's introduction. He was about thirty, dressed in a simple black frock coat of velvet and a vest of gold thread. His clothing gave off a scent of rosewater, but on his breath I detected a strong odor of the rolled tobacco leaves known as Sevillas.

"Would Madame de Mozart do me the honor of accompanying me into the concert hall?" Lichnowsky bowed and took my hand. He moved as though his limbs were hinged like the puppets in the emperor's marionette theater at Schönbrunn.

He led me through white double doors into a lavish hall. Pink and gray marble rose in a stucco relief up the walls, to give the effect of classical columns. The Grecian figures of the ceiling fresco represented the academic disciplines studied at the university.

The hall filled with the conversation of perhaps four hundred people. Many were of the highest society, holding themselves on their upright chairs with a listless rigidity that reminded me of the kings and queens for whom I had played as a girl. I noted much greater animation among those who wore plainer attire. These were probably wealthy merchants. Wolfgang had often said that aristocrats no longer had sufficient funds for household orchestras and so he had gathered groups of businessmen to support his concerts. These had come tonight to show that the pleasure of his music hadn't died with him.

Lichnowsky guided me to the front row. He bowed from the waist to some of those seated around us.

Everyone on the front row shifted to see who had arrived. Except one man. The Baron van Swieten stared ahead, silent and still. Looking sideways toward his seat at the center of the first row, I scrutinized him, unseen.

He was a broad man. His frock coat was embroidered with silver on a frosty gray fabric. His hands rested on a silver-topped stick that he held upright, its tip on the marble floor. Perhaps a decade older than me, he had very black hair. The shadow of his beard was thick on his cheeks and chin.

Swieten ignored the chatter around him, gazing at the piano with a look of puzzlement and pain. I had the impression he was trying to will Wolfgang back into existence so that he might hear him play once more. He bore himself with the air of one so powerful that he was used to having his wishes granted. His stare intensified, vexed to find this single, profound desire beyond his command.

Lichnowsky touched my elbow and gestured to my seat.

When we settled, the prince spoke so softly in the direction of the elaborate crystal lantern beside the stage that at first I failed to understand he was addressing me. "I consider myself to have been a close friend of your brother, madame," he said. "As close as is possible between two men of such different station, you understand."

"No doubt my brother was mindful of the honor you did him, my prince."

"I might even say I was his companion. We traveled together."

Wolfgang took to the road only when he was assured of paid recitals at the end of his journey, so I admit that I forgot to whom I was speaking. "You performed with him?"

Lichnowsky's eyebrow quivered in annoyance. Like all aristocrats, he thought of the public performance of music as a task fit only for servants. "We made a trip to Berlin together," he said.

"Rather a long journey."

"Which brought us into close companionship."

I recalled that Magdalena's husband had lent my brother money for that trip. I wondered why he had needed extra funds, if he had traveled with a prince.

"My brother went to Berlin in search of a position at the court of the Prussian king. May I ask why you went?"

"My family has estates in the Prussian province of Silesia. There were some rental issues to resolve."

"Do your estates take you to Berlin often?"

"Not at all." Lichnowsky spoke so sharply that, in the orchestra, a double bass player and two cellists looked up from their tuning in surprise.

The prince waited, to be sure that the musicians had returned their attention to their instruments. "I suppose I could've avoided the trip had it been solely to manage my estates. I chose to accompany Wolfgang for other reasons."

"As a brother Mason?"

He faked a cough, to disguise my words.

I would've questioned him more, but Maestro Salieri, the court composer, entered the hall from an antechamber. The orchestra rose.

Salieri acknowledged the applause. The room grew quiet. Salieri gathered himself, his mouth tight, his eyes full of suffering. He raised his arms and began the Allegro vivace of Wolfgang's last symphony.

It was the first time I had heard it. It carried me away with a complexity and majesty I hadn't encountered in his earlier symphonies.

By the time Salieri drove his arms high to end the fugue of the Molto allegro finale, all power had drained from my body. I had known my brother as a prodigy, then as a man of extraordinary talent at the keyboard who possessed a sensitive compositional technique. Until this moment I had failed to comprehend the staggering extent of his gifts.

My mouth opened and I cried low, while those around me rose to applaud. When he had been merely my brother, I had mourned Wolfgang's death. Now that I saw him as a man of such stupefying musical genius, I felt his loss so much more greatly. It was this which kept me in my chair, shivering.

Lichnowsky regarded me in puzzlement, as though embarrassed by my emotion. "Madame?"

I brushed a finger below my tearful eyes and smiled. I wished to divert him, to alleviate his discomfiture. I touched his wrist. "You were telling me about the trip to Berlin. How was the journey?"

"Wolfgang and I went slowly to Berlin, by way of Leipzig. Your brother made a study there of the works of Johann Sebastian Bach." His lip twitched and he stroked his nose. "We progressed to Berlin and attended upon the king of Prussia at the Sanssouci Palace. It's a most delightful place. The gardens are the best of it. While we waited, we walked through the terraces and into a pleasant grotto behind a waterfall."

"A grotto?"

He faltered over my interruption. "Quite so. A little cave. A cool place to sit during the hot summer months. The king was also constructing an Egyptian garden, with statues in the pharaonic style and mystical pyramids."

I slipped my hand into the pocket of my dress and touched Wolfgang's note. The Grotto. I closed my eyes.

The prince leaned toward me. "Are you unwell?"

Applause, once more.

"Your sister-in-law is about to perform," he said.

Constanze sang "Ah, I was in love," and her sister followed her with a virtuoso aria that, Lichnowsky informed me, she was performing in *The Magic Flute* at Schikaneder's theater.

But I heard little. I was overcome with confusion. Lichnowsky's mention of a grotto in Berlin, Stadler's fury over the letter, Gieseke's strange numerical rant. I tried to slow my thoughts. I needed to clear my mind before I performed.

My fingers were crooked and cramped. Staring at them, I feared I'd disappoint the audience. As a girl, I had often waited to perform while Wolfgang ran through his tricks and delighted everyone, playing blindfolded and improvising on demand. He frequently went on so long and to such acclaim that there was no time left for me to play. I would watch, downcast, as the dukes and princes wandered away to their dinners without hearing me. I wished that this would be my fate today. One after the other, Vienna's best musicians displayed their interpretations of my brother's genius. Soon I was to demonstrate that the name of Mozart might attach to mediocrity, too.

Mademoiselle von Paradies completed her recital of a piano sonata by Wolfgang in B-flat major with a vigorous cadenza. She came to her feet, breathing hard, defiant and triumphant. Her rolling, blind eyes seemed to seek me out in the audience.

As the applause for Paradies subsided, the orchestra tuned

up once more. Maestro Salieri bowed to me, gesturing toward the piano.

I stared at him, my vision out of focus, a chill in my belly. I had never been frightened in front of an audience. Neither was I now. I was scared of Wolfgang. What would he think of me?

My legs shook. I would not stand. I heard the coughing and muttering of the spectators as though I were listening with my head submerged in a washbowl.

I couldn't do it. Wolfgang would be ashamed of me.

"Madame de Mozart?"

I looked up. Baron van Swieten extended his hand. A long spray of white lace fell from his cuff, but the hand was thick and black hair ran along the backs of his fingers.

A delicate tug from that strong hand, and I arose. He led me to the piano, the tapping of his cane on the floor the only sound in the room.

I sat before the piano and watched him step to his seat in the front row.

As the soloist, I was to double as the conductor. But I found I couldn't lift my hands. A few of the musicians cleared their throats. Someone in the audience snickered.

The baron snapped his fingers to get the attention of the violas and cellos. Like me, the musicians saw the command in his face. He twisted his wrist to count the beats and conducted the orchestra into the march at the opening of the Allegro.

I stared at the hands in my lap. The keyboard seemed so far away from them. When I looked up at the baron, I felt the sting of tears in my eyes and a shaking in my jaw. He smiled and nodded encouragement, then he gestured for the woodwinds to answer the theme.

We approached the moment for me to play. I raised my hands and brought them through the brief scales with which the piano enters the concerto. By the time I neared the conclusion of the opening movement, I sensed a new strength in my fingers and through my shoulders. I improvised an intricate, exhilarating cadenza. My body felt weightless, drifting above the floor and the stool, connected to nothing but the keyboard.

I took in a long breath and lifted my head toward the baron. He led the orchestra into the serene second movement.

The music soothed me. Every note spoke to me like the voice of my brother when we had been children rattling from town to town in the coach my father bought for our longest tours. Wolfgang's smile beamed from the keyboard and his laughter reached out of the body of the piano.

In the final movement, I grew exhilarated by the speed of the arpeggios and scales. The joyous theme carried me to a sense of such complete triumph and life that I barely heard the applause.

Baron van Swieten gestured for me to stand.

I bounced on my toes with excitement. Constanze wept against her sister's shoulder.

In a strong baritone, the baron called, "Brava." He rose, and the crowd followed him.

I laughed when I caught his eye. My delight was pure and childish. But it was because of the music, not the applause.

He stepped forward and raised the silver head of his cane to quiet the crowd.

"Our dear Maestro Mozart has departed from us," he said. "He left the astonishing power of his music, whose secrets we amateurs might only guess at. But he understood, as until this moment we did not, that someone remained who might reveal those mysteries to us." He reached for my hand. "Thank you, Madame de Mozart, for restoring to us the great spirit of your lost brother."

I lifted my lower teeth over my upper lip and grinned. It wasn't the most sophisticated of gestures, but after all no one knew as well as I how lost my brother's spirit had appeared to be—nor how strongly it had returned to me.

As the audience applauded again, I vowed that I'd repay Wolfgang for this moment, no matter the cost to my soul or my body. I had rejoined him in his music. Once more we were together.

9.

*B*aron van Swieten concentrated on his cane, as though its tip clicked out a message in an obscure code on the floorboards. The muscles of his face were tight. I saw he struggled to overcome a strong emotion, but his voice revealed it. "It was as though Wolfgang performed for us here this evening."

"You flatter me, sir."

He rubbed his finger beneath his nose. "Oh, I'm really not given to flattery."

"It's something I've never learned, either. So you'll believe me when I say that Wolfgang wrote of you very often and most fondly."

"Less of me, I imagine, than of the concerts he gave among my friends. I host small musical gatherings each Sunday afternoon in the great hall of the Imperial Library. We used to sing around the piano, and Wolfgang would play and sing and correct our harmonies all at once. It's as if a beloved son has been taken from me." Swieten's eyes lifted from the floor and brightened. "Will you join us tomorrow for our little musical salon? You'd honor us."

Perhaps, in Swieten's library, I'd find others who had been close to Wolfgang. They might know more about the mysterious Grotto, or at least assuage my doubts about his death. "I should be delighted. I hope my playing won't disappoint you and your guests."

"After hearing you this evening, I'm sure it shan't."

"The audience was most distinguished. It was a lovely evening of music all around."

Swieten glanced at the aristocrats and merchants promenading about the hall. "These people are stinking and corrupt. Their unwashed bodies reek beneath this tide of cologne on the air. But you're right, the music was lovely."

Though I wished only to relish the thrill of my success, I was sensitive to his evident preoccupation. "Something is amiss, my lord?"

"Let's say I have some troublesome duties at the palace. In addition to the library, I head the emperor's censorship office. But I find that I don't believe in censorship. I would have everyone free to say and write just what they wish." His smile was bitter. "I'm forever at war with those in the emperor's service who'd ban all but the Bible."

Lichnowsky came to Swieten's shoulder with Stadler and Constanze.

My sister-in-law took my hand. "You played so beautifully," she said.

"The concerto was divine, Madame de Mozart," Lichnowsky said. "Wolfgang was so much ahead of his time, almost not of this world, an angel. One might say he was too much for us. That's why he died—to enter a heaven fit for him."

Swieten rapped the floor with his cane. "Nonsense, my prince. Wolfgang was of this time more than any of us. He represented its new ideas of enlightenment and freedom and equality, of scientific and intellectual inquiry. You'll find all these things in his songs and in the themes of his operas. If there are some who'd prevent the course of progress, it's they who truly drove him to his death." He looked about as though he might find such people nearby and wished to confront them. He radiated a potency that was at odds with the lace and embroidery of his costume.

"But Wolfgang's ideas can't be killed off," he continued. "He never allowed his fears to silence his art."

I caught a glance between Lichnowsky and Stadler that carried a warning. I wondered about Swieten's last words. What had Wolfgang had to fear?

"So Maestro Mozart was free of fear? If so, it was a fault." A smooth, cultured voice behind us. "'Fear should sit as the guardian of the soul, forcing it to wisdom.'"

Our group turned toward a gentleman in a green coat who smiled at Baron van Swieten, twirling the curl of his periwig above his ear.

"But Aeschylus goes on to add that mercy should take precedence over harsh judgment," Swieten said. "Your classical learning is faulty, sir."

"If only I might ruminate all my days in your Imperial Library, I'd correct this fault. Alas, my duties are of a more practical nature."

Swieten squared his jaw, but was silent.

The newcomer opened a gold box, tapped some snuff onto his knuckle, and sniffed it into each nostril. "I overheard the prince calling Mozart an angel. Perhaps our departed maestro has, indeed, become a myth. After all, he's now in the realms beyond earthly power." He lowered his voice. "Even if none of *us* has yet escaped it."

Lichnowsky took a step backward. His eyes registered fear. "An angel? I meant it as a figure of speech. I—"

"There's too much unthinking speech nowadays and not enough reverence for the way things are." The gentleman bowed to me. "Madame de Mozart."

His manner made me hostile and pedantic. "I ought to correct you, sir. I'm Madame Berchtold von Sonnenburg, to be precise," I said.

"Oh, I'm aware of that." His expression was devout and insouciant, like a priest before a cowering sinner, pleased by the knowledge that secrets could never be hidden from him.

Under that gaze, I felt a quiver of disquiet, as though by mentioning my husband's name I had implicated him in some conspiracy as yet unknown to me.

Swieten grimaced. "Madame de Mozart, may I introduce to you the Count von Pergen, our Imperial Minister of Police."

I curtsied.

"I didn't take you for a music lover, sir," Swieten said.

Pergen toyed again with the curl of his wig. "I'm a great devotee of Maestro Salieri. Even when the court composer conducts the music of someone else. I must commend you, Herr Stadler, on the choice of music."

Stadler straightened like a guilty boy before a stern schoolmaster. "Thank you, your Honor."

"You didn't include any of Maestro Mozart's more tactless compositions."

"Tactless?" I said.

"The count refers to *The Marriage of Figaro*," Swieten said. "He disapproves of the opera because it portrays a servant triumphing over his master, I assume."

"No doubt your brother was deceived by the Italian reprobate who wrote the text of that opera," Pergen said. "A Jew, no less."

"A convert to Christianity," Swieten said.

"I fear the conversion never really took hold. But the fellow is gone. Let's hope we hear no more of this seditious work."

Now it was my turn to be tactless. "I thought *Figaro* was an exquisite opera."

Pergen snorted a scornful little laugh. "Dear lady, if a poison tasted vile, it would be harmless—no one would ever swallow it. The poisoner gives it the flavor of fruit or sugar to seduce us to our doom. Your brother's beautiful music was the seduction, and *Figaro*'s outrageous philosophy was the poison. One might say the same of Freemasonry, for example." He glanced around our group.

Lichnowsky and Stadler cast their eyes down. Swieten sighed.

"Young men are drawn into Masonry with promises of equality and other fine ideas," Pergen said. "Only then, when they have given their mortal oath to be brothers, do they learn that they must pursue an agenda that undermines our state."

I thought of Wolfgang's letter. "Can the Masons really be so dangerous?"

"The Revolution in America was led by a cabal of Masons. You've heard the names Washington, Jefferson, Franklin? All committed to the overthrow of the natural order of government and monarchy. All Freemasons. They're condemned by His Holiness the Pope."

"But Wolfgang was just—"

Pergen raised an eyebrow. "Continue."

"Just a musician." I felt feeble before him. "I can't imagine Wolfgang engaging in subversion."

"Maestro Mozart had his first great success some years ago with *The Abduction from the Seraglio*. You recall the opera?"

"Naturally."

"Its theme of reconciliation between the nations and races is to be applauded. Unless one understands that it may have been the work of a member of the Illuminati."

"Come now," Swieten said.

"Who?" I asked.

Swieten scoffed again, but Pergen spoke to him with an archness that silenced him. "Baron, you can explain the Illuminati's purpose so much better than I."

Swieten shifted on his feet, like a man I had seen once at a prizefight in the village fair, balancing to take another blow but knowing he might not stand it.

"Please," Pergen said, "do explain to the lady."

"It's a secret society founded in Bavaria. Its aim is to end religious and national prejudices." Swieten recovered himself and turned to Pergen. "Hatreds fostered by priests and government ministers."

"You may call them religious animosities and national enmities. I call them simply religion and nations, which ought never to be overthrown," Pergen said.

Constanze took a small step toward the count. "Wolfgang wasn't opposed to religion, and he loved his emperor."

"He named the leading character in that dangerous Illuminist opera Konstanze, did he not?" Pergen said. "Don't think I'm fooled by the alteration of an initial letter, madame."

Constanze gasped and rocked on her heels.

"You go too far, sir. You can't suspect the maestro's wife," Swieten said. "The Illuminati are men, as are all Masons."

Pergen shrugged. "At least Maestro Mozart's little Masonic compositions weren't a part of tonight's fare. I much prefer the music he wrote when under the influence of a natural fear."

Wolfgang's fears again. "What inspired such dread emotions in him, my lord?" I said.

"Death and final judgment. I was in St. Michael's Church a few days ago for Maestro Mozart's memorial service."

Swieten supported Constanze by the elbow. She seemed faint. "We performed Wolfgang's Requiem Mass there," he told me. "He had been writing it at the very moment of his death."

"A wonderful composition. It was inspired by the awesome majesty of God," Pergen said. "This was greater music than the petty bickering of spiteful servants in a despicable operatic farce."

"Were you at the church to hear the music, or were you visiting your dead?" Swieten drew himself to his full height and flared his nostrils.

"It's true that the Pergen family tomb is set into the floor in the aisle of St. Michael's." Pergen took another pinch of snuff. "But I've no need to visit them. The dead are always with us."

"Indeed." Swieten's grimace was sarcastic and impatient.

"I see them walking among us even now. Sometimes I find it hard to tell the difference between a living man and a ghost." Pergen reached out to stroke the embroidery of Swieten's silver coat. "Until I touch him."

Constanze's knees gave out and she collapsed onto Swieten's arm. During the fuss to revive her, Pergen made a deep bow to me. He stepped back with his left leg, flourished his hand, and folded himself low over his right knee. His extended leg seemed to curve inward in its silk stocking, giving him the look of a flunky in a satirical cartoon.

He sauntered away at a measured pace.

We descended the stairs of the Academy and waited by the brazier as the carriages pulled up to take people into the night. Swieten climbed into his coach with a tip of his hat to me. Lichnowsky was so pale after his encounter with the police minister that he appeared to shine in the interior of his carriage like a thin slice of the moon. Stadler left without a word.

Vienna had seemed to be weeping for my brother's death. But there was self-pity and terror in the mourning of his friends. It was as though they expected something just as dreadful to happen to them. I had intended to go in the morning to Wolfgang's grave, but the conversations in the concert hall convinced me to delay. Before I went to pay my last respects, I needed to be sure of what had happened to him. In our lives, we had become silent to each other. At his graveside, I would allow that there be no more secrets between us.

Constanze stared into the dark side streets as we returned

from the Academy. The police minister's suspicions terrified the poor woman. I restrained my enthusiasm for our performances. It was no time for celebration.

Still, my joy in the music I had played that night overpowered even Pergen's intimidations. I was thrilled to have performed Wolfgang's compositions before such a distinguished audience, to have felt the presence of the brother I had thought so lost to me.

I bade Constanze good night and watched her carriage rattle toward Kärntner Street. I breathed deeply of the silence in Flour Market Square and perched at the edge of the pool around the Fountain of Providence. Dangling my fingertips in the freezing water at the feet of the goddess, I hummed the melody of Wolfgang's concerto and wondered about the private life of the Baron van Swieten.

10.

*T*he morning light sparkled on the old, warped glass of the windows and shone through a gap in the curtain around my bed. The sunshine was silver, like the pure light that emanates from a saint in a vision. Silver like Baron van Swieten's coat. I stretched my arms above my head and kicked off the heavy winter covers. The excitement of my performance at the Academy still warmed me.

Lenerl tied the curtains to the bedpost and curtsied. "*Guten Morgen*, madame."

I sat up and pulled my knees close to my chest under my nightdress. "Morning, my dear."

"You were very excited when you came back last night, I must say, madame. The concert must've been wonderful."

"It was a night I've dreamed of for so long. I suppose I'd given up hope that anything like that would ever happen to me."

The girl grinned and held up my dressing gown. "You couldn't even get a sentence out. You danced into bed like you were dreaming."

I stepped into my slippers and let her wrap me.

Lenerl poured a hot chocolate from the breakfast tray at the dresser. I tasted it with such pleasure that I shuddered.

"I shall perform again today, Lenerl," I said. "For the Society of Associated Cavaliers."

"Very fine gentlemen, no doubt, madame. You're making the most of Vienna."

I heard a shadow of disapproval in the girl's voice. She was simple and religious, and she would have expected me to spend the week on my knees beside Wolfgang's grave. But I was in no mood to discipline her. "There's a lot for me to accomplish here," I said.

Heavy clogs ascended the stairs. A knock at the door. Lenerl eased it back with care, so that I shouldn't be seen undressed. She held out her hand, red with housework, received a letter, and brought it to me.

I recognized the crest impressed in the wax seal. I had seen it on Baron van Swieten's coach as I walked to Magdalena Hofdemel's home. I caught my bottom lip between my teeth.

The baron's letter confirmed that I should play for his Associated Cavaliers that afternoon. He requested that I join him for lunch first. He had something in particular he wished to share with me alone, he wrote. His language was formal and impersonal, but it excited in me an enthusiasm I knew to be unseemly.

"Give me my writing case," I said. "I have to reply right away. Then you may dress me for a lunch with the baron."

Lenerl unscrewed the lid of a pot of ink. On the edge of the dresser I wrote a brief note to the baron accepting his invitation.

"Imagine, lunch with a baron, madame. Have you met him before?"

"I encountered him last night at the Academy."

"A baron. No wonder you were so dreamy when you came back here."

"Don't think I'm so impressed by the title of a baron, my girl," I said. "I've performed at the keyboard for kings and empresses."

Her head inclined a touch. I saw she was thinking that playing the piano and taking lunch were two different things. I sealed the note and found a few kreuzers in my purse.

"Take this downstairs. Have the landlord send a boy to the Imperial Library to deliver it."

Lenerl curtsied and left.

I stroked my hair where it fell blond across my collarbone. With both hands I lifted it so that it sat above my head.

I wanted to be on my way to the baron now. I reached for the bag in which Lenerl had packed ribbons for my hair, and I pushed aside the breakfast tray. My stomach was tremulous and excited. I had no more appetite for chocolate.

Before I set down the bag of ribbons, I noticed another letter on the dresser. It had been concealed beneath the tray. In the small, jagged characters of my husband's handwriting, it was addressed to me.

I cut it open with my thumb. Berchtold must have written it less than two days after I left for it to have arrived so soon. I read the first line, but I was too distracted to take in its meaning. I chose for the moment not to examine why that might be. I started once again at the beginning.

My dear lady,
Madame, I trust you have arrived in good
health in Vienna and that you have paid your
respects to the widow of your brother. You may
be sure that your children and mine desire your
swift return and await you in a state of noisy
agitation that is most disturbing to my office
and duties. I very much hope your initial purpose
in traveling to Vienna has been swiftly disposed
of. Such things as murder, of course, occur
among the disreputable elements of Viennese
society, but I trust you have uncovered a more
natural explanation for your brother's passing.

The vivacity with which I had awoken drained away. In the mirror on the dresser, my expression was sheepish, like a catechism pupil scolded by a nun.

Your son, the letter went on,

doesn't neglect his studies at the piano, though
I have noticed that his childish playing is
somewhat enervating when my offended ears are
not later compensated with the greater skills at
the keyboard of his mother.

I imagined little Leopold at the piano and smiled to think that my husband suffered the boy's music with my own performances in mind. That he recalled with pleasure the times when I played for him was as close to intimacy as he would allow himself to come in writing.

The door opened and Lenerl entered. "The boy's on his way to the baron, madame," she said.

I looked down at my husband's letter with a shock of remorse for the pleasure I had taken in the baron's attention. I thought of my religion and the vows I had made before God. I had always been devoted to Our Savior and the Virgin Mother. On Good Fridays I made a tour of Salzburg's churches, praying in more than a dozen of them and climbing the steps to St. Kajetan's on my knees.

Lenerl stared at the letter in my hand. Her face tightened with guilt.

"Sorry, madame, I forgot all about that letter. It came last night," she said. "You returned so late and you were in such fine spirits. I didn't want to spoil things."

"Why should this letter have spoiled my mood?"

"Well, it's from—you know." She wrung her apron in her hands. "Isn't it? From him?"

Servants had been a trouble to me all my life. My dear father always said I was too harsh on them. Perhaps it was so, but I couldn't allow this affront to pass. I widened my eyes and pursed my lips to deliver a rebuke. Then I saw her eyes tearing, and I pitied her.

But for some chance, it might've been me quaking before a displeased mistress. When Wolfgang left Salzburg for Vienna, I had collapsed into an emotional confusion and taken to my bed in tears. With my brother gone, I had feared I'd have no one to support me, if my father passed away. Papa used to say that a woman left alone would be forced to enter domestic service. I wouldn't have been a lady's maid like Lenerl, but even as a child's governess I'd have been miserable. I liked it little enough when compelled to care for my stepchildren. My character wasn't given to servitude. My father knew that and was anxious about it until he found a husband for me.

I folded the letter and made my voice forgiving. "My clothes, Lenerl."

She went to my traveling chest.

"The mauve dress with the lace over the bodice," I said.

"Of course, madame."

I slipped my husband's letter into my writing case. Later I'd write to him of my invitation to the baron's Society of Associated Cavaliers. Berchtold would be pleased that I was received by a high imperial official. He needn't know that I hoped to learn more from Swieten about Wolfgang's last days, nor that an emotion I preferred not to name moved in me when I first saw the baron outside the Collalto Palace.

Lenerl laid out the dress on my bed. She took my underwear from the drawer. The bones in my corset rattled when she held it up. I slipped off my nightgown and let her wrap the stays around me.

"Have you seen a little of Vienna while I've been making my visits?" I said.

She tightened the laces. I breathed out and she pulled them harder.

"I had a little walk up to the cathedral, madame," she said. "To pray there for my mother's soul. Such a place."

"You like Vienna?"

She took the dress from the bed and lifted it over my head. "It's got a bit more going for it than St. Gilgen, madame."

Over my shoulder, she caught my eye in the mirror. She lowered her eyes to the laces at the back of my dress. "No barons back home, either."

She was right. No one in my village was like Baron van Swieten.

11.

I entered Library Square past the field-green façade of the Palffy Palace, where Wolfgang had often played for his aristocratic sponsors. I whispered a prayer for my brother and hummed one of his arias.

Across the broad square, the monumental limestone of the Imperial Library shone in the crisp midday sunlight. My pulse sharpened, the old kick of excitement that used to come over me as a child whenever I entered a palace. I whistled Wolfgang's aria through my teeth.

The porter directed me to an alabaster staircase whose windows enhanced the golden light of the day, rather than filtering it. As I climbed, I didn't merely leave behind the dirt and noise of the streets. I ascended to a place where it seemed everything might be illuminated.

At the head of the stairs, a door of polished chestnut opened onto a breathtaking hall. Oak bookcases rose in two decks, high over the cream marble floor. Roman numerals in gold leaf designated their place in the library's catalogue. Thick ivory-colored pillars reached up to a bright fresco on the ceiling.

A librarian came down a stepladder with a pile of volumes under his arm. I asked him to lead me to Baron van Swieten. He shoved at the shelves behind his ladder. A segment of the bookcase pivoted, opening into a hidden room big enough for little more than a single desk.

The baron perched on the windowsill with a manuscript across his lap.

"Madame de Mozart." Laying the manuscript on the desk with care, he dismissed the librarian. "Thank you, Strafinger."

He wore a black frock coat with mother-of-pearl buttons and an embroidered blue vest. He dropped into a bow, my hand to his lips.

I glanced at the open manuscript. His eyes followed mine, and he smiled.

"Parchment. A map of the Roman emperor's postal system. Look here." He stepped to his desk and beckoned for me to come close. "See there, the tip of Italy. Here is Serbia, Albania, Greece."

The map was as long as my arm. Its irregular edges were a deep brown with age. "How old is it?"

"It was copied sometime around the fifth century."

I caught the scent of dry sweat that adheres to parchment.

"Isn't it beautiful?" he said.

"Truly."

"Beyond beautiful, really. Stunning." He gestured toward the door. "Let me show you something else."

From a desk in the library's main hall, he pulled out a wide, shallow drawer. "As a native of Salzburg and a musician, you'll enjoy this."

I looked down on a page of primitive musical notation, the red lines of the stave marked with crosses for the notes. A Latin text ran beneath the music.

"Can you read it? Look." The baron sang through the first line in a breathy baritone. "One of the privileges of heading the library is that no one may tell me to be quiet. This is the story of the death of St. Benedict. It's intended to be sung as part of the church liturgy. It was copied in your hometown six hundred years ago."

"Astonishing."

The baron beamed like a proud parent. Absently he spun a globe almost as tall as me that charted the constellations. "Astonishing, yes. But also outdated and of little use to a musician today."

"I suppose so."

"Unlike Wolfgang's music. He'll still be full of life to musicians born six hundred years from now."

The thought of Wolfgang's work seemed to fill the baron with energy. He swung his arms wide, catching his elbow on the stepladder. His librarian, on the highest step, grabbed a column for balance. Swieten glanced up at the startled man and moved along the hall.

Under the grand fresco of the central cupola, he held his hands behind his back and spoke toward the polished marble of the floor.

"Had I known you were coming to Vienna, I would've delayed the funeral, madame," he said.

"Please don't apologize. I understand that you organized and paid for the rites. I feel only gratitude to you, sir."

"You know the current custom—it was a simple funeral.

An ordinary grave which will be plowed over in ten years to save space."

"Of course."

"It's a little inhuman, perhaps," he said, "but the spirit of the departed is more important than his bones, don't you think?"

"Surely."

He brought his hands in front of his chest as though in prayer. "I would have you know, madame, that I examined Wolfgang's body before his doctors took it away to the cathedral for his funeral service."

My fingers grew numb and cold, as if Wolfgang's ghost reached out from Swieten's palm to grip them now.

"My father was physician to the Empress Maria Theresia," Swieten said. "Ever since my birth I've been surrounded by men of science. I still keep up with the latest research. In medicine, too. So I consulted a doctor in whom I have some confidence. I told him I had . . . doubts about your brother's death."

I seemed to suffocate with tension, as though the bones in my corset drew tighter over my ribs. "What did he tell you?"

The baron stared into the sunlight that shimmered through the high windows. "He disagreed with the diagnosis given by Wolfgang's doctor."

I turned from him to hide the excitement and apprehension in my face. "But Wolfgang's doctor discovered a rash on the skin that confirmed the cause of death as a fever."

"That same doctor opened Wolfgang's veins to try to cure him, as if we still lived in medieval times. He ascribed

Wolfgang's sickness to an excess of black bile and phlegm."
The baron slapped his hands together. "The man is a fool."

"Then what killed my brother?"

Swieten stroked his neck. "The doctor I consulted also attended Wolfgang at the end. His name's Sallaba. I respect his research."

"It was he who differed as to the diagnosis?"

"It was."

Swieten hadn't been the only one of Wolfgang's friends to doubt the cause of death. Yet while the others were terrified of the truth, the baron had sought it out. His love for my brother and his belief in justice drew me to him more strongly even than the sympathy he had shown for my nervousness at the Academy the previous night.

He went to a stone spiral of stairs. I followed him up to a gallery along the second level of bookshelves. Behind a pink marble bust of an old emperor with a long flowing wig and empty eyes, he waited for me. Below us, the library was silent, except for the pacing of Strafinger as he replaced some volumes from a trolley.

"Early in the year, when Maestro Haydn departed to give some concerts in London," Swieten whispered, "Wolfgang embraced him and said that he feared they would never see each other again. Haydn's getting on a bit. I assumed at the time that Wolfgang meant the journey or the effects of the London rain might kill the old fellow. I now think I misread his comment."

"You believe *Wolfgang* expected to be the one to die?"

Swieten grasped the base of the bust. His fingernails whitened with the force of his hold. He drew a heavy volume in light brown leather from the nearest shelf. He leafed through the book, turned it toward me, and jabbed at the page with his finger. "*Acqua toffana.*"

The poison Wolfgang believed had been administered to him.

The Italian text described a poison developed by a Sicilian lady named Signora Toffana in the sixteenth century. She sold it to women who wished to dispose of their husbands without leaving traces.

"A blend of arsenic, deadly nightshade, and lead," Swieten said. "It's colorless and has no taste when mixed with water."

I glanced down the page. The symptoms of the poison were hallucinations and delusions, agitation and obsession with death, stomach pains, failure of the kidneys, swelling, and— I came to a halt. "Skin rashes."

Swieten bit at his lip. "Each of those symptoms was manifested in Wolfgang."

"Delusions?"

"He saw enemies everywhere. When I came upon him in the street not long ago, he lifted a finger to his lips to quiet me, looking around as though someone dangerous were tracking him." Swieten took back the book. "But perhaps it was no delusion."

"Wolfgang's letters to me never mentioned that he was threatened by anyone."

"Vienna has changed in the last few years, madame. Years when—you'll forgive me for mentioning it—you and Wolfgang weren't in touch. Viennese artists used to be free to express themselves. People conversed without restraint, even about politics."

"But now?"

At the end of the gallery a door opened. A page in a red jerkin stepped through. "Lunch is ready, my lord," he said.

Swieten slipped the book back into its shelf. "These days nobody can afford to make a mistake."

I followed him along the gallery. As the page shut the door behind me, I thought I caught the sound of whispering in the library. I paused, but I heard nothing more. I decided it had been merely the brushing of my skirts against the bookshelves.

12.

*I*n the baron's apartment, thick, leather-bound volumes and musical scores weighted the lid of the clavichord. I glanced at some sheets of music propped before the keyboard. Incomplete and with many corrections, they had been scribbled beneath the title *The Lost Master*. Swieten grabbed them, shuffled them together, and hid them beneath a treatise on Hungarian agriculture.

"Your own composition?" I asked.

"I wished to express something of my feelings about Wolfgang's death," he said.

"May I see it?"

He shook his head. "Like all my music, it's as stiff as I am."

I thought of my husband, silent and upright at his accounts. "I'm used to searching for the softness beneath a rigid surface. I'd like to play it."

His face grew open and vulnerable, then he grimaced. "It would offend your hands to touch such a combination of notes," he said. "I'm content to perform as an amateur among friends. My compositions I must keep in this room. My guilty secrets."

He traced his hand over a yellow arabesque painted on the dark green wall. With a shrug, he extended his arm and led me through the door to a dining room decorated in blue and white damask.

The chamberlain poured an emerald white wine. Swieten raised his glass. "A fine old Smaragd, from the Wachau, just along the Danube from Vienna," he said. "About twenty years old. Very rich. Excellent."

"I've grown unaccustomed to fine wine."

"When you live in the mountains, it's natural to drink the pure lake water. Here in Vienna the water's so tainted it'd kill you in a week. You must choose between wine, beer, or the graveyard." The mention of death halted the glass on its way to Swieten's mouth. He rolled his lip as though offended by the bouquet.

I drank. "The wine's very good, your Grace."

"I apologize for my somber mood," he said. "I shouldn't have revealed my doubts about Wolfgang's passing. They're probably nothing more than the result of too many years in the palace. Conspiracies are everywhere here."

"Don't think that I came to Vienna merely to mourn at Wolfgang's grave, sir. I, too, have my doubts about the way he died."

"Do you?" He spoke with eagerness and relief.

"Indeed, I do." I ran my finger around the lip of my glass. "I see that his passing affects you deeply."

He tapped at the tabletop. "I found all my inspiration in Wolfgang's music. Now he's gone, I'm in despair. Not only personal despair, but despair for our entire Empire."

The servant laid a bowl of beef broth before me.

"The Empire?" I said.

"New ideas of equality and freedom have transformed intellectual life across Europe. I persuaded the emperor to base his policies on this spirit of enlightenment." Swieten circled his spoon through his broth, but ate nothing. "Then came the Revolution in France. Our emperor started to fear an uprising in the Austrian Lands."

"Is a revolution really possible here?"

"The other great monarchs of Europe have faced the impossible. King George felt the sting of defeat in his American colonies less than two decades ago. King Louis was thrown out out of Versailles itself only a few months past. Still, I doubt it'll happen here."

"Thank God."

"Of course, it's easy for me to be so relaxed about it. I have less to lose than the emperor." He stared at his spoon and laid it on the table. "Our monarch pays no heed to my reforms now. He fears my liberality might allow radical ideas to enter Austria. Have you finished your *Rindsuppe*? Take this away."

The servant removed the dishes and brought a steaming ceramic pot from the sideboard.

"These days the emperor listens to the suspicions of Count Pergen, whom you met at the concert last night. The Minister of Police, as you may have noticed, is no liberal."

From the pot, the servant drew out a slice of boiled beef with a thick band of fat and ladled some potatoes onto my plate.

Swieten watched the servant set a plate before him and frowned. "I'm losing my battle against Pergen. The battle to preserve a place in our society for progress and free thought."

When I had entertained noblemen on the harpsichord as a child, I had known nothing of their struggles to promote their ideas and to make the state in the image of themselves. Listening to the baron, I felt foolish to have been so concerned with the color of my ribbons and the dressing of my hair. All around me had been conflict over issues of great importance, yet I had tinkled out a gavotte or a minuet.

"Wolfgang's music allowed me to believe this battle would soon be over," the baron said. "His art embraced these new ideas and gave me the feeling that they were unstoppable. Even Count Pergen would tap his foot to one of Wolfgang's contredanses. Your brother's compositions were irresistible in a way that my arguments in the emperor's council could never be."

"I'm sure that only your grief for Wolfgang makes you see things so darkly." I heard the emptiness of my words and so did the baron.

"Without him, my failures are highlighted rather too brightly," he said. "Perhaps it's because I miss Wolfgang's inspiration that I've turned to desperate speculations about how he met his end. I beg you to put them aside."

"In only three days in Vienna, I've learned some curious things about Wolfgang's death. I don't know what to make of them, but they're more than mere speculations."

I drew the paper from my pocket and unfolded it. I saw that Swieten recognized the handwriting as my brother's even across the table. His features were instantly alert. He laid down his knife and fork, and reached for the page. I passed it to him.

"What was Wolfgang's Grotto?" I asked.

The baron flicked his wrist for the servant to remove his plate. "Grotto?"

"He appeared to have in mind some new Masonic lodge at the time of his death."

Swieten read over the two paragraphs of Wolfgang's writing.

The servant hovered, waiting for the baron to remove his free hand from the rim of his plate. He stood back when he saw his master's preoccupation.

"A new lodge?" the baron said. "How did you—?"

"Constanze found it among Wolfgang's papers."

He shoved his plate away. He whispered Wolfgang's name, as though admonishing a child.

"Herr Stadler seems to believe that this put my brother in danger," I said.

"You'd think that with so many aristocrats among the Masons, Wolfgang would see it as a pleasant debate club. You know, just a way to meet influential patrons," Swieten said. "Indeed, it was—for a time. Until our emperor concluded that the Masons spread radical ideas, and placed restrictions on them."

"So people are afraid to be known as Masons now?"

"Terrified. Most of the Masons simply resigned from their lodges. They've no wish to risk a confrontation with the emperor."

I drew in my breath. I knew my brother's dissident temperament. "But not Wolfgang."

The baron stared at the paper I had given him. "Wolfgang became one of the most prominent men in the remaining Viennese lodges. He wrote music for their meetings."

"And he allowed his participation to be widely known?"

"He didn't hide it."

"Did he put his life at risk?"

Swieten watched the sunlight, green through his wine-glass. "You haven't seen *The Magic Flute* yet?"

"With respect, my lord, is that the answer to my question? Did *The Magic Flute* endanger Wolfgang?"

"I'd be delighted to accompany you to a performance."

"I heard that it's full of the symbols used by Masons in their secret practices."

"So it is."

"Could Wolfgang have been threatened by Freemasons angry that their secrets were revealed?"

Swieten tipped his head. "I don't know. But I'm sure Wolfgang only wanted to show the emperor that Masonry aims to create a brotherhood of mankind. That it's no threat to his power as ruler."

The naïveté of the project sounded true to my brother. "You believe another Mason murdered Wolfgang, don't you?"

"The Masons live in a state of mutual suspicion," he said. "They're infiltrated by Pergen's agents. They fear to be accused of treachery against the emperor so much that they become traitors to each other."

He handed the Grotto note to me. I returned it to my pocket, as he went into his study. Through the door, I saw him draw a file from a pile of manuscripts and open it. He came back to the doorway.

"Listen to this. 'The police are charged with observing what people are saying about the monarch and his government, what the general attitude of the people is concerning the government, whether there are any malcontents or even agitators at work among the upper or lower classes, all of which is to be regularly reported to headquarters.' This is a secret decree of the emperor granting new powers to Pergen to employ agents at every level of society. No one may speak freely anymore."

"But one may *sing* freely?"

He raised his finger. "Wolfgang believed so."

"Was he wrong?"

"When people speak out against the state, only a few radicals on the fringe of society pay attention."

"But when Wolfgang played his music—"

"Everybody listened."

The bells sounded the Angelus, three strokes followed by a pause for prayer, repeated three times. I whispered a Hail Mary between each set of chimes.

When the chimes stopped, Swieten cleared his throat, as though prayer were an embarrassment. "My guests will be arriving. It's almost time for your performance."

13.

*T*wo dozen gentlemen of the Society of Associated Cavaliers chattered and swigged from their cups of hot wine, as the footmen lit the lamps in the Imperial Library. Across the courtyard, the lanterns of the emperor's ceremonial apartments glimmered amber through the double-glazed windows.

I took my seat at the piano. Baron van Swieten stared at the men until they quieted like guilty schoolboys on their gilded chairs.

"Madame de Mozart," he said, with a bow.

For the occasion, I had practiced one of Wolfgang's fugues, because I remembered he had written of Swieten's liking for that style of composition. It was a complex piece by a mature musician. But these men already knew that Wolfgang. I wished to show them the Wolfgang I had known. I closed my eyes and recalled a room at an inn in Amsterdam when I was fifteen.

Wolfgang would've been ten years old. My mother was

reading a new English novel, though she managed to learn little of that language despite our year in London. Our father was writing another of his letters to our landlord in Salzburg enumerating our many successes. I was at the piano, while Wolfgang scratched his quill over the notebook he used for composing, humming a bland little melody.

Even as I lifted my hands to the keyboard in the Imperial Library, I recalled the way my brother and I had laughed as he forced his way onto the piano stool, bumping his hip against mine, so that he might try out the set of variations he had written. They were based on a song by the prince of Orange's court composer.

So, instead of the fugue, I went into that trilling Dutch theme. I continued through the syncopated variation, the triplets, the shorter notes, the Adagio.

I became that fifteen-year-old girl once more, happy and playful, her family around her. Within the music I created a fantasy life in which I hadn't lost touch with my brother. In this fiction, I had spoken to my mother and father as I had wished to speak, rather than as I thought they'd prefer to hear me. These fictional parents duly consented that I should follow a musical career, like Wolfgang.

While I played his music, I imagined that he hadn't died.

Then the variations were at an end. I was in the Imperial Library once more. The cupola resounded to the applause of some of the most powerful men in Vienna.

And Wolfgang was dead.

The florid faces around me beamed at one another in enjoyment. Anger tightened my hands into fists. When I played Wolfgang's music it was as though he were alive. How could they hear the piece reach its end without experiencing once more the tragedy of his death?

Baron van Swieten's lips were firm, not smiling. I saw that for him, too, Wolfgang died every time he heard his music. We watched each other until the applause ended.

Someone cleared his throat as if in embarrassment. Swieten collected himself. "Herr Gieseke, please."

I hadn't noticed the actor when I entered. He came to stand before the piano. I gave him a smile of surprise and recognition, which he didn't return. He wore the same black coat I had seen on him in the pavilion at the Freihaus Theater. He had scrubbed the milky stain from its hem. His cravat was high around his neck and he had brushed his thinning hair into a romantic sweep back from his brow. I took a chair beside Swieten.

Gieseke declaimed the opening lines of an ode by the scandalous poet Schiller. I had heard that it portrayed ordinary men as equal in station to their monarchs. Yet the aristocrats smiled approval as they listened to the actor.

"Anger and revenge shall be forgotten. Our deadly enemy shall be forgiven."

The strength of Gieseke's voice surprised me. When I met him, he had been sneering and shrill. I wondered if an actor speaking lines might be transformed as I was when I sat before the keyboard.

"Delivery from the chains of tyrants."

Swieten's chin quivered, moved by the poem.

"A serene hour of farewell. Sweet rest in the shroud."

Gieseke paused.

In the silence, he caught his breath with a hiss and lifted

his eyes, expectant and fearful, toward the cherubs and sages painted in the dome above.

He raised his arms high. "Brothers, a mild sentence from the mouth of the final judge."

"Bravo." Swieten shot to his feet and applauded.

As the other cavaliers followed the baron, Gieseke dropped into a brief bow. A tightness across his brow looked like doubt. Was he unsure that his own sentence would be as forgiving as the poet suggested?

Swieten clapped Gieseke on the shoulder and thanked him. The actor shuffled toward the punch bowl.

"More music," the baron called.

Maestro Salieri took the piano, Swieten and two others the vocal parts, to perform an oratorio by Handel.

A heavy man in a blue coat with gold edging and white breeches settled on the chair beside me. His brows were low, and his face gave the impression of an eager wolf dog, jocular and predatory.

"Your performance was excellent, madame," he said, straightening his short, white wig.

"Thank you, sir."

"I had the pleasure of a close brotherhood with Maestro Mozart." He smiled in the direction of the singers and spoke without moving his lips. He glanced to the side to take me in. Though he was at home in the palace, his eyes had a feral meanness that belonged in the slums.

"I'm at the disadvantage of not hearing your name, sir," I said.

"The Baron Konstant von Jacobi, madame." His accent was harsh and clipped, northern German.

A close brotherhood with Wolfgang. I recalled his name and the triangles he had signed after it in Stadler's souvenir book. Another Freemason.

"A pleasure to meet your Honor. I detect by your voice that you're not Viennese. What brings you to this city?"

"Duty. I'm the ambassador of the Prussian king."

"Had you shared your—your brotherhood with Wolfgang a long time?"

"Since his visit to Berlin two years ago. We renewed our acquaintance soon after, when I took up my post here."

"In Berlin. So you first saw him with the Prince Lichnowsky?"

The prince sat across the room, stiff and upright, his back not touching the support of the chair.

"Yes, with that scoundrel." The ambassador flicked his hand in dismissal in the direction of Lichnowsky.

I found myself offended by this attack on a friend of Wolfgang. "He seems to me a fine gentleman."

"You think so? He's like one of the barges floating down the Danube toward Hungary. He travels well in the direction of the current, but he can't make the return journey against the tide. A trimmer, you understand, who follows other men. Without principle." The Prussian licked his lips and grinned. "He ought to be broken up for firewood, as those barges are when they reach their destination. Quite a scoundrel."

"But also a brother, is he not?"

He saw the inference and watched me as though amused by my deduction. "One can never be sure of escaping wickedness, even in the most brotherly of circles."

I had no wish to debate Lichnowsky's character. I returned

to Wolfgang. "On your first meeting with Wolfgang, he sought a position at the court in Berlin."

Jacobi puffed out his cheeks. "The king wished to employ him and, therefore, extended the invitation. But there were cabals in the king's service opposed to Maestro Mozart. Threatened by his talent, no doubt. It was, in the end, beyond my lord's power."

"He decided not to impose his will?"

"Political matters extend beyond the drawing of borders and the deployment of troops, madame. Those who covet important jobs at court are much given to maneuvering. Musicians are no exception, although your brother was naïve in such things."

I knew this to be true enough. On our travels, our father had always taken care of the flattery that gained our entrance to palaces and salons. Perhaps Wolfgang never learned the skill.

"I've been commanded to buy certain of Maestro Mozart's manuscripts for shipment to Berlin," Jacobi said. "You'll understand this is a sign of the esteem in which your brother was held by the king. I'll visit the widow soon to make my selection."

I didn't question that Constanze would be willing to sell. I thought I might go through Wolfgang's scores first to claim a few of my favorites. I also recalled that he often wrote notes to himself in the margins of his compositions—reminders of issues and ideas unconnected to music. Having received no letter from him since shortly after our father's death, I wished to search in those scribblings for some of what he might have experienced in the years that were lost to me.

The singing concluded. Maestro Salieri conversed with Baron van Swieten while he improvised on a tune with a Turkish flavor.

Prince Lichnowsky bowed before me. Rising, the Prussian ambassador shook the hand of the man he deemed a scoundrel. He sauntered to the punch bowl, where I noticed Gieseke putting away a goblet of wine in a single draft. The actor glared at me, his eyes and skin shining as they had when I first met him.

Prince Lichnowsky's Tokay swirled, scarlet and amber, in his glass as he perched on the next chair.

"A fine performance, madame. I always admired the classical symmetry of Wolfgang's music."

"I'd call that a surface appearance," I said. "Wolfgang creates a strain in each piece. Our pleasure is in his inspired resolution of that tension."

The prince rolled the Tokay in his mouth. I saw that I had contradicted him too frankly.

"It's not in looks alone that you resemble your brother. He, too, couldn't let a foolish remark pass on the subject of music."

"I didn't say it was foolish, just—"

"Wrong."

Fast footsteps approached and Gieseke stood over my chair. Close enough that I picked out the remnants of the stain he had tried to scrub from his coat.

"The Baron van Swieten urges that I accompany you to your lodging, madame." His voice was louder than necessary, as though he intended to quash any objection by the prince.

As Gieseke extended his hand to me, Lichnowsky shrugged and swallowed the last of his Tokay.

14.

*G*ieseke's coat flew open as he crossed Library Square. In the twilight, his wide eyes were jaundiced by the lanterns in the palace windows. He reached for my elbow. "Madame, I beg of you to hurry."

He rushed me past the Augustinian Church, repository of the hearts of the Habsburg dead. I struggled for balance on the icy cobbles. On Dorotheer Lane, he dragged me into the entryway of an apartment house.

"I warn you, you're in great danger here," Gieseke whispered. "I told you how Wolfgang met his end."

His fervor scared me, but I forced my mind to slow down, to concentrate in spite of my nerves, as I did when I performed.

"You told me how you think he died, but not who killed him," I said. "For all I know it could've been Hofdemel, and he's dead, so he can hardly be a threat to me now."

Gieseke tightened his hold on my arm. "Why do you mention Hofdemel?"

I dropped my eyes.

"Oh, the affair with his wife," he said, distracted and somehow relieved.

I wriggled against his grip.

He watched the corner of the street, as though to see if we had been followed. His clammy hand rested on my wrist, where he had pulled me toward our hiding place.

"If you really think you're safe," he said, "why is your pulse beating like a frightened bird's?"

I wrenched my arm from his grasp and walked into the quiet street, heading away from the palace toward my lodging. He followed, staying close to the wall and keeping an eye on the spray of lantern light at the corner.

We turned toward the Flour Market. The street was narrow, unlit, and empty.

My foot slipped in the manure of a horse. Gieseke grabbed me to prevent my fall.

"Thank you, I—"

He pushed me against the wall. I caught the scent of the hot punch he had drunk at Baron van Swieten's salon. I cried out, but he covered my mouth with his hand.

He brought his face close to mine. Though it was obscured by the dull light of the day's end, I saw an imploring desperation there. If I was in peril, it wasn't from this man.

"Don't you care?" he whispered. "Don't you care that you endanger others?"

I pulled my face away from his hand. "Whom do I endanger?"

"Those who know the truth about your brother."

"Why should that be dangerous?"

"Don't play dumb. I explained it to you."

"All those ridiculous combinations of the number eighteen?"

I pushed at him, but he held me to the wall. The rough edge of a brick bit at my back.

"You pretend it's ridiculous, but if you didn't suspect something wrong in the way Wolfgang died you wouldn't be here," he whispered. "You didn't come to Vienna just to trot out a few tunes for his aristocratic patrons."

I ceased to resist him.

"I'm right, aren't I," he said. "What else do you know? Who else has told you of the way Wolfgang died?"

I thought of the baron and his book of Italian poisons. "What am I to do, Herr Gieseke? You tell me that Wolfgang was murdered, but you don't want me to stir things up?"

Low voices approached the corner. Two men turned into the street.

Gieseke pressed his hand to my mouth again. "Pretend you're a whore," he said.

I grunted a protest into his palm, but he thrust himself toward me and lifted me against the wall.

The men paused as they passed us. One of them chuckled and voiced some encouragement to Gieseke, before he moved on. The other waited. He hissed to his companion and came closer.

Silhouetted against the pale walls across the street, he lifted his arm. A knife glinted, icy and gray.

I screamed into Gieseke's hand. He spun and went at the man low, taking him down.

Gieseke rolled and was back on his feet. He kicked at the attacker's arm. The knife tinkled across the cobbles.

The second man landed a blow against Gieseke's head, but the actor twisted and wrestled him into a doorway.

"Get away, madame," he called.

Gieseke groaned as the first man rejoined the attack, butting him in the small of his back.

I made to move farther along the street.

"Not to your lodging. They'll look for you there," Gieseke shouted. "Back to the palace."

I hurried down Dorotheer Lane and across the square. The door of the library was barred and the lights had been extinguished within. I ran along the wall to the carriageway beneath the imperial ballrooms.

Rushing into the lamplight, I was sure I'd find guards who might come to Gieseke's aid. But I saw no one.

I went on, past the high, stained-glass windows at the rear of the palace chapel, fearing that I'd be too late. Then I heard a voice from the darkness.

"Madame, you're distressed."

I turned. Prince Lichnowsky came into the lamplight. He wore a high fur collar and a tall sable hat.

He frowned. "Madame de Mozart?"

I grabbed at his glove. "Do you carry a weapon, my prince?"

"A sword, but—"

"You must come with me."

I dragged him across the square. With the little breath I had, I explained that Gieseke was in danger. The prince picked up his pace, opening his coat and drawing his sword. I recalled the Prussian ambassador's accusation against Lichnowsky. Yet he seemed brave and noble, neither a coward nor a scoundrel.

The street was empty. The doorway where Gieseke had fought the two men was quiet. Lichnowsky slid his sword into its scabbard.

I stood in the doorway and relived the moment in which I had glimpsed the knife. I felt sure it had been coming at me, not Gieseke.

"Allow me to accompany you to your inn, madame." Lichnowsky extended his elbow.

I recalled Gieseke's warning not to return to my lodgings. I wished to give myself time to think. "I'd prefer to walk awhile—among a crowd of people. To make me feel safe, not so isolated. It'd calm me down. Do you mind?"

His lips tightened with a hint of impatience. He bowed. "An honor."

I took his arm.

"I have a meeting I must attend. I mean to say, it's a social obligation, you understand," he said.

"I don't wish to detain you."

"Perhaps you may rest and recover yourself in an anteroom, while I conduct my business."

"I thought it was a social affair?"

His mouth hardened once again. "The Graben is a short distance this way," he said. "Even on an evening as cold as this, it'll be full of carriages on their way to the theaters. I'm sure you'll find it most diverting, and you'll be quite safe with me."

15

*W*e came onto the Graben at the Plague Column. The lamps of passing carriages flickered over the memorial to those who died of the Black Death. Nine carved choirs of angels ascended toward its gilded peak. To me, it seemed the cherubs were slipping down to Hell, grasping in vain for the elusive light of salvation above them. I prayed for the faith to see the sculpture as it had been intended.

The street was loud with the hammering of horses' hooves and the bellowing of coachmen, spurring on their teams and warning pedestrians. Lichnowsky kept close to the walls of the houses, clear of the carriages.

"I'm concerned for Herr Gieseke," I said.

He looked about to be sure that no one listened, though it was barely possible for me even to hear my own words over the chaotic traffic.

"There's nothing to worry about," he said, holding my arm close to his side as we walked. "Don't be fooled by an actor's fine diction. He's sure to be acquainted with many disreputable fellows. Believe me, he'd know just how to deal with them."

Had I turned and left the pavilion of the theater when I first encountered Gieseke, I might have allowed that the prince's assessment was true. The actor had seemed nothing more than a disheveled lout. But I had stayed. Now I couldn't forget what he had told me and with what genuine terror he had spoken. "Herr Gieseke believes—"

"What?"

"That Wolfgang was poisoned."

"The man's just repeating wild rumors."

"Wolfgang thought he had been poisoned, too."

Lichnowsky stared at the Holy Trinity on top of the Plague Column. "The poor man," he murmured.

"He never confided this in you?" I asked.

The prince lowered his head.

"Will you help me?" I said.

"At your service, my dear madame."

"I must know if it's true."

He returned his gaze to the monument. I wondered if he was thinking of those who had been saved from the plague, or of those who had succumbed to it.

"Please." I brought my hand out of my fur ruff and laid it on his wrist.

"What if it *were* true, dear lady?"

I confess I hadn't considered how I might act once the truth was uncovered.

He noticed that I was at a loss. "There's more of Wolfgang in you than is at first apparent," he said. "I saw how you bounced on your heels after your performance at the Academy of Science. You would've cavorted with joy just as he used to do, had you not held yourself back out of shyness in front of new acquaintances."

"What does this have to do with—?"

"Your naïveté, too, is like Wolfgang's. It was this which placed him in a dangerous position."

"So you, too, believe he was murdered?"

"No, I don't." He smiled his reassurance, fleeting but kind. It was strange to see his inert features even so briefly animated. We had embarked upon a topic which perhaps robbed him of his habitual rigid control.

"There are dangerous people in this city," he continued, "who had reason to dislike Wolfgang. If you persist in questioning the manner of his death, they may conclude that you'll blame them for it."

"But I'd never accuse—"

"And attempt to silence you before you can slander them as his killers." He leaned close to me. "Wolfgang never quite grew up. Your brother believed he could behave exactly as he did as a little boy, when he played at the palace and jumped into the lap of the empress. He didn't notice how Vienna was changing. Don't be fooled by the gentility of Baron van Swieten's Society of Associated Cavaliers. This is a bloody town of vicious passions."

A coachman bawled an insult at a man who had attempted to cross the street on foot, cracking the whip over his horses and making the poor fellow run to avoid a trampling. I watched the relieved pedestrian hurry into a side street.

The prince lifted his hand to point along the road. "Look down there. Before the cathedral spire. Four years ago a murderer was broken on the wheel in that square. Tied up and tortured. Each of his bones was smashed with a mallet, one by one. Then he was hung. The good people of Vienna, our great city of art and culture, turned out in their thousands to enjoy it. They're no more civilized than anyone else."

I covered my face with my hand. No doubt Lichnowsky thought I was merely a squeamish woman. Yet that wasn't all. I was thinking of my husband and the small tortures he decreed as official punishment for those convicted of smuggling and poaching.

Lichnowsky continued, "The city's intellectuals, including some of those you met at Swieten's salon, were there to savor the prisoner's agony, too."

I felt the horror of the execution, as though my own bones were being crushed. My legs weakened and I dropped against Lichnowsky's chest.

He brought his hands under my arms to support me. "I've spoken too roughly, madame. Forgive me. You must have time to gather yourself." He led me through the traffic. "Across the way here, it's the house where I must meet my—my friends. Let's step inside."

I caught only glimpses of the street through my dizziness. The long, white heads of a team of carriage horses dipping in unison as they trotted by. The feathered brown flanks of a passing mount brushing against me. A heavy door opening. A well-appointed hallway. The butler's eyes, dark hollows, as he bowed before Lichnowsky.

16.

*U*p a flight of broad stone stairs, Lichnowsky led me into a large chamber. I blinked hard, but the walls remained a blur of bright colors. He sat me on a divan.

"A glass of punch will revive you, madame." He snapped his fingers at a footman.

"Where are we?"

A piano played in the room above us. Wolfgang's variations on a minuet by the director of royal chamber music in Berlin. Very well executed.

"We've arrived before the others come for the meeting," Lichnowsky said. "But you mustn't be seen by them, I implore you."

The footman approached with a cup of warm punch on a silver tray. I took a long sip.

The images on the walls of the chamber took shape. They were painted in the Venetian style, sensuous and shocking. Animals and naked men and women lounged across rocks, draping themselves in vines and dining on vivid fruits.

Footsteps ascended the stairs, with a rumble of jocular male conversation. The men went into another room and closed the door.

"What is this place?" I said.

"Madame, I believe those were the guests arriving for my meeting. You must rest here. I'll return as soon as certain affairs are completed." Lichnowsky patted my wrist and went onto the landing. He gestured to someone farther up the stairs.

I heard a few measured paces across the floor above. The piano stopped playing. Lichnowsky continued across the hallway.

I drank the remainder of my punch. The footman took away the empty cup and shut the door behind him with care.

The nudes on the walls taunted me with their carefree pleasure. I frowned at these representations of Paradise, innocent and pure. Closing my eyes, I was back on the dark street as Gieseke wrestled our attackers.

Music sounded across the hall. A small orchestra of perhaps eight instruments.

I stepped through the door onto the empty landing.

Men shouted, and I started in fright. The voices continued in song. The cry had been merely the song's opening phrase.

"Loudly let the instruments sound," they sang, "announcing our joy."

The music came from behind double doors across the hall. In E-flat major. The men's chorus gave way to a single tenor and two bass singers.

It was impossible not to recognize the style, disciplined and graceful, the melody clear over the complex counterpoint. This was my brother's composition.

The tenor sang of a "great mystery." Then he added, "Sweet are the Masons' feelings on such a festive day."

Lichnowsky's "business" was with his brother Masons.

As I laid my hand on the knob of the double doors, I recalled that Gieseke had said dire punishments were imposed upon those who revealed the secrets of the Brotherhood. What would they do to a woman eavesdropping on their rites?

The chorus joined in with the tenor. Under cover of the louder group singing, I edged the door open.

I entered a large, long hall. The corner nearest the door was unlit. I could remain here without detection, provided no one left the room.

The Masons sat along the walls on velvet benches, perhaps thirty of them, their swords at their sides. I noticed Stadler seated not far from me. The musicians played at the far end of the hall.

Behind the orchestra was a raised stage. On a painted backdrop, a triangle veiled the sun. Its glowing outline was blocked in with stones. I saw that it was a pyramid, such as ancient Egyptian rulers constructed for their burials.

Lichnowsky had told me the king of Prussia built an Egyptian garden at his palace in Berlin. Perhaps its architecture resembled the design of this hall. The symbols daubed across the stage surely represented secret mysteries of the Masons, like the triangles in Stadler's souvenir book. I wondered at the Egyptian connection. Could the king of Prussia be a Mason?

On a table in the middle of the stage lay an unsheathed sword and an open volume the size of a family Bible. Upon the book, a skull.

A man walked into the lamplight on the stage. It was Lichnowsky. He wore a white apron around his midriff.

"Esteemed brothers in the Craft, it has pleased the everlasting Master Builder to tear our beloved brother from the chain of our Brotherhood." His voice was loud and slow. "Who did not know him? Who did not value him? Who did not love him, our worthy brother Mozart?"

Lichnowsky examined the gathered men. His expression was hostile, as though his eulogy were an accusation. Did he expect someone to confess that he hadn't loved or valued Wolfgang?

"Only a few weeks ago he stood in our midst and with magic tones added beauty to the dedication of our Masonic Temple. We have heard his music again tonight. He was a most enthusiastic follower of our order. He was a husband, father, friend to his friends, and a brother to his brethren."

Lichnowsky returned to his seat.

One of the men rose from his bench. He was the librarian I had seen when I visited Baron van Swieten.

Stadler crossed the floor, blindfolded the man, and led him to the center of the room. He called on him to introduce himself for his initiation into the lodge.

"Petitioner Josef Strafinger, son of Michael, twenty-seven years old." His voice was low and probing, as though he were searching through the darkness of the room from behind his blindfold. "Born on May first in Rohrau, Austria. Of Roman Catholic faith. A commoner. By occupation, assistant to the imperial librarian."

Stadler lifted his sword. "A warning, and your oath. Swear to speak to no one of the secrets of the Brotherhood or the practice of our Royal Art, nor to write or engrave the least syllable or character of them on any surface beneath the canopy of heaven. Should you do so, swear by the Grand Architect that you know your penalty shall be for your throat to be slit ear to ear and your tongue to be torn from your mouth."

The blindfolded initiate repeated the oath. His mouth was solemn and hard, when he had finished.

I imagined this moment in Wolfgang's own initiation. I was overcome by a sense of the danger that had closed around him. I covered my eyes. When I lowered my hand, I seemed to see Death rush past me into the room, tearing the blindfold from the initiate's head.

But the features revealed weren't those of the librarian. It was my brother's face. I gasped. The words of the bloodthirsty oath echoed in my ears. Wolfgang's voice acknowledged the murderous fate of a traitor. He turned to me, a bloodless, blue corpse, grinning like the skull on the stage.

I heard a shriek, and I backed toward the door. The Masons turned to the entrance of the hall. I realized that it had been I who called out.

I ran. The men came after me.

Lichnowsky caught my arm and hurried me down the stairs. He pulled the apron from his waist and shoved it into the arms of a footman.

As we went into the street, the brothers gathered on the staircase. The blindfold was up over Strafinger's brow. His expression was of mortification, as though I had seen him undressing. One of the men called out, "A woman? Who brought a woman?"

The chill of the night froze me. Lichnowsky held my upper

arm as we went along the Graben. "Now you know that I'm a Mason."

I shook my head. "I already knew that. I saw the triangles you drew in Stadler's souvenir book. But I didn't know the horrors to which Masons swear."

"It's just an oath. It means nothing. It's a bit of theater, that's all."

"You were Wolfgang's brother? This was his lodge?"

"For seven years."

"Did he swear such an oath?"

"I must insist that this subject is dangerous."

"Did he?" I raised my voice. "Did he swear?"

"Stop this. It's too risky to talk about it."

We came to the steps of St. Peter's Church. He squeezed my fingers. "You're very cold. Let's go inside."

17.

*I*n the quiet half light of St. Peter's, the prince sat me in the rearmost pew. He drew a flask from his coat and raised it to my lips.

I coughed on the cognac and let my head drop back in exhaustion, staring into the shadows of the cupola. High above the altar, the angels crowned Maria. *Let them surround* me, *too*, I thought.

I took another taste from the flask.

Before the high altar, three nuns knelt in prayer. A priest came from the sacristy and murmured to them.

Lichnowsky stared at the priest. "Wolfgang's sister-in-law came to these precious men of God. To ask them to give the last rites to him."

Relief warmed my chest like the alcohol. "I'm happy to hear it. I was worried that he hadn't received absolution. Constanze's letter didn't mention—"

"The priests didn't come."

Lichnowsky spoke the words, but I thought I heard the

voice of Wolfgang whisper them in unison, pleading and lost, wandering the church, his sins unforgiven. I looked around for him, but felt only the chill on the air.

The door of the sacristy slammed shut. I turned with a start. The priest was gone.

"Why didn't they come?" I said.

"Perhaps you've heard that the Masons are a godless bunch."

"But that's not true, surely. Not Wolfgang."

"Of course not. But since when did a priest feel compelled to listen to anyone's explanations. Most of the brothers are deeply religious. Yet in the opinion of the priests, all of us are as opposed to the church as the Illuminati."

Lichnowsky rubbed his knuckle against his front teeth. "Everyone suspects the Masons. If it isn't the priests, it's Pergen. He has agents inside the Brotherhood. We must obtain permits from the police minister for new lodges and pledge our loyalty to the emperor. All this we've done."

"But the Illuminati?"

"They remain underground. No one knows who they are. Even Pergen, I believe. If he discovered a member of the Illuminati, he'd—"

I touched the prince's arm. "Go on."

"The penalty for membership in the Illuminati," he said, "is death."

I swallowed a long draft of the cognac and returned the flask to the prince.

"Did Wolfgang join the Illuminati in Berlin?" I asked.

"Berlin." The skin beneath Lichnowsky's eye twitched. He watched the nuns depart. When the door closed behind them, he drank from his flask and put it in his coat.

"I remember the performance he gave before the Prussian king," he said. "He played magnificently."

"Yet the Prussian king disappointed him. He didn't give him a position."

Lichnowsky stared at the altar. "There never was a position."

"The king deceived him?"

He braced his arms against the next pew and sighed as though he were exhausted. "I have tried, madame, to persuade you of the threats that surround you. You question the death of Maestro Mozart, a prominent man who had access to the salons of the most powerful nobles in the Empire, to the imperial court itself. A Mason who refused to adhere to the new regulations governing our Brotherhood."

I shook my head. "He wanted only to make music."

"He lies buried in a simple grave—next to a baker and a seamstress, for all I know—but his life was complicated and it touched upon issues that powerful people might wish to keep hidden."

He stared at me with such intensity that I dropped my eyes to my hands.

"For your own protection, madame, I'll tell you this much, in the hope it'll convince you to pursue this no further. Wolfgang wasn't discontented with his journey to Berlin. He accomplished the mission on which he was sent."

"Mission?"

"Our lodge here in Vienna sent him to communicate with King Friedrich Wilhelm of Prussia."

I saw the danger, though I barely understood it, just as I sensed the interior of the whole church from the few columns and buttresses visible in the evening light. "The pyramids painted in your lodge. The king of Prussia's Egyptian garden."

The prince held up his hand to still me. "Yes, damn it, woman. The king of Prussia is a Mason. He's a member of a lodge twinned with the one Wolfgang and I joined."

A cloud must have passed, because a new shaft of moonlight dropped through the turreted window at the center of the cupola. It glinted on the ornate golden pulpit. I flinched, thinking someone moved there.

Lichnowsky gripped my wrist hard. "Your brother died a death of natural causes. Throughout his life he was weakened by disease, you know that. But if you persist with your questions, your doubts shall come to the attention of the emperor's secret police. They'll wonder if there was, after all, something suspicious about Wolfgang's death. They'll investigate. They'll find no proof of murder. Yet in the course of their inquiries they might uncover the true purpose of Wolfgang's journey to Berlin. How do you think that would look for the rest of us in the lodge?"

"Like espionage," I said. "Like treason."

"Dealings with the king of Prussia, our emperor's greatest enemy. By a secret organization which already stands under severe legal restriction. Yes indeed, treason."

We left the church. The chaos of carriages on the Graben had diminished. Lichnowsky walked me past the Plague Column. Sweat glinted on his lip.

"To your inn, madame?" he said.

The thugs who assaulted me in the street might've gone on to my lodgings. Lenerl would be safe among the crowd in the barroom. Still, I ought to stay away. "I'd prefer to go to my sister-in-law."

The habitual stiffness of Lichnowsky's face had returned, but I detected a tremor beneath it.

At the gate of Constanze's courtyard, the prince lifted his hat. "You may find me most mornings at Jahn's coffeehouse, around the corner on Himmelpfort Lane. Just beyond the old Winter Palace of Prince Eugene."

"I shall be sure to see you there."

"I shall be delighted." He went back along Rauhenstein Lane.

One of Wolfgang's simplest minuets came down into the street from the apartment upstairs. A child was at the keyboard, or at least someone who played like a child. The tempo was irregular and the notes were picked out with little certainty.

At the stairs, it occurred to me that I hadn't asked Lichnowsky the purpose of Wolfgang's mission to Prussia. What had his Viennese lodge hoped to gain by sending him?

I hurried back through the entrance, but the prince had turned the corner and was gone. The street was empty and silent, except for the false notes sounding upstairs on my brother's piano.

18.

*C*onstanze greeted me with a distracted smile. She ordered her maid to prepare a hot cup of *glühwein* for me and led me into the studio.

Little Karl stumbled through the minuet at the keyboard. As I approached, he slipped from the piano stool and disappeared behind the couch.

A heavy man was bent over Wolfgang's standing desk, his boot resting on the rail. With a groan and a hand in the small of his back, he straightened and turned to me. The Prussian ambassador's grin once more had something of the joyful huntsman to it.

"Madame de Mozart." He bowed.

Constanze twitched her head toward me, surprised.

"I met the Baron Jacobi this afternoon at Baron van Swieten's salon," I explained.

The ambassador came across the room, spreading his chest. A musical score dangled from his hand and I saw that he had been examining still more pages piled on the desk.

"I decided to begin my selection of Maestro Mozart's scores right away," he said. "My sovereign is eager that he should obtain the rights to the greatest of these pieces. I thought it best not to delay. Someone else may bid for them."

The maid entered with a cup of hot wine on a silver tray. Jacobi exclaimed with pleasure, reached out and took it. As he drank, Constanze made a circle with her finger, signaling the maid to bring another.

"Excellent," Jacobi said. "Hungarian?"

"Purchased from Herr Hammer at the Red Hedgehog," Constanze concurred.

"The best, the very best." Jacobi drained the cup.

Constanze averted her eyes. I assumed it embarrassed her to be seen serving an expensive wine even as she was selling off the rights to my brother's work.

"During the winter months, Wolfgang would partake of a little of this wine, sir," she said, filling her voice with a liveliness that wasn't matched by her eyes. She was, after all, an actress who could sing of pleasure when she felt pain. "It kept his blood flowing as he worked late into the night. He often composed until two in the morning."

"Whenever inspiration came to him, no doubt," the Prussian said.

"And also when it didn't. Even a genius like my Wolfgang had to work hard at his craft."

I stepped to the desk and fanned out the first few manuscript pages. His craft, yes, and his beautiful, difficult soul were in every light stroke of the quill across the musical staves before me.

The maid brought another *glühwein*, which Jacobi again grabbed with a cry of delight.

Beside the scores lay a writing case embroidered with scenes from a garden. I lifted the silk cover. The case contained letters in Wolfgang's hand. The first was a copy of a note addressed to Lichnowsky, begging for money. The folder's spine was jammed into the pile of scores, as if the Prussian had been searching through my brother's correspondence while he bent over Wolfgang's music.

I sensed Jacobi at my shoulder. I closed the writing case.

He lifted the score that he held in his hand and slapped it onto the top of the pile on the desk. His thick fingers sprouted red hairs. He spread them across the manuscript covetously, like a drunk I had witnessed fondling a waitress in a roadside tavern on my journey to Vienna.

"Your performance this afternoon at Swieten's salon was excellent, madame," he said.

"I'm most dedicated to preserving my brother's work." I noticed that Constanze had left the room. I heard her speaking to the maid and calling for her elder son.

Jacobi wiped his nose on the back of his hand and glanced at the scores on the desk. "In that, you have a friend in my lord the king of Prussia."

"Is it for the sake of friendship that your king wishes to purchase Wolfgang's scores?"

Jacobi slipped a finger beneath his wig and scratched at his scalp. "He seeks also to guard the honor of the maestro's family, too. Naturally."

"So this purchase is more of a charitable donation."

The ambassador smirked with subdued pride, like one of my mischievous stepsons caught in an act which ought to have made him ashamed.

I stared at him hard. "Or might we call it payment for a mission accomplished?"

He righted his wig and sucked at his teeth.

"I know that Wolfgang didn't go to Berlin for a position at court. He was on a mission to your king."

"Who told you that?"

I lifted my chin.

Jacobi held his hands out wide. "A mission? To what possible end?"

That much I didn't yet know. "It was for his lodge. You're a Mason, too. Why don't *you* tell me?"

"It's a mistake common among those excluded from power and position to think that because a man is a member of a secret society he must be privy to all the hidden knowledge in the world," he said. "I don't know what you're talking about."

Constanze returned with another cup of hot wine. She brought it directly to me. "Here, sister. So that you may be as warm as our friend the ambassador." She smiled at her joke, a glimpse of the playfulness Wolfgang had loved in her.

"*Zum Wohl,*" I said. "Your health."

"*Zum Wohl.*" Jacobi took Constanze's elbow and brought her to the desk. He dropped his fist onto the pile of manuscript pages. "These, Madame de Mozart. I will take these."

Before Constanze could answer him, I lifted a hand to cover my eyes and stumbled against the desk, spilling some of my wine. I made a show of whimpering and let tears come to my eyes.

"I'm sorry, sir," I said. "You'll think me hopelessly sensitive. I was overcome by the thought of losing my dear brother's creations. It's as though he still lives in these pages, you see."

"I understand completely, madame," he said.

His voice was grudging, but Constanze fussed around me and I knew that I would secure what I wanted.

"If only you'd leave them here a few days, sir, so that I might copy them," I said. "Purely for my own purposes."

The ambassador glanced at the manuscripts. He swallowed like a card player with a bad hand staring at the pot he's about to lose. "Well—"

"Of course, sister," Constanze said. "I'll help you to copy them. I'm sure his Grace the ambassador won't object."

The Prussian drummed his fingers on the edge of the desk. "I suppose—"

Constanze took hold of one of the buttons on his tunic. "Your Grace, do relent. My dear sister's request won't delay your plans so very much."

Baron Jacobi gave a low, slow bow, exhaling through his nostrils. He made his voice cheerful. "I must go now, to meet a friend for supper," he said, slapping his heavy belly. "Music, alas, is not the only food I require."

In the door, he passed close to Constanze and dropped a purse into her hand. When he saw that I had observed their transaction, the huntsman's glint in his eyes disappeared. They darted like prey. He went along the hall with Constanze.

I flipped through the manuscripts, searching for something that might signal what the Prussian had found in them. I could discern no pattern. String quartets, a violin concerto, a piano sonata, some songs, the unfinished Requiem Mass.

I didn't doubt that they were worth whatever the Prussian had agreed to pay, and more. But when I thought of Wolfgang's secret purpose in Berlin, I felt sure Jacobi had been seeking something other than musical excellence.

From the window, I watched the ambassador emerge into the street.

He clapped his hands. A whip snapped in the dark, and a carriage rattled over the cobbles toward him. A footman in a blue coat jumped down. He helped Jacobi haul his bulk into the cab, and leaped onto the seat beside the driver, hugging himself against the cold.

A cavalry patrol clattered down the street, signaling that the hour approached eleven. The captain of the horsemen saluted Jacobi's carriage as he passed.

Constanze returned. "He has bought the Requiem, sister, the funeral Mass," she said. "I feel as though he has purchased Wolfgang's death."

And you have sold it, I thought. Right away I felt sorry for my harshness. I hugged her thin shoulders.

19.

*W*hen we broke our embrace, the Prussian's coins rat-tled in the purse. Constanze caught her bottom lip between her childish white teeth.

"One hundred ducats," she said. "For each composition. A total of eight hundred ducats."

I murmured a noncommittal acknowledgment and glanced at the scores on the desk.

In the kitchen, the maid yelped and Constanze's little dog scampered over the bare floorboards. Gaukerl arrived with a roll between his jaws. He dropped the bread at Constanze's feet.

"He snatched it from my hand, madame," the maid said.

Constanze laughed, slipped Jacobi's purse into her sleeve, and picked up the dog. "It's all right, Sabine. He can have a munch of bread for supper. Can't you, little trickster." She ripped the roll and dangled it before the eager dog.

She twirled on her toes with her pet pressed against her neck. "Sister, I'm in high spirits. Let's have some billiards."

"I haven't played in a long time."

"Wolfgang and I had a game every day. He used to smoke his long pipe and hum a silly ditty to himself. I'd have to tell him to be silent while I took my shots. The next time I'd hear the tune, it'd be a wonderful symphony." She squeezed the dog and set it down.

The burst of happiness which had come over her was infectious. I followed her into the next room. We pushed the chairs against the wall, so that there'd be room for our billiard cues.

Constanze took the first shot. She caromed her ball off the red and into mine.

"Your point," I said.

She gave a cheer and pretended to blow a trumpet.

All evening I had been preoccupied with strange revelations about Wolfgang. I still felt the terror of the knife attack, too. It was an extra beat that slipped into the rhythm of my pulse, making it irregular and frenetic. With relief, I laughed at Constanze.

She sent her ball toward mine, striking below the center with the tip of her cue so that the spin brought her back to clip the red. She whooped and shook her hips in excitement. "Bagatelle," she called.

Her exuberance was liberating. The room seemed warm, despite the frost in the window mullions.

When I took my shot, I scuffed the end of my cue into the baize. My ball trickled toward the cushion.

"You'd do better if you simply drove the ball across the table by farting at it." Constanze laughed, but was suddenly silent. She stared at me, fearful that I'd disapprove. Embarrassed points of color rose on her cheeks.

I turned my back to the table, pushed out my backside, and blew a raspberry. "Bagatelle," I cried. We hugged, giggling.

Constanze lined up her next shot, but before she struck the ball she dropped her cue onto the table. "What am I to do, sister?" She folded her hands over her face and sobbed.

It was as though there had never been a happy embrace between us. Now that she was miserable, I found I couldn't touch her. I had cried as hard as this when she married my brother, knowing that I would have to be my father's nursemaid in his old age. I hardened myself to her grief, because it recalled my own.

"Debts. Only debts," she cried. "That's all he left me."

"You have eight hundred ducats to keep you from the poorhouse." I heard the lack of sympathy strangling my voice. "It's clear Wolfgang must've made a wonderful impression on his visit to the Prussian court."

She sniffled and rubbed at her eyes.

"I mean, for him to command such a sum from the king there," I said. Back to the subject of Berlin. Just when I had started to relax.

Resentment crossed Constanze's face. The color rose on her cheeks again, but this time it was not from embarrassment. She bent over the billiard table, made another carom, and moved into position for the next shot even before the balls were still.

"Eight hundred ducats is poor return for the amount Wolfgang spent on his trip to Prussia," she said.

The balls clicked and she lined up another shot.

"All the Prussians gave him when he was alive was a gold snuffbox. With the king's crest on it." This time, it was she who made the sound of passing gas with her pursed lips. There was no humor to it.

She scratched chalk onto the end of her cue to give it grip on the ball. Concentrating on the table, she sucked her upper lip and was silent.

The easy mood was gone, so I ventured a question. "Did Wolfgang find no other way of profiting from the trip?"

Constanze missed her shot and cursed under her breath.

I bent to the table and played. My ball clipped the red and rolled aimlessly off the banks. It came to a halt with the slightest kiss against Constanze's ball.

"A lucky shot," I said.

Constanze let her head drop. "I suspected another woman."

I rested the butt of my cue on the floor and reached for her arm.

She shrugged away my consoling touch and looked into the courtyard. She spoke as though she were whispering to the darkest corners of the stable below, addressing shapes which might barely be seen. "He dallied in Prague and then in Leipzig on the way to Berlin. I believe he was detained by a—a lady."

"I can't agree."

She waved away my objection. "Disappointment always cast him into a black mood. He said he had been promised a post in Berlin. He found no employment there. Yet he wasn't dejected. He returned to Vienna as cheerful as ever I saw him."

I sought to reassure Constanze without telling her what I knew of Wolfgang's mission. "If he was happy, then he must've accomplished something else. Something that made him contented or hopeful."

Constanze cursed under her breath. "Take your shot, sister."

The cue slipped over my knuckles and skewed my ball wide of its target. It was a nervous shot, shaking with the secret that I struggled to keep. I glanced at her, but she hadn't noticed. She examined the chalk on the tip of her stick.

"When he traveled, he always sent me letters with his news. He wrote almost nothing to me while he was on that trip," she said. Her ball chipped against the others and she watched it bounce off the cushions. "Something was going on, I know it."

I took this as confirmation of what Lichnowsky had told me. Wolfgang went to Berlin with no intention of securing a position at the court. He had returned with his mission accomplished, whatever it was, and had been happy for that.

That didn't mean Constanze was incorrect about the other woman. I thought of the scars on Magdalena Hofdemel's face, given by a jealous husband. I considered that Wolfgang might have fallen into sin on more than one occasion. But I preferred to believe that he had hidden a less wicked truth from his wife, one based on a pledge to his Masonic brothers rather than to a secret lover. He might have offended his emperor, but I still hoped he hadn't wronged his God. I didn't pause to consider which violation would be more dangerous in Vienna.

When Wolfgang was young, he had been so naïve that he was often unable to fathom the jealousy and intrigue of others. I wondered if he had learned deception in the imperial capital, fawning and flattering in aristocratic salons. Was his mission to Berlin so important that he would allow his wife to suspect adultery, rather than reveal the truth to her?

"Believe me, Constanze, I know this can't be true. It surely wasn't adultery which delayed him in Berlin."

My sister-in-law laid her cue on the table. I saw that she took the indecision in my voice for disapproval.

"If he was unfaithful, you'd blame me, wouldn't you?" she snapped. "It'd be my fault for being a bad wife."

I retreated a step from the force of her anger.

"You never liked me. You and your father." Her hands were fists at her sides. "You shunned me when we visited Salzburg after the wedding and you ignored your only brother throughout the last, difficult years of his life."

"I've wronged you, I know, but—"

She pulled the purse from her sleeve and threw it onto the billiard table. "I saw how you looked at me when Jacobi gave me this money. If the king of Prussia's buying, I'm selling. That's the legacy your brother left me. You think I care too much for money? Let me remind you that you refused to share your father's bequest with Wolfgang."

"It was Papa's will—"

"And who cared more about cash than that wicked old miser?"

I started to speak, to tell her that my father had only wanted to protect me from poverty. But I knew it wasn't true. I shut my mouth and lowered my eyes. My father's denial of Wolfgang's inheritance had been the spite of an old man who felt rejected by his brilliant son.

Constanze went into Wolfgang's study and rattled back the lid of the roll-top desk.

I came to the door. Behind me, the maid whispered for Karl to follow her to the kitchen. In his crib, little Wolfgang grizzled.

When she turned from the desk, Constanze's black curls

fell across her face. She brandished a single sheet of paper and came toward me, pushing her chin forward. "Look at this. The inventory of his estate. That damned billiard table is the most valuable possession he left to me."

I scanned the penciled columns of numbers and the scribbled descriptions of every object in the apartment.

"More valuable than anything—except his scores," she said. "You understand me?"

I blinked and nodded.

"He could've made a lot more money than he did," she said. "He charged six ducats a month for lessons, but he only took a few pupils because he preferred to be composing."

Six ducats was a tremendous fee even for a famous musician like Wolfgang. I wondered again how Magdalena's husband, the court clerk, had paid for such an extravagance.

"Did I ever complain that he should compose less and teach more, for the sake of money? Never. Not me." Constanze shoved the inventory into my hands and pushed past me.

She bent over a chest at her bedside and pulled out a few jackets and breeches, tossing them onto the divan. She pressed a red frock coat to her, and she sobbed.

"He wore this at the premieres of his operas. At all his most important concerts." She ran her hand over the fabric and played with one of the buttons. It was mother-of-pearl with a red stone at its center. "A gift from the Baroness Thun. He loved it."

I held her arm and guided her to the bed. Laying her down, I folded the covers over her. She rolled toward the wall, spent with the desperation of bereavement and poverty. I stroked the hair at the nape of her neck. Then I returned the red coat to the chest.

In the doorway, the maid stood with her ruddy hands on Karl's shoulders. The boy watched his mother's shivering back.

"Bedtime, little Karl," I said.

The maid rocked the baby's cradle, while Karl undressed.

I went into Wolfgang's studio.

In the candlelight, I looked over his bookshelves. Full of memories. I picked a book of Metastasio's librettos from the shelf and touched my finger along the title page. The Turin edition of the famous court poet's works, in a set of nine volumes. It had been a gift from Count Firmian in Milan after Wolfgang played for him. My brother had been fourteen years old.

I sat in an armchair by the window, unfolded a blanket over my legs, and set the book in my lap.

Outside, players were leaving the court on Ball Lane after a late-night game of *jeu de paume*. They bade their boisterous farewells, with their shoulders hunched against the chill.

The street emptied. The darkness in the doorways rippled and shifted, as though it were a lingering thief buffeted by the wind.

The keyboard of Wolfgang's piano was blue in the moonlight. I shut the lid over the keys and went to sleep.

20.

I awoke before dawn, stiff and cold in the armchair, my hand locked in a claw around Metastasio's book. I trembled to see the night lingering outside. It hid the men who had tried to kill me and it shrouded the vicious secrets of Vienna that Prince Lichnowsky had warned me of.

I rolled my neck and told myself not to be afraid of the coming day. At this very window, Wolfgang must have yearned to see a new morning begin, pleading with the Lord to let it come, as he felt the poison work its destruction on him. He was close to me always now, whether in the light of day or in the furtive, threatening night. I decided to welcome the dawn and to pray for his soul at early Mass.

Gathering my cloak and gloves, I crept toward the door. The clock on Wolfgang's desk showed five-thirty. Constanze sprawled across her bed with the dog curled beneath her arm.

Karl sat up in his nightshirt. His dark eyes were sad, his face as pale as the glimmers of moonlight outside. I put a finger to my lips and went through the kitchen, past the sleeping maid, and out into the freezing end of the night.

At St. Stephen's, my candle flickered away into the vaults of the ceiling, beyond the ornate copper lanterns hanging from their long chains. I had grown accustomed to the intimate village church at home in St. Gilgen. The unlit spaces high above me in the cathedral felt heavy and crushing.

I took my place in the shivering crowd of worshippers. Dropping a little wax onto the back of the pew before me, I jabbed the end of the candle into it so that it'd stand.

The clergymen passed down the aisle singing a Latin antiphon and swinging incense on a jangling chain. Two of them helped the oldest priest to his knees, so that he might reverence before the altar, and then they lifted him into a chair. They draped him in his vestments, and he announced the name of the Trinity. His thin voice proclaimed our gratitude for the Lord bringing us out of another night.

I closed my eyes, thanked God for saving me from my attackers, and prayed for Gieseke's safety.

The priest sprinkled holy water on the air before him. In Greek, we asked Our Lord for His mercy three times: *Kyrie, eleison. Kyrie, eleison. Kyrie, eleison.*

"The Kyrie was, I thought, the most impressive part of Maestro Mozart's Requiem."

Shadows obscured the face of the man who spoke to me from the aisle. I stared at him in confusion.

He removed his hat, laid it on the bench, and sat beside me. With a gentle touch of his periwig to be sure it sat straight, Count Pergen turned his secretive smile on me. His eye wept a little from the cold wind outside. A tear traced over the broken veins in his cheek.

I was as surprised to find that his eyes could cry, even if only from the cold, as I was to see him at my side.

"The performance of the Requiem at St. Michael's was superb," he said.

The congregation sang the Gloria. Pergen's voice was a sharp baritone, though not unpleasant. He stared at the crucifix above the altar with a trace of suffering on his face, as though he knew the agony of that execution.

When the hymn was done, Pergen lifted an eyebrow and smiled. "What was the Prussian ambassador doing at your brother's apartment last night?" he said.

I looked at him with eyes wide. He flicked his wrist as though it were not worth explaining how he knew such a thing.

"You followed me here?" I said.

"I come to early Mass every day. I have a healthy fear of Our Lord, and anyway I sleep little. Nonetheless, I usually sit in a pew at the front. You're correct that it's not by coincidence that I find myself in this humbler seating this morning." He held out his palm. "You were about to tell me of the Prussian ambassador, madame?"

I found my throat dry and I coughed. "He was buying some of Wolfgang's scores."

"Only his scores? Nothing else?"

"What else could there be?"

"Dear lady, your brother's pranks and his silly laugh may have fooled some people into thinking of him as a harmless buffoon. But it's my job to know a man's true self. Your brother's intellect was considerable. Sadly it led him to absorb an unfortunate philosophy and to keep dangerous friends." Pergen pinched the bridge of his nose as though his sinuses ached. "Why were *you* there, at your sister's home?"

"For safety."

A lady in the next pew turned to stare down the chatterers behind her. Pergen leaned toward his candle so that she might see his face. She swallowed hard and returned her gaze to the missal in her hands.

"So you took refuge at your brother's house. Do continue." The count let his head drop to the side. A question.

"From an assault," I said. "An attempt against my life and the life of a gentleman after we left Baron van Swieten's salon at the Imperial Library."

Pergen showed no perturbation at the news of the attack.

I saw that his closed mouth was a tactic, forcing me to fill the gaps. Only the guilty fear silence, but I was compelled to run on. "I was with Herr Gieseke. I fled and now I have no idea what became of the poor man."

"Gieseke? The actor? No doubt it wasn't his first brawl of the day," Pergen said.

We responded to the choir's chorus of Alleluia.

"Did you know Gieseke wrote some of the text for *The Magic Flute*?" he said.

"But Herr Schikaneder—"

"Wrote the first draft. Your brother edited it. Then Gieseke added some verses."

The count leered, satisfied that he had shocked me. I thought of Gieseke's fear, Schikaneder's warning for him to restrain his tongue, the knife in the twilight as it descended. I had believed it was aimed at me, but perhaps Gieseke had broken a Masonic bond of secrecy and was sentenced to death.

As Wolfgang had been.

The priest started his sermon. Pergen stood and held his elbow out for me. "The monsignor's homilies are less than instructive, madame. Will you accompany me?"

"I came to hear Mass."

"We'll return for the Eucharist. I assure you I have things to tell you that have more bearing on your salvation than this priest's sermon."

He took me to the quiet transept and into the baptismal chapel. I shielded the flame of my candle with my hand. The dawn showed only its first, thin glow, white on the water of the font.

"Your brother, madame, tried to make himself a friend of the Prussians," Pergen said. "That was against the wishes of our emperor."

My features registered astonishment, but not at Wolfgang's actions. Did this man know everyone's secrets in their entirety?

Pergen bent over the font. The light reflected off the water, shadowing his face. "Your nephews and nieces were all baptized right here, you know." Gaunt and gray, his skin was wrinkled less by age than by the lack of fat that softens cheeks and chin. The lines deepened into a grim smile, as though he were crumbling to shards like shattered terra-cotta. "Including the ones who died."

I crossed myself and whispered a prayer for Wolfgang's lost children and for my little Babette, who had been taken from me. I pulled my cloak closer.

"Do you not sense their ghosts here?" His eyes scanned

the shadows, and his hand gripped hard at the rim of the font. "I see them in the holy water, washing themselves. But nothing can cleanse the diseases that took them from us."

I was quite still. It seemed that to him I was less present than the ghosts of the babies crowded around the font. He spoke to himself, or perhaps to the spirits of the lost children.

"You can't wash away a death, even with the blessing of the pope himself," he whispered. "Neither can a funeral for a godless man secure his place in heaven. His ghost will wander among us, seeking revenge."

"Godless?" The candle flickered in my trembling hands.

He looked about him with momentary urgency. Did he feel the same touch now as I had done when I sat at Wolfgang's piano, icy and light against my hand and across the back of my neck? A ghostly presence.

"Do you suggest that my brother—?"

"His funeral was in the Chapel of the Cross, on the other side of the church." His thin smile glimmered and he appeared to return to the world. The ghosts had left him. "I doubt that there has ever been such a gathering of atheists in our venerable cathedral."

I was shocked. "Sir, please."

"Masons, the lot of them. Men who wish to undermine our entire society."

"I'm sure they only wished to mark the passing of a wonderful musician."

"They gathered to wish him on his way to the place they call 'the Grand Lodge Above.' Even Heaven must bow down to the rule of these Masons, it seems. They're gripped with a mania to overthrow our government." He slapped the sandstone rim of the font. "They wish to put themselves in power, a secret elite to govern us all in *their* interests."

"Wolfgang loved the Empire." Only as I spoke these words did I realize how much I had started to question them. "I'm sure of it."

Pergen raised his chin. He seemed to perceive my doubt. He waited, like a schoolteacher before a hesitant pupil.

I tried to justify what I had discovered of Wolfgang's final months, as much for my own benefit as for Pergen. "How could the Masons be committed to the overthrow of the government? Their membership includes prominent aristocrats."

"Who better to dream of power than men already close to it? Do you know what they call the secret knowledge they guard among themselves? The Royal Art. What royalty? A few misguided aristocrats, yes, but otherwise tradesmen, merchants, musicians, and actors." Pergen crooked his arm once more and led me out of the chapel. "Your brother was a member of a Masonic lodge of the Rosicrucian type."

I struggled to remember what Gieseke had said of the Rosy Cross. I recalled the number eighteen and its connection to Wolfgang's death. I had no idea what lay behind the numbers. "I'm unfamiliar with such things."

"The Prussian king is a member of that kind of lodge. Did you know that?" Pergen laid his fingers upon my wrist as though he might measure a lie in my pulse. "Have you read through your brother's compositions for Masonic meetings?"

"I haven't seen them."

"One of them was called 'You, Our New Leaders.' As if our emperor isn't leader enough for us."

"I'm sure it must've been a poetic image. About moral or

spiritual leadership, not real power." In spite of myself, I was shocked. With all I had learned of Wolfgang's connections in Vienna, I was forced to consider that he might've been a danger to the state.

We returned to our pew as those at the front of the congregation received Communion.

"Your friend Baron van Swieten was our ambassador to Berlin some years ago," Pergen whispered.

My candle spilled wax onto my hand. I winced.

"He joined a Berlin lodge of Masons. He became very close to the Prussian royal family. One of their princesses was rather taken with him."

My jealousy was as sharp as the sting of the hot wax. I struggled to set it aside. What Pergen told me of Wolfgang was confusing enough. I couldn't allow a sinful attraction to the baron to distract me from my purpose.

"Surely you don't suspect him. The baron is appointed by our emperor, as are you," I said. "His apartments are in the palace."

"What did I just say about men close to power?" Pergen stood aside for me. "Swieten is the head of censorship for our emperor, yet he allows many dangerous books to be published."

I went up the aisle. As I received the host on my tongue, Pergen knelt beside me. The priest proffered another disc of bread. The count licked it into his mouth like a lizard catching a fly.

The deacon mumbled that the Communion wine was the blood of a man. It was as cold as ice. Pergen shut his eyes as he sipped it.

Signing the cross, the old priest bade us go in peace.

"Thanks be to God," I mumbled with the other congregants.

Pergen followed me along the aisle to the door.

"Don't be fooled by Maestro Mozart's friends, madame," he said. "It's a Viennese tradition to criticize a man while he's alive, only to laud him once he's dead."

"I believe that's a universal trait."

"How cynical, dear lady."

"Not cynical. Forgiving."

"Here they call such criticism 'graveyard courtesy.' You may wonder why your brother had such financial trouble while he lived, when all his companions were rich men. Naturally it's because they're much better friends to the memory of a poor sainted fellow who died young than they were to a real, live composer with a family to feed. Whatever he believed, Maestro Mozart was a pawn."

Pergen stopped in the main entrance of the cathedral. "He has been sacrificed," he said. "I'm sure you want to know by whom."

"Do I?"

"You've come a long way in the midwinter, if all you aimed to do was watch men like Gieseke brawl."

In the square outside the cathedral, a constable drove a line of prostitutes to sweep the cobbles. A raw wind rustled their thin skirts. Their heads had been shaved in punishment for their lewd trade. They brushed the manure and vegetable leaves across the ground with their brooms, shaking in the cold, their scalps bloodied by the careless shearing at the police barracks.

The first traders lay their baskets on the ground, where the harlots had passed. Pergen snapped his fingers at a woman selling almond candy. She deposited a little sack in his hand with a humble bend of the knee, reaching up to accept his coin without raising her eyes. He put a piece between his back teeth and crunched into it. A white trace of adulterated sugar smeared the corner of his lip. He licked it away with a bloodless tongue and strolled to his carriage.

The dawn striped the low clouds purple, as though they were bruised by the rooftops. The sky promised rain sharp enough to cut me like the pale skin of the whores' skulls.

21.

At my inn, I found Lenerl in the taproom playing a game of tarock with three other maids. A hungover breakfaster glanced up at me from his table with resentment on his ashen face. A woman with a bruised cheek and thin, bitter lips watched in silence as her husband spooned thin gruel into his mouth.

Lenerl laid a card, laughing, and took a draft of beer. Her partners threw down their hands. One of them noticed me and inclined her head to Lenerl.

The girl rose, straightening her bonnet. "Madame, *guten Morgen.*"

I raised an eyebrow. I had wondered if the men who attacked me had, as Gieseke expected, continued to my inn to track me down. From my maid's blithe demeanor I assumed that, if so, they had displayed gentler manners toward her than toward me. I was also none too pleased to see her gaming at cards when the sun was barely arisen.

The innkeeper came from the cellar, bottles of red wine

under his arm. The hungover diner greeted him with a desperate gurgle of pleasure. It was early in the day for a man to partake of wine, even in a city where the water wasn't fit to drink. Yet when one lodges at a public inn, one confronts such low types.

"I'll take my breakfast over here by the clavichord, if you please," I called.

The innkeeper bowed.

I snapped my fingers at Lenerl and went to the corner of the room. The lid of the old clavichord was open. Splashes of brown beer and gravy stained the white sharps and flats. The wood of the casing was scratched with the initials of bored drunks.

"How did you pass the night, my girl?" I said.

Lenerl's expression suggested she wished to ask me the same question. "I was here in the restaurant. With the other maids and some gentlemen."

The man who had received his bottle of wine belched, held his stomach, and groaned.

"Most elevating, I'm sure," I said.

Lenerl grinned at the uncomfortable man. "Nobody's themselves first thing in the morning, madame."

I thought of Pergen at the cathedral. The thin dawn reflecting off the font into his gaunt face as he whispered of ghosts. Had that been a moment of early-morning weakness, like the queasiness of the drunk in this taproom?

"Quite so," I said.

"And you, madame? The recital at the Imperial Library was a success?"

"Indeed, it was." I thought to tell Lenerl what had befallen me with Gieseke. But I decided that if the attackers hadn't come to the inn it would be better if the girl knew nothing of it. "Afterwards I encountered some—some gentlemen in the street, but we were separated. Did they come to look for me here?"

"No gentlemen, madame. Only a lady. And a couple of ruffians," she said.

The innkeeper brought a pastry and a pot of chocolate. Lenerl poured me a cup.

"No doubt those ruffians were the men to which I referred."

"But you said—"

"I was too polite, girl. They were no gentlemen."

"They were asking for you here in the bar. I was playing cards and I was about to speak up, but Joachim took a look at them—"

"Who's Joachim?"

"The innkeeper, madame. He looked them up and down, and he put his hand on my shoulder to keep me in my seat. He feared they might harm me. He told them they wouldn't find you here. They went off looking very angry."

I needed two hands to keep my cup of chocolate steady on the way to my mouth. I affected to dismiss the news of the men searching for me. "You said a lady came, too?"

"A Madame Hofdemel. She asked Joachim for you, so he brought me to her. It was late in the evening. I told her you'd have finished your concert and must've gone on to dinner."

"Did she leave a message?"

"She said to tell you she had come to repent."

I tore a corner off the pastry. "Repent?"

"Perhaps it isn't my place to say this, but she seemed a bit disturbed. Her face was covered. Even so, it was obvious that she'd been attacked. Cut up, I mean."

"Her husband."

Lenerl sucked in a breath through tight lips and bit at a fingernail. "I hope he pays for it, then."

"His punishment is ensured."

She took her lower lip between her teeth. I saw that she was aching to know where I had spent the night.

"After the recital, I went to my brother's house," I said. "I comforted my widowed sister-in-law and slept there. This morning I was at early Mass."

She let go of her lip. "Very good, madame."

"I didn't see you at the cathedral."

"I thought I ought to wait for you here, madame. I said all my prayers at the foot of your bed."

I chewed on the pastry. Lenerl lifted the pot to refill my cup of chocolate, but I held up a hand to stop her. The drunk slumped over his morning wine could've felt no more nauseated than I.

Wolfgang was dead. But how? At the hand of someone connected to his illegal Brotherhood of Masons? Or of the men who assaulted me in the street? Perhaps it had, after all, been the husband of Magdalena Hofdemel, avenging an adulterous affair. Why else would she come to my maid speaking of contrition?

I wondered if my brother had died with something to repent.

22

J rested in my room until midmorning, when I descended the stairs to practice at the clavichord in the corner of the taproom. I played a sonata by the Neapolitan maestro Scarlatti. The instrument had been inferior when new. Years of spilled food made the keys stick. The first diners arrived for lunch, chattering over my music. I struck a heavy, ugly chord in frustration and returned to my room.

As Lenerl dressed my hair, she picked at a knot in one long tress. I grabbed the comb from her hand and yanked at the tangle until my eyes teared. I pulled it through with a moan of pain and anger, and threw the comb onto the dresser.

Lenerl scrutinized me sidelong in the mirror. I wished to explain why I was so tense, but I couldn't confide in a servant about the dramas of the last day. Someone else would have to help me unravel my confusion.

I wandered into the Flour Market with little idea where I would go. Lenerl followed along Kärntner Street until I hissed at her to wait for me at the inn.

I regretted my outburst right away. My maid could hardly be spying on me. Yet the dimensions of the conspiracy surrounding my dead brother seemed sufficiently broad that there might even be an informer in my room. It was bad enough that the police minister had sought me out before dawn to warn me—or perhaps to enlist me as an agent, I wasn't sure. But Pergen had made me doubt those I would've trusted, like Lenerl, just as I now started to suspect those closest to Wolfgang.

I lunched at the Blue Bottle on the Staff-in-Iron Square. The room was large and noisy. A red-faced waiter with pale, thick arms laid a loaf on my table. I picked at the bread, but ate little of the soup or the beef that came next. My attitude must have seemed so doleful that the waiter brought me a glass of Tokay, after I had laid down eight kreuzers for the meal.

"On the house, madame," he said.

"That's very kind of you, sir."

"It'll warm you up." He smiled. "Though I expect you're used to the cold. Salzburg you're from, is it?"

I had never believed that I spoke with the accent of my region. Perhaps years in the village had turned the yokel speech of Salzburg from a joke shared with Wolfgang into my true manner of talking. "That's right," I said.

"Missing home, I expect."

"No doubt."

"Still, there're lots of sights to see in Vienna before you leave." He pointed a pasty finger through the window.

I followed his gesture and saw a bulky post in the center of the square. It was ringed by a heavy padlock.

"What's that?" I said.

"A couple of hundred years ago, an apprentice locksmith sold his soul to the Devil to make a lock that no one could open. His master gave him his freedom, because he'd shown himself to be a great craftsman. But then the Devil claimed him and dragged his soul down to Hell."

"A most moral reminder to the public."

"Apprentices hammer nails into the post to remember the lad who sold his soul."

I sipped my sweet Tokay. "Or to remember the Devil."

"Maybe that," he said. His smile wavered, and he snatched the kreuzers from my table and tugged his fair hair.

On the Graben, the air felt clear. Pergen had tried to undermine my impression of Swieten by mentioning his membership in the Masons and his connection to the court in Berlin. But it was to the baron that my thoughts returned when I looked for comfort and safety. In the hours since I had seen him, I had experienced only danger, menace, and mystery. I recalled the way he had calmed me before I played at the Academy of Science—without words, by the inclination of his head and the confidence of his smile.

I turned along the Cabbage Market toward the palace. The afternoon light grew stronger the closer I came to Swieten, until the Imperial Library burst into my sight, its walls white and gleaming.

As I climbed the sweeping turns of the marble staircase, I heard a single violin. I stopped outside the door of the library's great hall and listened. It was a solo by Johann Sebastian Bach, the master from Leipzig and a favorite of Wolfgang's.

Baron van Swieten stood at the center of the library with a

violin beneath his chin. The lofty cupola seemed to accentuate his height. Eyes shut, he rocked to the tempo of the music on legs that were strong and elegant.

Strafinger noticed me from the gallery. The clerk gave me a short bow and went toward the cupola. When Swieten finished his piece, Strafinger cleared his throat and inclined his head toward the door. Swieten twisted with the violin still at his throat.

With a smile, I applauded.

The baron laid his instrument on a pile of books and picked up his coat. He came toward me, shrugging his wide shoulders into it.

"I like to play in that very spot," he said. "Wolfgang always said it had perfect acoustics."

His face was fresh and alive with the music. To my confusion, I felt once more jealous of the Prussian princess whom Pergen said had shared an affection with the baron. An awkwardness came upon me. He took it for disapproval of his remark or of his musicianship perhaps, because he cleared his throat and added: "Wolfgang never needed perfect acoustics to produce perfection. In my case, even that cupola can't rescue me from mediocrity."

A lock of his hair had escaped the black ribbon with which he tied it at the back. It must've come loose as he played. I lifted my hand as though I might push it away from his face, but I checked myself. He noticed the motion and gathered the strand of hair himself, his eyes on the floor between us.

I glanced around at the tall bookshelves and the busts of old emperors. "Baron, it isn't music that brings me here," I said. "I need your counsel."

He led me behind the shelves to his office. He shoved the door shut and poked at the dwindling fire in the grate.

Outside the window, in the park behind the palace, a man in a yellow suit embroidered with golden thread walked at a stately pace along a path of limestone chips. Servants and ladies, noblemen, hounds and lapdogs trailed him in a pack, jockeying to be near him. He paid no attention to them.

The emperor, I thought. Alone with his fears and suspicions. I searched for Pergen among the jostling courtiers, but I couldn't make out faces from such a distance.

"I believe Wolfgang may've been involved in dangerous things," I said. "So dangerous that your suspicions about his death appear more and more valid."

The baron lifted the vent of his coat to let the fire warm the backs of his legs. "What has happened?"

"Men with knives attacked me and Herr Gieseke last night."

"Where?"

I noted that he was the first to hear of Gieseke's involvement without suggesting that it had been merely a brawl among low-living actors. "Not far from here," I said. I recalled the knife in the night, and I heard the shrillness in my voice. "Then Count Pergen came to me at early Mass—"

"Pergen himself?"

"He made me suspect all Wolfgang's best friends."

"Including me?"

I bit my lip.

"It's quite understandable, Madame de Mozart. I, too, am responsible for these dire thoughts of yours. It was I who told you Wolfgang was poisoned." He smiled. "What did Pergen say about me?"

"He was talking about the Masons, the danger they pose to the emperor."

Swieten shook his head.

"He said you were a Mason," I told him.

"True," he said. "I thought you had guessed it. Is it so damning?"

I thought of the Prussian princess. She had hit a raw point in me, but I saw nothing that connected her to Wolfgang's death and I didn't wish to introduce the question of romance to my discussion with Swieten. "Pergen said you had a particular bond to the king of Prussia, our emperor's enemy."

The baron crossed the small office and beckoned to me. Taking a key from his vest pocket, he opened a drawer beneath the bookshelf.

At the center of the drawer, a turquoise sash with a red border was embroidered with golden leaves and sunbursts shining out from four symbols. They were letters from an alphabet I had seen many years ago on the exterior of a synagogue in the Netherlands. A triangle of garnets surrounded them. Next to the sash lay a small paper-covered book bearing the two legs of a compass in its design.

"I shan't hide it from you, madame," Swieten said. "The crest on this sash attests that I'm a brother Mason. I can show you the secret handshake if you wish, but you'll find that it's not for such trivialities that we enter our noble lodges. Neither was it for such fetishes as you see in this drawer that Wolfgang joined our Brotherhood."

"Why *did* Wolfgang join?"

"To be among men who recognized his true nobility. To be the equal of those who paid him to perform his music. To be at peace with the world. In any case, my years in Berlin were spent in the service of our emperor. Pergen wastes his time in suspecting me."

"You were a personal friend of Prussian royalty."

He locked the drawer and pulled a thick volume out of the shelf above. "My father made this study of vampires in Moravia at the request of the Empress Maria Theresia." He opened the book and showed me the title page. "But that didn't make him a vampire."

"Did it make him a believer in vampires, though?"

"My father reported that the whole thing was peasant superstition." Swieten shut the book and slid it into place on the shelf. "When Wolfgang was upset or preoccupied, he found music soothed him. And you?"

I thought of my frustration at the clavichord that morning. "Usually."

"Then perhaps we might talk more after you've played for me?"

"Perhaps it'll help me see things clearer," I said.

"I'm quite certain of it." He took my arm and led me back under the cupola.

I sat at his piano.

The baron laid his hand on my shoulder. His touch flickered with heat like a naked flame. For a moment, I felt that I couldn't breathe.

"Would you sing for me?" he said.

"Very well."

"An aria. 'I wish to explain to you.' Wolfgang wrote it to be inserted into a production of an opera by Anfossi."

"I know it. He sent a copy to me."

I relaxed the muscles of my throat and played the introductory passage. This aria always touched me, with its secret pleading to a lover who's promised to another. The baron had been correct about the acoustic effect of the cupola. My soprano held in the air with all the longing my brother had written into the song.

> *I wish to explain to you, O God,*
> *what my grief is.*
> *But fate condemns me*
> *to weep and stay silent.*

Swieten held his hands behind his back and stared toward the ceiling. I let my voice ring around the cupola, so that we were encircled by Wolfgang's music, by my breath.

When I reached the high D that signals the approaching end of the piece, the baron turned away and his shoulders shuddered. I wondered if he was thinking of the genius so recently lost to us.

> *Part from me, run from me.*
> *Of love, do not speak.*

I concluded the aria. The joy of music making felt so great that I thought I might float up into the dome.

The baron's eyes glistened. He bowed with great solemnity and held out his hand. He took me to a staircase in the corner of the cupola.

I entered the spiral steps first, but I noticed that he looked about the library before he followed, as though he wanted to be sure we were alone.

His breathing was heavy and deep, as he came behind me. I held my skirts to clear each step. We climbed for some minutes. I felt perspiration on my lip.

We reached a narrow gallery high in the cupola itself, close enough to touch the ceiling fresco. The paintings were distorted by the foreshortening that would make them seem natural when viewed from the floor of the library. Famous men of science peered at maps of new lands, directing their telescopes at the farthest horizon. The shading of their robes was made with gold crosshatching. They leaned against columns painted like soapy marble.

I glanced a hundred feet down. Fear stabbed in my stomach. I put my hand to my eyes and swayed against the balustrade.

The baron took my wrist. "No, you must look, or you'll fall," he said.

I stumbled and found I was close to him.

"I apologize," I whispered. "I feel such tension."

"Because of the height?"

"Not only that. These things I've learned about Wolfgang's death. If he was involved in a mission to Prussia—"

"A mission?" He narrowed his eyes.

I leaned over the balustrade again and lurid colors overcame my sight. I shut my eyes. "It might concern ruthless men.

I don't know if I can safely investigate further. But I must, I owe it to Wolfgang."

I barely knew it, but he had taken my other hand, too, and drawn me to face him.

"Madame," he said.

I opened my eyes. The gold buttons on his simple waistcoat angled to the light with each of his breaths, glinting.

"The emotions your singing evoked in me——" he said. "You understand? I——"

It had been love that almost lifted me into the air when I finished the aria. I couldn't pretend it was otherwise.

Still I tugged my hands from his grasp and hurried to the staircase. With my foot on the first step, I turned. He smiled distantly, as though recalling some long-ago happiness.

I descended the stairs, breathing harder than I had on the way up. I thought of my children on the shore of the Abersee. I wished that these steps, which seemed to go down forever, would open onto the village square on the day before Wolfgang died, and I might again be Frau Berchtold and not the woman who had survived an assault in the street and who was filled with fear and who loved a baron in the Imperial Palace.

Under the cupola, I turned a circle, looking for Swieten in the gallery high above me. I wanted to see him there, to feel his smile reach me.

Without a sound, he was before me. I lifted my foot to approach him. I would've thrown myself into his arms, had he not spoken, had he only reached for me.

"Tonight I will take you to hear *The Magic Flute*."

His voice was formal, as though on this floor he was the imperial librarian, rather than the man who had stammered about his feelings at the top of the stairs. But his eyes were gentle, and so only for a moment was I disconcerted.

"Yes," I said.

"First I want you to come with me. There's someone you ought to meet."

23.

*T*he baron's carriage turned into the entry of a well-appointed house on Bäcker Street. In a fresco above the gate, an unsuspecting cow rested beside a vicious wolf, a propaganda remnant of the wars between us Catholics and the Protestant heretics. As the carriage passed under the entrance, I seemed to hear the painted predator snarl.

Swieten stepped down to the courtyard and held out his hand for me. When I took it, I shed the fear that had come over me with the wolf. On the wall behind him, two carved angels placed a gilded crown on a stone Madonna. Her blank face was accusing as I stood beside a man who had all but declared his love for me.

The baron led me up the steps to the seigneurial apartment. An external gallery ran from the stairs to the door, decorated with curling black wrought iron. He tugged on the bellpull. A peephole in the door slid back, and a pale, rheumy eye frowned through.

Swieten jerked his chin in command. The bolt went back

and an old manservant ushered us into a dingy kitchen. I coughed at the foul odor in the room.

The manservant shuffled toward the front of the apartment. As we followed, the sting of sulfur grew stronger in the air.

We came to a darkened room which, I assumed, would have overlooked the street had the shutters been open. My eyes were adjusting to the blackness, when there was a burst of green light.

I cried out, and the baron's hand was on my arm once again. He removed it almost as quickly as the light faded. His touch shivered through me just as the brief flash had found every corner of the room.

The manservant opened a window to push the shutters back. The sulfurous scent cleared, replaced by the reek of animal feces and damp fodder. The salon was crowded with glass bottles and bubbling liquids.

A short man stepped into the shaft of light from the window. He wore an old-fashioned shoulder-length wig, its white curls framing a plump face that appeared younger than the headpiece. His stubby hands rubbed at a pair of spectacles with a cloth. His eyes bulged from their sockets, as though he were in the last moments of strangulation. He set the glasses on his nose, and his eyes disappeared into the thick lenses.

"Ah, my dear Baron van Swieten," the man said. "I apologize for any shock I may have caused."

"What was that eruption?" Swieten said.

"I'm trying to find a cure for toothache."

"With explosives?" Swieten leaned over the dishes and bottles on the table.

"With light."

The manservant shoved open the final shutter. Under the table, a dozen rabbits lounged in a cage on a layer of dirty straw.

"Everything is light and nothing more. Your tooth, too," the short man said, pushing his spectacles higher on his nose. " 'Let there be light.' Our Holy Bible tells us there was no existence before light, except for the spirit of God. This wall, this bench, you yourself—all just condensed light."

"Hence this experiment?"

"Ah, well, but that flash just now was an extraordinary effect I hadn't anticipated. It didn't happen last time, not to that extent. Odd, most odd." The man reached under his wig and scratched at his neck.

Swieten inclined his head toward me. The little man rushed to kiss my hand.

"Dr. Matthias Sallaba, at your service, madame," he said. His cheeks were a lurid pink. Dry skin peeled in flakes the size of a thumbnail around his mouth. His face looked like the wall of a poor man's basement, its plaster peeling away to reveal the brick beneath, mottled by neglect. He saw that I noticed these imperfections and he rubbed his neck again. "I've a little mercury poisoning, madame. Don't worry. It's not catching. The result of some experiments here in my laboratory."

"You must halt your experiments, then," I said.

He laughed and glanced at Swieten, who returned the smile.

"Then I'd never cure the toothache." Sallaba opened his mouth wide and pointed to his teeth. They were blotched with silvery gray lumps. "Dental amalgams, madame. I preserve my own teeth in my head and, therefore, may eat the sweetest foods with impunity."

Swieten dropped his hand onto the doctor's narrow shoulder. "In a few years, my dear Sallaba, you'll succumb to the poison. But we'll bury you with all your own teeth."

The doctor laughed hard, then shivered as though a spasm had gripped him. He clapped his hands. "You've come for your brother's death mask, madame?"

I stared at him. He took my silence for surprise that he had recognized me.

"I didn't get to know Maestro Mozart until his final days, when his face had puffed up a bit and he wasn't at his best," the doctor said, "but it's clear enough who you are."

He beckoned me to the corner of the room.

Beside a dangling skeleton, a gray plaster cast of Wolfgang's face rested on the sideboard. It showed more weight beneath his chin than I remembered, but I noticed the depression between his brows that I shared. The long nose, a little too wide at the end, was like mine, too. He was quiet now, his eyes shut and at peace, but the cast couldn't mask the suffering he had endured at the end. Suddenly I seemed to see the eyes open and the jaw spring wide to cry out in pain.

I clutched at my chest.

The doctor bent close to the death mask. Swieten laid his hand on my elbow in reassurance.

"I'm quite sure I could've helped you, my poor fellow." Sallaba stroked the mask with a gentle, discolored finger. "They didn't call me in until the end. By then, it was too late for you."

"You could've helped me?" I said.

"What?" the doctor replied.

"Him, I mean. You could've helped *him*."

"It wouldn't have been easy, but his regular doctor, Closset, wasn't up to the job. He's more or less a medieval physician, like most doctors in Vienna. No idea about new treatments, no real science. All he knew to do was bleeding and cupping. Opened the poor fellow's veins, weakening him critically, just when he needed all his strength. Tortured him by placing the rims of hot cups on his flesh—drawing forth the bad vapors, he would've claimed."

The death mask called out its pain to me again.

"Dr. Closset attested that my brother expired of 'acute heated miliary fever,'" I said.

Sallaba grinned. "He also told me Herr Mozart had an excess of black bile building up. Our bodies, according to the ancient doctrine of Hippocrates, are balanced between blood, phlegm, and yellow and black bile. Too much of any one of these and we fall sick. Closset decided Maestro Mozart's black bile was building up in a deposit on his brain. That's why he bled him and gave him powders that would cause him to throw up—so that the black bile would stop moving to his brain."

"He made Wolfgang vomit?" I stammered.

"A big jet of it."

I whimpered. Swieten clicked his tongue and glared at Sallaba.

The doctor scuffed his shoe against the floor, embarrassed. "He died right afterward. You might say Dr. Closset killed him. But there was probably nothing Closset could do. Because of his limited experience with poisons."

The doctor dribbled a few drops from a stone jar into a pan of liquid that had just come to the boil. The sulfurous smell returned.

"So Wolfgang was— He died by poison?" I said.

"Oh yes, most certainly," he said. "It's my specialty, you see. I've made a study of poisons, in my capacity as chair of forensic medicine at the university."

"How was he poisoned?"

"Well, not by mercury. Even Closset could've spotted that. Foul breath, cloudy urine, sweats. The same symptoms you find in the average syphilitic who's had too many doses of quicksilver in his member to counter the pox."

"Doctor, there's a lady present," Swieten said.

Sallaba looked up from the boiling pan, as though he had forgotten I was there. "Quite, quite," he said. "Poor Mozart was hallucinating at the end. He thought he was at a performance of *The Magic Flute*. He said, 'Quiet, the Queen of the Night is taking the high F. Listen, she's singing her second aria. How powerfully she hits the B-flat and holds it.' All the time staring off beyond the bed as though he were in a theater rather than a death room. Poor fellow."

"Doctor, how was he poisoned?"

"*Acqua toffana.* Arsenic, lead, and belladonna," Sallaba said. "Tasteless, colorless. Deadly."

"How can you be sure?" I asked.

"Well, there was no autopsy, but the observable pathology points to poisoning."

"And the miliary fever?"

"My manservant has had one of those for some days now. He seems to be all right." The doctor called down the hallway.

"Ignaz, have you been hallucinating? Burning pain in your mouth or throat?"

The rumbling voice of the servant came from the kitchen. "No, sir."

"Abdominal pain? Muscle spasms?" The doctor turned to me. "I can vouch that he has had no spasms. The old fellow barely moves a muscle. However, if you look at his skin, you'll see the rash like millet seeds that Dr. Closset entered in the Black List for your brother."

"The Black List?"

"The death register." Swieten coughed. "Doctor, something in here irritates my breathing."

Sallaba sniffed at the boiling liquid in his pan. "Really, that's interesting."

"What is it?"

"Just something I'm investigating. It bothers your lungs, does it?"

"Yes. Very much."

"Good, good. You know it's quite poisonous over a long period. But I'm intrigued that it had such an immediate effect on you—"

I rushed out of the room, past the doctor's disheveled bed, toward the kitchen and the door.

"Wait," the doctor called. "Don't you want the death mask?"

I leaned over the gallery outside and clutched at my stomach. An eddy of cold wind spiraled down through the courtyard, but the diabolical scent of Sallaba's poisons clung to my cloak. Swieten's coachman slouched against the flanks of his lead horse with a pipe in his mouth.

The baron came onto the gallery. "Madame, I apologize for the distress," he said. "I merely wanted to—"

"I'd like to pray for Wolfgang." I felt as though the gas circulating in the doctor's laboratory had filled me with the vapors of Hell itself. What scent enveloped the soul of my poor dead brother? "Take me to the cathedral."

24.

*T*he painted faces of the saints shone with sacred clarity from the niches of the Franciscan Monastery. In the gloomy twilight on Bäcker Street, I wondered if the luminous portraits were an illusion, some symptom of Dr. Sallaba's poisonous gas.

Swieten made to speak, but he turned his face to the window of his carriage, instead. I struggled against the urge to touch his hand, pulling back my arm as though restraining an excitable pet.

"I don't like to leave you by yourself," Swieten said. "It isn't safe. The men who attacked you in the street last night—"

"No one knows I'm here. I need to be alone for this."

At the cathedral, the footman gave me his arm. I stepped down into the square. He swung onto the step at the rear of the carriage.

From the window, the baron peered into the half darkness. "I'll collect you at your inn, madame, at seven," he said.

"We'll proceed to the Freihaus Theater. They're giving *The Magic Flute* tonight."

I inclined my head in assent. "Your Grace is most generous."

The silver knob of his cane glimmered in the diffuse light from the lantern dangling beside the driver's seat. He pointed with the stick and his voice became curt. "Through the main door and to the left, by the tomb of Prince Eugene."

The coach clattered away past the cathedral's North Tower.

I kept to the shadows as I passed through the high doorway of Vienna's mother church. I slipped away from the nave to the place where Wolfgang's funeral Mass had been held.

The sandy brown stone of the Chapel of the Cross was blackened by generations of candles. Behind the altar, a tormented Christ arched away from His cross, struggling against the nails in His hands and feet. He was almost the size of a real man, His head rimmed with thorns made of the same cherrywood as His body. Hair cut from a human beard had been glued to Our Lord's chin, but its dryness made it more lifeless than the wood.

A draft swept the chapel. It set the lanterns swinging. They lit Our Savior's face, illuminating His agony, then dropped away to leave Him in shadow, over and over. Like a fairground trick, the light animated the carving. I crossed myself twice.

The stone floor was cold when I lowered my knees to it. I couldn't hold Christ's tortured gaze. Where had Wolfgang's coffin lain when Swieten and Constanze brought my poor brother here for the funeral service? Years of guilt pulsed through every part of me. I shivered with a quiet sob.

For my greed and for the sin of jealousy, I begged forgiveness. Begged the Christ on the cross. Begged Wolfgang.

After our father's death, I had inherited all the money saved from the tours of Europe Wolfgang and I made as children. Our father had invested well, and it was a substantial sum. He also left expensive furnishings, musical instruments, and a hoard of gold watches and jeweled snuffboxes that were gifts from the nobility of all Europe.

Wolfgang had been the main attraction during those early tours. He ought to have had his share. Though our father disinherited him, even so I could've sent half the money to Wolfgang. Yet I begrudged my brother his freedom. I convinced myself he should pay for it with his inheritance. He had left Salzburg for a life of accomplishment and fulfillment in the imperial capital. He had abandoned me, my talents ignored and my prospects for a good marriage dimming as I entered my late twenties. We had been close as children, but I had cut myself off from him.

I looked up at the crucifix. I betrayed Wolfgang for money, as Judas had sold one greater than him who had loved him.

I twisted the rosary of dried seeds from the Holy Land. Did I deprive Wolfgang of money that could've made him secure? I thought of the debts Constanze mentioned. Wolfgang had been living beyond his means, but I knew it wasn't our financial dispute that had hurt my brother. I had done something much worse than to cheat him out of a few thousand florints. I had denied him the last remnant of the family that had nurtured his talent and taught him about love.

Another sob caught at my chest. *Intercede for me, Virgin, with your son, my Savior*, I thought.

The lamplight rocked across the face of Christ. I saw His pain, as He called to His Father whom He thought had forsaken Him. His passion was alive and it was my sacred duty to bear it, like the agony on the gray death mask Dr. Sallaba displayed in his room of poisons.

I told Holy Mary my vow: to face any suffering, any hazard, so that I might make amends to my brother. I crossed myself as I rose to leave the chapel.

Outside in the square, someone exclaimed at the new degree of chill in the air. Another man laughed at his companion's discomfort.

It was night now. But I had no thought of the danger that had seemed to hang in the darkness after I was attacked with Gieseke. I was calm and decided.

A shepherd drove a small herd of sheep past the cathedral. He called to a shaggy, lumbering wolf dog, which nudged the bleating animals toward Schuler Street. Then I was alone in the drifting lantern light.

I pulled my cloak around me and set out for my inn. My thoughts were clear now. I had spoken to Wolfgang in prayer. That night at the opera I felt sure he would reply.

25

*C*enerl dressed my hair by the window overlooking the empty Flour Market. The cobbles were shiny and damp around the statue of Providence. Blinking with each tug of the brush, I watched for the lanterns of the baron's coach.

As I waited, I thought of love. Not of husbands and of duties.

Only of love.

In Salzburg when I was in my twenties, I had fallen for D'Ippold, an army captain who headed a school for boys of noble birth. He didn't satisfy my father's ambition to marry me into the aristocracy. His suit was rejected. I obliged my father many years later by pledging myself to Berchtold, who had one foot on the lowest rung of the nobility. Perhaps Papa thought that, in his search for a husband of high birth, he was merely matching me with a man appropriate to my aspirations. After all, I had always refused to pull my hair back in a cap and instead wore it up like a woman of rank. With all my years of prodigy behind me I finally had the comfortable home and children that my unexceptional friends had long enjoyed.

A coach clattered past the Capuchin Church and halted outside the inn. The baron's face appeared in the window. I saw why love had preoccupied me. I trembled with guilt.

"The emperor will attend tonight's performance," Swieten said, as I settled onto the bench opposite him in the carriage.

I thought of the haughty, slow walk of the man I had seen trailed by his courtiers across the park at the palace that afternoon. "I recall him as a child, when I played for his mother, the empress, at Schönbrunn."

Swieten murmured something I couldn't hear. I sensed a heaviness in him.

"Will I think him much changed?"

"Leopold? Out of all recognition. It's hard to imagine the emperor was ever a child."

At the Freihaus, carriages crowded the road. Baron van Swieten tipped his hat to the ladies and gentlemen as we crossed the courtyard to the theater.

I bounced on my toes with anticipation. Except for one trip to Munich, I had only ever seen Wolfgang's operas performed in Salzburg—in halls with which I was familiar to the point of extreme weariness.

The marble entrance of the theater was as dazzling as the costumes of the wealthy Viennese in the lobby. I heard Wolfgang's name on every pair of painted lips.

Swieten gestured across the lamplit foyer toward the stairs. "I must attend upon the emperor's arrival, madame," he said. "You'll find my box in the first tier. I shan't be detained long, I hope."

He maneuvered through the lobby. The crowd jostled for a good position from which to coax a nod of acknowledgment from the emperor. I mounted the stairs.

When Wolfgang and I played at the palace, the future emperor had made no great impression. Leopold hadn't been first in line to the throne. One would've assumed him well made for some provincial dukedom. By contrast, his sister Maria Antonia had run about the royal chambers with us, giggling. Now she lived under arrest in Paris with her husband, the French king. Perhaps a lively convivial nature clashed with the demands of the world. It had certainly been the case with Wolfgang.

At the head of the stairs, the usher directed me toward Swieten's seats. I came into a long gallery. Lichnowsky paced the empty corridor. He glared at the baron's box, as though he might conjure someone from its emptiness by the force of his impatience.

I called to him. The expression he turned upon me was that of a man preparing for a duel, sharp and alert. With an effort he softened his face.

"Are you looking for Baron van Swieten, my prince?" I said.

"Where is he?" His voice was low and strangled.

"He attends the emperor in the foyer."

He put a finger to the corner of his eye. The gesture was like a dark blot on a page of fine penmanship, so evidently was it a sign of the disturbance beneath his placid expression.

"Haven't you seen this opera yet, my prince?" I asked. "You, a great patron of my brother?"

"I was at the premiere, madame." A noise from along the

corridor. His eyes snapped toward it. "I find it a most excellent work, of course."

"I'm told Wolfgang considered it his finest."

"I don't believe it surpasses his *Don Giovanni*."

"Why's that?"

"In *The Magic Flute*, you'll see that the hero and heroine discover the essence of life in some kind of holy union. Don Giovanni realizes that one can learn the truth about the world only when forced to take a journey to Hell."

"Perhaps Wolfgang learned that Hell isn't one's destiny," I said. "It can be escaped, by prayer and goodness."

He shook his head and seemed about to contradict me, but he heard the orchestra tuning up. He bowed and went down the stairs, shoving past the couples coming up from their obsequies to the emperor in the lobby.

I entered Swieten's box and glanced over the balcony toward the stalls. The musicians in the orchestra laughed and joked with the easy confidence of men who knew they had a hit.

"You?"

I turned to the voice. Hiding behind the open door, Gieseke waited.

"Are you unharmed, sir? Thank heavens, I see that you are," I said.

He was in costume for the night's performance, a long white robe. His face was painted into a stern glare with thick stripes of black grease.

"Where's Swieten?" he said.

A round of applause started and the orchestra stood. The violinists tapped their bows against their music stands. The emperor proceeded down the aisle to his seat, followed by a retinue in clothing so fine the fabric shone like suits of armor. Leopold moved with a deliberate grace. His puffy, grim face was frozen and aloof.

"Of course, Swieten's down *there*." Gieseke remained in the darkness at the rear of the box. "Sucking up to the emperor with the rest of them."

"Watch your tongue," I said. "The baron is worthy of respect."

The actor held himself poised by the open door, an eye on the corridor.

I stepped toward him.

"Leave me alone." His voice grated through his throat as though it had been burned. "I didn't know you'd be here. It's dangerous to be close to you."

"What do you mean?"

"After you ran away, I was nearly stabbed to death." Under the theatrical makeup, there were traces of purple bruises. He lifted his hand. The palm was bound around with a grubby cloth. "I had to grab the knife by the blade to pull it away from that thug."

"You think those men wanted to hurt *me*, not you?"

"I'll keep quiet about Wolfgang's poisoning. *You* won't. Of course they wanted you."

"But they let me get away. Maybe they wanted you, after all."

His eyes disappeared into the thick greasepaint. He nodded, slow and appalled. He saw that I was right. What did he know that made him dangerous enough to kill?

"You saw it done," I said.

"Done? What?"

"The poison. You saw it administered, didn't you? When?"

He bit at the bandage where it crossed the back of his hand. "At the Masonic hall. After they performed the cantata I wrote with Wolfgang."

"Who did it? Who poisoned my brother?"

"I'll only tell a man with whom I share other secrets."

The bond of brothers. "A Mason?"

"That's right."

"Why not a woman?"

He grabbed my shoulders. "What did you say?"

I struggled free, stumbling against the rococo woodwork of the balcony. The emperor had taken his seat. The conductor came to his podium to loud acclaim. Until then I hadn't noticed how large the theater was. The burst of applause from five tiers of boxes was jolting.

Gieseke stepped through the door and rushed away.

A heavy chord from the trombones started the overture, as the door shut behind him. I flinched at the sudden volume.

A second and third chord. In E-flat major. The same key as the music I had overheard at the Masonic lodge. Wolfgang never used key signatures randomly. They always signaled a mood or some other information to the listener. With these first three bars of the overture, I already knew that this was a Masonic opera, just as Gieseke and Schikaneder had told me.

As the fugue developed, I peered through the lamplight across the theater. Count Pergen sat in the front row a few seats from the emperor, his legs crossed and his buckled shoe dipping in time to the rhythm of the overture.

In the box opposite me, Prince Lichnowsky sat beside a

pretty, dark-haired woman. She leaned forward to the edge of the balcony and danced her fingers in the air as though she played the melody on a piano.

Swieten hurried to the chair next to me, resting both his hands on the knob of his stick as he had done when he listened to me play at the Academy of Science. He turned to me with a smile for the music. He must have noticed the disturbance on my face, because he reached out for my hand.

On the stage, the action commenced. Tamino fled a giant serpent. "Help me," he cried.

Swieten swiveled toward the exclamation and withdrew his hand.

Before Tamino's first aria was over I was lost in the beauty of my brother's creation. Schikaneder had said the opera was intended to promote Masonic values, but to me it was full of Wolfgang's pure playfulness.

So entranced was I that when two men entered our box, I hardly noticed. At first Swieten, too, paid them no attention. They lingered in the doorway, irresolute and confused. With a sigh of irritation, the baron stared them down.

The men were ill-dressed and rough. They avoided the baron's glare, but didn't retreat.

He took a step toward them, pulling back his broad shoulders and lifting the heavy, jeweled end of his stick like a cudgel. The men touched the brims of their hats and left.

Swieten paced the box for several minutes before he returned to his seat.

Onstage, the Queen of the Night appeared on a throne gilded with stars. She sang of her lost child. Tears of pity came to my eyes. The diva was Constanze's sister, the voluble Josefa whom I had met at the Academy of Science. Her aria moved into G minor, which Wolfgang so often used to convey grief, as she recounted her daughter's kidnapping and beseeched Tamino to rescue the girl.

There was soon a respite from such tragic emotion with the low comedy of Schikaneder as the Bird Man, and the delightful Three Boys, young sopranos who swung over the action in a magical flying barge.

Gieseke strode across the stage with the rest of the priests. He had a minor role, but he spoke his lines well. His voice, which had seemed to rip through his throat when he stood before me in the box, was smooth and resonant.

In the finale to act one, he lurked among the ranks of the priests at the edge of the stage. My eyes happened to be upon him when the frightened Bird Man asked the kidnapped princess what he might say to explain himself to the approaching High Priest. "The truth, the truth!" she called. "Even if it be a crime." Gieseke spun and took two steps toward her. His movement on the crowded stage went unnoticed by the audience. But the girl who sang the role of the princess flinched, as though she had seen some threat in the advancing actor's eyes.

The intermission began. Wolfgang's music played on in my head. I experienced a rapture so powerful that I wanted to skip onto the stage and dance.

When Swieten stood to make his way to the royal party I grasped his hand and squeezed it in joy. He responded with a similar pressure from his fingers. The beads woven into his jacket glimmered like stars.

He descended to greet the nobles who hovered about the

emperor. The orchestra was tuning up for the second act when he returned.

Constanze's sister pulled off the high coloratura of her final aria with such accomplishment that it sounded more like a wind instrument than a human voice. Schikaneder played his magic bells to summon his beloved and sang a playful duet with her. I smiled through tears of delight.

Swieten brought a handkerchief from his sleeve. I held it close to my face longer than was necessary to dry my eyes. I breathed in the scent of his jasmine cologne on the lace.

26

*T*he princess had been refused entry to the priesthood at first, insulted as a weak, gossiping woman. By the end of the opera, her determination and rectitude won over the priests, who allowed her to enter their order. As the curtain came down, I spoke to Swieten above the applause. "All the most profound utterances were made by the princess."

He sucked his upper lip. "Quite so."

The prince and princess slipped through the curtain and accepted the ovation with Schikaneder and his bird-woman bride.

The door of our box opened. Stadler entered. His eyes signaled urgency, but he paused when he noticed me.

Swieten shifted in his seat to face the clarinetist. "Stadler, *guten Abend*."

Stadler ran his hand over his close-cropped hair and bowed to me. He hesitated in the doorway.

"It was a wonderful performance, Stadler," Swieten said. "Was it not?"

Another silence, before Stadler stammered: "Truly, most astonishing."

"It acts powerfully on the emotions," I said.

"What does?" Stadler's reply was quick this time.

"Wolfgang's opera." I inclined my head, curious at his agitation.

Constanze's sister joined the other four singers on the stage and brought the audience to its feet. She flounced down into a deep curtsy, her head almost bowed to the stage and her hand on her breast, as though she had been consumed and exhausted by her performance.

Stadler sat on the edge of a gilt chair behind Swieten. He rubbed his palms on his breeches.

In the first row of the theater, Emperor Leopold clapped delicately, but, it seemed to me, without enthusiasm.

"Can it be that the opera doesn't meet with the emperor's approval?" I asked.

Stadler craned over the baron's shoulder. His cheek twitched as he registered the reserve in the emperor's applause.

Swieten took Stadler's wrist between both his hands. "Dear Stadler, something is amiss?"

"What do you mean?"

"It's clear you came to see me with urgent news. Don't let Madame de Mozart's presence put you off. I can assure you, she's privy to everything I know."

"About what?"

"Come on." Swieten leaned close. "Wolfgang. His death."

On the stage, the singers started the encores. Schikaneder led them with a bumptious reprise of his introductory aria, "The Birdcatcher am I."

With the ovation suspended for the singing, Stadler lowered his voice. "Gieseke has information."

Swieten raised his chin, as though the scent of unseen food had wafted by him.

"He knows who poisoned Wolfgang," Stadler said. "But he's scared. He'll reveal the name of the killer only to you. He wants your protection."

The baron shook his head. "God help him."

He went to the door. "I'll go and look for this poor fellow," he said to Stadler. "Stay with Madame de Mozart."

Stadler protested, but the baron gave a look of warning. "Don't leave her until I return," he said.

As the door shut, Stadler slumped into his chair.

Applause for Schikaneder. Then the princess took center stage for her encore. While the orchestra introduced her aria, I recalled a line of hers from act two. "A woman who does not fear night and death is worthy and will be initiated," I whispered.

Stadler stared at me with his jaw quivering. I had an idea now of the missing paragraphs from the page Wolfgang had written, which lay in the pocket of my skirt.

"The Grotto, Herr Stadler," I said. "Wolfgang shared the secret of that new Masonic lodge with you, did he not?"

"He—he did." Stadler spoke as though with his final breath.

"He left the essay unfinished in which he described his plans for the Grotto. But this opera completes the scheme as clearly as if he were to have written it out himself in plain prose."

On the stage, the princess took her bow.

"Wolfgang intended to allow women to join his lodge," I said. "Look how this princess is tested and given membership of the priesthood. That's what Wolfgang wanted to do—to accord the same rights to women as to men. No doubt he saw it as the natural development of his ideas of equality, his belief in the new Enlightenment. Correct, Herr Stadler?"

He gave the slightest of nods, as the Queen of the Night opened her aria. Vengeance, she sang again, boiled in her heart.

"But his ideas were dangerous?" I said.

Stadler grabbed at his face and doubled over, rocking on his seat. "We take fearful oaths when we join the Brotherhood. There're dreadful punishments for those who break the rules."

"I heard the oath."

"So you did, when you—"

"Wolfgang tried to break the rule that excludes women from the Masons. He's dead. But who else is at risk, Herr Stadler?" I said. "Who else was involved in the new lodge? You? Gieseke?"

He groaned his acknowledgment. "Lichnowsky, too. He backed Wolfgang in founding the new lodge."

I wondered why Lichnowsky had ventured into so hazardous a project. I looked across the theater to the prince's seats. The woman with the piano-playing fingers leaned her head against the edge of the box, enraptured. Lichnowsky's face was as empty of emotion as hers was awash with it.

The encores of the primary singers were at an end. The heavy scarlet curtains drew back. The entire cast appeared onstage among the classical columns of the set for a curtain call. I couldn't see Gieseke among the white-robed priests.

The door of the box opened. The baron entered.

"Gieseke?" I asked.

"Not a sign of him," he said. "Perhaps he'll come to me if I wait here."

Gieseke had only to have spoken a single word to me, the guilty name. But he had fled. It was as if the identity of the killer had been written out in water, plain before my eyes and yet elusive. I rose to my feet in confusion.

From backstage came a loud crack, like a heavy rope severed.

The barge from which the Three Boys had sung their advice to the Bird Man swung out under the proscenium. As it rocked back and forth, a gasp spread through the audience. A man dangled headfirst from the boat, high above the stage.

Something spattered down from the barge onto Schikaneder. He wiped it from the shoulders of his feathery costume.

As the barge swung back, its motion dislodged the hanging man. He plunged to the stage. Schikaneder pulled the screaming Queen of the Night out of the way.

The body lay twisted on the boards, blood spreading over its white robes. Schikaneder lifted the prostrate man's head.

"My God," he cried, in the penetrating baritone that we had applauded moments before. "It's Gieseke. He's dead."

In his box across the theater, Lichnowsky came to his feet. The pretty young woman spun in horror and pressed her face to his midriff. He looked toward Swieten's seats. The baron stared at the stage, his hands closed into fists. Lichnowsky went quickly from his box, and the sobbing woman hurried after him.

27

I mounted the stairway to Jahn's coffeehouse. Ahead of me, I heard the click of billiard balls and two voices. One said, "Well played, Prince." The other: "Pure luck, Lichnowsky, you bastard."

As I reached the head of the stairs, I saw the tall figure of Prince Lichnowsky, his arm extended and his palm held out. A stout man, dressed in the fashionable simplicity of the English style, pulled his wallet from his coat and slid out two banknotes. He slapped them into Lichnowsky's hand with a grimace.

"You're lucky that you're of a lower class than me, Hoffmann," the prince said, as he put the money away. "Otherwise I'd demand satisfaction for your insults."

"I'd be happy to take you on. Choose your weapons."

"I wouldn't dignify you with the honor of a duel. But you'd better watch your mouth, or I'll thrash you in the Graben outside my house like an insolent servant."

When the third man rose from his table, I saw that it was Stadler. He imposed himself between the two men, a hand on each of their chests, and laughed. "Neither a duel nor a brawl would bring much honor to either of you," he said.

The loser of the game dropped onto a sofa. Hoffmann waved his hand toward a man in a white apron, who nodded and drew a pot of coffee from a brass urn.

Lichnowsky pinched some snuff beneath his nose. "It's early in the day for the coffee to have made you so quarrelsome, Hoffmann," he said. "Usually you don't challenge me to a duel before lunchtime."

"Most of the people who know you for a scoundrel are the kind to lie in bed until late, so ordinarily the field is mine until noon." He lifted a shaky hand toward me. "Today I had to beat the rush."

The prince spun on the heel of his boot with an expression of shock. When he saw me, his face turned to anger, but he composed himself. "Hoffmann, you dishonor this lady."

"Not before you did, surely."

"This is Madame de Mozart."

"Wolfgang's sister?"

The pot of coffee arrived. The seated man busied himself with pouring from it, trying to cover his embarrassment. Stadler hid behind a news sheet.

Lichnowsky took my hand. He led me to a table in the corner of the room.

"You told that man your home is on the Graben, my prince. The meeting of the Masonic lodge. It was held at your house, wasn't it?"

He covered his mouth with his hand and coughed. He held up two fingers to the man in the apron.

Jahn's was one of the most popular coffeehouses in Vienna, but at midmorning Lichnowsky's companions at the billiard table had it to themselves. It was comfortably furnished with snug booths of red velvet along the walls. The news sheets hung on wooden rails beside the bar. The air was charged with the aroma of crushed coffee beans.

Lichnowsky lit a long Sevilla. His breath shivered between his lips as he blew out the smoke. "Wolfgang played many of his public concerts here," he said. "Financially your brother did quite well in this place."

I glanced at the piano beside the bar. A coffeehouse seemed a poor venue for Wolfgang's beautiful music compared to the palaces in which he had appeared. But perhaps it was my own experience in making music for cash that made Jahn's seem low. Our family once lingered too long in London and money ran short. We children had been reduced to afternoon shows in a beer hall at a penny a ticket.

The fellow in the apron brought a tray with a porcelain coffeepot, cups, and two slices of cake. He poured a coffee for each of us and set the cake on our table with a bow.

"This is Herr Jahn's invention." Lichnowsky handed me a fork and pushed my plate of cake toward me.

Jahn bowed with pride and returned to his bar.

"Try it," Lichnowsky said, exhaling a blue stream of cigar smoke. "It's wonderful."

Though I had breakfasted at my inn after early Mass, I had eaten little. I had been troubled still by the shock of Gieseke's death at the theater the previous night. I took a piece of the cake. It was an apple torte, brown and crusty, soft sliced fruit within. Poppy seeds spread across my tongue, bitter like the grounds of coffee.

I said, "That night when you found me in distress after the attack—"

"I was honored to be of aid to you."

"You told me Wolfgang's death wasn't suspicious. You were wrong. He was poisoned."

"Come now, madame—"

"But you were correct about one thing."

"Was I?"

"You said his enemies might strike against his surviving friends. It has happened. Poor Herr Gieseke."

Lichnowsky tapped his fork against the crust of his torte. His face bore the impatience of a reckless youth who must listen in silence to an admonishing parent, though he knows his own acquaintance with risk to be greater than that of the one who lectures him about it.

"There's more that you haven't told me, I'm sure of it," I said. "You can't pretend you aren't deeply involved in this intrigue, my prince."

He cut away a piece of cake with the edge of his fork and divided that once more into two.

"The Grotto. You were to take part in this new lodge," I said.

With the back of his fork, Lichnowsky mashed the slices of apple on his plate. "I told you this subject was best left alone."

"It's like a melody that plays over in my head. I can't ignore it."

His eyes, when they looked at me sideways, were probing, sharp, and resentful.

"Tell me the truth about Wolfgang's secret mission to Berlin," I said. "Why does it scare everyone? His friends are terrified. One of them is dead."

"So far."

I had expected to see fear in Lichnowsky's face. Instead, his features were piqued, like a child thwarted at his play. As his anger subsided, it came to me just what that game had been. "When you visited Berlin, it was you who was on the secret mission," I said. "You're the spy, not Wolfgang."

He drummed his fingers on the table. I had sensed that Wolfgang lacked the guile to be an agent. I saw that I had been right.

"Wolfgang's presence was a cover for my journey to Berlin, but I'm no spy," Lichnowsky whispered.

Stadler rattled his news sheet to straighten the page. Hoffmann snored on his sofa.

"There was never a job at the palace in Berlin for Wolfgang?" I said.

"We told everyone Wolfgang expected a position there, so no one would suspect my reasons for visiting an enemy capital."

"You'd appear to be just the maestro's traveling companion."

"That's the idea."

"What was your true purpose?"

Lichnowsky's eyes became distant. They flickered with doubt. I wondered if espionage took a man so far into deceit that he might lose track of the genuine impulse that had started him on his cheating course.

"The king of Prussia observes the same Masonic principles as our lodge," he said. "He's a member of the Rosicrucian order."

"So your trip was a brotherly visit?"

"The king craved more than fellowship. He wanted his own lodge in Vienna. Secret and outside the restrictions of Count Pergen's police."

"To what end?"

Lichnowsky slapped his hand on the table. "You really ought to—"

"To what end?" I spoke through my teeth, low and hard.

"The king of Prussia's not interested in our Masonic principles. He wants connections."

"Spies?" My fingers touched an arpeggio across my skirt. I hid them beneath the table, but I let them continue their silent exercises for the sake of my concentration.

"Informants, in the highest circles of Viennese society," Lichnowsky said. "Under the control of Prussia."

"You went to Berlin to receive orders from the king. You were to return to Vienna to recruit these highly placed spies. That was your plan?"

The prince raised his voice. "No, no." Stadler shifted behind his news sheet. Lichnowsky collected himself. "I went to dissuade the king, to beg him not to carry out his plan."

"Really?" My sarcasm surprised me as much as it offended the prince.

"If our emperor learned that a Prussian lodge had been planted in his capital it would endanger every Mason here. He's already suspicious of us. If he linked us to his greatest enemy, who knows how we'd be punished."

"But the king of Prussia refused to abandon his plan?"

"Not at all. When I presented my case, the king agreed it'd endanger his—his friends in Vienna. But Wolfgang spoiled everything."

"Wolfgang?"

"After he played for the king in Berlin, he suggested the idea of a Masonic opera."

"*The Magic Flute*."

"Your brother was only looking for funding for his production. He spoke with such animation that the king once more determined to involve himself in Vienna, in our Masonic life. It was Wolfgang's fault that this mess came down upon us." Sweat stood on the prince's lip.

"But there's no Prussian lodge?" I said.

"There is not."

"Then why does the danger persist? Why is Gieseke dead?"

"There are powerful men with much to lose. Great men of state, Wolfgang's Masonic brothers, whose positions would be at risk if they were suspected of links to Prussia. The Count Küfstein, the Court Chancellor. Count Thun, my father-in-law, and many others. I believe someone wishes to make known the story of the Grotto, so that these worthy men will lose their positions. Austria would be destabilized. Our state would be made vulnerable to a Prussian attack."

"War? Perhaps that was the king's intention. Not to set up a cadre of spies, but to sow discord in the palace. To weaken our government."

"You may be correct."

"But surely Wolfgang's purpose was simpler? He wanted to allow women into the Masons."

Lichnowsky took a draft of his coffee. "That stupid idea."

"Why stupid?"

He took me in as though he only now noticed that I was a woman and that this fact made me ridiculous. "It's utterly absurd."

"Yet for this reason he wrote *The Magic Flute*. And that isn't absurd. It's the most beautiful of his creations."

"The music, maybe. The ideas are silly." He swilled some coffee in his cheek and stubbed out his cigar. "It meant a lot to him, I suppose, this notion of women in the Brotherhood. He broached it in Berlin, too. Perhaps the king agreed because he wanted to enlist the wives of powerful men in his lodge. They might've supplied him with information from their husbands. Either way, the king was using Wolfgang."

"Wolfgang managed to get *The Magic Flute* produced. How do you know *he* wasn't using the king?"

Lichnowsky spat coffee grounds into his cup and dabbed his lips with the lace of his cuff. "Because Wolfgang is dead."

28.

A hay cart passed the entrance to the coffeehouse, turned up Rauhenstein Lane, and trundled toward Wolfgang's apartment. I imagined the comfort I might find there. It would be a welcome contrast to the edgy banter of the men at the billiard table. I saw why Wolfgang had been determined to marry after he arrived in Vienna. He played music with men, but he created it beneath the pink marble stucco and the painted relief of the goddess of flowers. With women.

I heard footsteps descend the stairs behind me. Then silence. An intense force quivered on the back of my neck like the touch of a feverish hand.

When I turned, Stadler beckoned from the doorway. I stepped toward him. He glanced along the street.

"I must beg you again to desist, madame," he said. "This business with—"

"With the women in Wolfgang's lodge?"

"I was weak with fear when I let that slip to you at the opera house. Lichnowsky will know that you heard it from me."

"You eavesdropped on my conversation with the prince?"

"Mention it to no one else, I implore you."

"Why're you scared of Lichnowsky?"

"I'm scared of every Mason just now."

"Your brothers?"

"My brothers. But *your* brother most of all." He scanned the street as though he expected to see Wolfgang's ghost weave through the passing traffic, calling out all his secrets now that he was beyond punishment for disclosing them. Stadler felt no such immunity.

"Wolfgang wanted women in his lodge," I said. "It's a violation of Masonic rules. But I don't see the great danger in—"

"Those are the Masonic rules in Austria. But not in France."

"In France, there're female Masons?"

"The Revolution brought equality for women, too. You understand? For God's sake, woman, whether he intended it or not, Wolfgang was introducing a revolutionary French idea at a time when those same French people have overthrown the aristocracy and appear poised to murder their queen." Stadler lifted his arms and let them fall to his sides. "Now do you see?"

The street was busy with carriages depositing players at the *jeu de paume* courts on Ball Lane. The wheels of a yellow trap cracked out a din on the cobbles, passing close to the door of the coffeehouse.

Stadler ducked back into the shadows of the hallway. When the trap moved on, the clarinetist was gone.

I went along the edge of the street.

The Revolution in France. The schemes of the king of Prussia. Even I, who was innocent of politics, could see that Wolfgang had taken dreadful risks. Yet I wasn't surprised. He had spotted a chance to produce a beautiful opera based on his cherished principles. Naturally he scorned the dangers.

I passed through the entryway of Wolfgang's building and climbed the spiral steps to Constanze's door.

My nephew was at the keyboard once again. This time I barely noticed his false notes. I took Karl's cheeks between my hands and kissed his forehead. He rubbed his brow and slid beneath the piano. His frown disguised a smile.

Constanze laughed at her son. "Sister, welcome." Taking my hands, she called to the maid: "Sabine, a hot punch. We need to warm you up."

"Hardly. I've just been drinking coffee. My heart flutters like a sparrow's wings."

"Then take some punch to soothe your nerves."

Little Wolfgang woke and howled in his crib. Constanze went to the next room to calm him with kisses.

I sat on the bench before the piano keyboard. The maid set a low brazier behind me. The heat of the coals seeped into the small of my back and I realized that I had been bent, as if by the weight of my uncertainty.

I sipped my rum punch and considered what I had learned of my brother's death. Of one conclusion I was in no doubt—Wolfgang hadn't died because of an affair with Magdalena Hofdemel. The rumor that Constanze had been so careful to deny in her letter to me was a calumny. It didn't fit the facts as I had uncovered them, neither the connections to the Masons nor the links to Prussia.

I thought of Hofdemel's poor widow, alone in her home with the wounds inflicted by her dead husband. I decided I must tell Magdalena that I knew she was without sin.

Constanze left her baby with the maid and sat beside me at the keyboard. She leafed through a pile of manuscript pages on top of the piano.

"These are the pieces the Prussian ambassador wishes to purchase for his king," she said. "Will you play one for me?"

Her smile was so guileless, I wondered that people thought of me as Wolfgang's double. In her simplicity, the resemblance between husband and wife appeared much stronger.

"Of course, my dear," I said. "Which one?"

She pulled a few sheets from the top of the pile. "This one, of course."

I peered at the music as she unfolded the pages along the stand. "Why 'of course'?"

"Don't you see the dedication?"

She ran her finger, stained black with ink from copying manuscripts, beneath a note at the top of the first page. It was scribbled in my brother's handwriting. "To my most dearly beloved sister, Maria Anna, my Nannerl." Then the curling parallel lines under our family name with which he signed his manuscripts.

I touched the signature and whispered his name. I glanced at the opening staves. The piece was a sonata for piano. "He used to send me his scores all the time. But I've not seen this one."

"It's new, isn't it?" Constanze's black eyes glinted from the aureoles of tired, gray skin around them. "Play it. I've never heard the piece, I'm sure."

As I settled myself to play, I wondered why the Prussian ambassador chose to buy this sonata, rather than one of Wolfgang's better-known compositions.

I wasn't far into the first movement before I noticed that it was one of my brother's most difficult sonatas. The broken arpeggios of the left hand moved fast beneath a testing, syncopated melody.

Constanze turned the pages for me with excitement. I completed the final Rondo with an exuberant cadenza, and grasped my sister-in-law's hand.

We spoke in unison. "It's wonderful." We laughed and embraced. At my feet little Karl hugged my legs. Constanze's spaniel hurried into the room and jumped into her lap. I regretted that we had never shared such a happy moment when my brother had been there to enjoy it.

Constanze tinkled out a few notes of the sonata's melody on the keyboard and said, "It's as though Wolfgang left this piece to welcome you here. His way of saying hello to you."

"But I might never have seen it."

"Oh, I expect he knew you'd come."

I caught the dog's ears and stroked them. He licked at my wrist. I read through the final bars of the sonata once more.

When I reached the end, I noticed something that had escaped me in the thrill of playing the piece. A few lines scrawled in the margin. In Wolfgang's hand.

I bent closer and read them aloud. " 'She repents her blindness, as she is always penitent. At the keyboard her notes run riot like demons cast out. I will be with her as a brother in the halls of Paradise, at her side as always I've been, though not as my father intended.' "

"It's one of Wolfgang's little riddles. What does it mean?" Constanze scratched at the dog's neck. "Do you remember the riddles he wrote for Carnival?"

"Quite vividly." Those puzzles had been smutty, as was appropriate for that festival of drink, dance, and lust. But this riddle disturbed me. The mention of repentance brought to mind the message Magdalena Hofdemel had left with my maid at the inn. "Blindness" and "Paradise" suggested Maria Theresia von Paradies, the brilliant pianist. So did the notes spilling from the keyboard like a riot. Yet surely the final reference— to his companion in Paradise, who wouldn't be the one chosen by our father—was connected to Constanze. Papa had disapproved of her until the end.

"Wolfgang was always too clever for me," Constanze said. "But he told me you understood his word games, Nannerl. Can you solve it?"

I considered the puzzle's mention of "a brother in the halls of Paradise." Did that suggest the solution would be the name of a woman chosen to enter Wolfgang's Grotto as a fellow Mason?

Constanze nudged me. "Well?"

"I'll need to give this great thought," I said. "I'm sure I'll work out the answer, sister."

I wondered if it had been for the riddle at its conclusion that the Prussian ambassador chose to buy this manuscript. No doubt Constanze was right—Wolfgang had set the puzzle for me. He had dedicated the sonata to his "most dearly beloved sister" and left this message at its end as a signal or a guide.

To what?

I shivered as I considered that there may have been something of Wolfgang's dangerous work that he knew would be left undone at his death. Had he decided that I'd be the one to complete it?

"Well, keep thinking about it." Constanze stood. "I'm putting all my hopes in you to figure it out."

I felt a tug at my skirt. Karl crawled from under the piano. He shoved a white leather ball into my hand and ran through the door. Down the corridor, he took up position behind a triangle of skittles.

"He hasn't played with anyone since—" Constanze broke off, her hand over her mouth.

I wound up my shot. "Here it comes, little Karl."

The ball bowled over the floorboards and into the ninepins. It ricocheted into the air, and Karl caught it. One skittle remained standing. The boy knocked it over with his foot, laughing, as I cheered my success.

The maid announced lunch. Constanze took my hand and drew me to the door.

"Let's get some food inside you. It'll be cold in the church," she said.

I watched Karl set up the skittles again. I wanted very much to stay and play with the child. It had been little more than a week since I left my village, but I missed even the arrogant smirks and indiscipline of my stepsons. Most of all I thought of my Leopold, who was almost the same age as Karl. "Church?"

"After lunch, it'll be time to go to the funeral Mass," Constanze said.

I stared at her blankly.

"For poor Gieseke."

"Yes, of course," I murmured. "Poor Gieseke."

Karl thrust the ball into my hand.

29

*B*eneath the angular medieval frescoes at the entrance to St. Michael's Church, Schikaneder recounted the story of Gieseke's death for a handful of mourners. He fretted at the shoulder of his black frock coat, as though brushing away the blood that poured from the actor's dangling corpse onto the Bird Man's costume during the encores. With his eyes fixed on the altar, its sculptural angels tumbling to earth, his arm traced the dead man's drop to the stage.

Constanze called to him. He advanced toward her. When he saw that it was I who was arm-in-arm with my brother's widow, he hesitated, but it was too late for him to return to his audience.

"My dear Constanze," he said. "We are to sing some sections of Wolfgang's Requiem Mass today. For our friend Gieseke, who died during the performance of one of your husband's most perfect works."

"It's as it should be, Emanuel." Constanze's eyes glistened in the candlelight.

The impresario gave a brief bow to me. "Madame de Mozart."

I bent my knee. "Herr Schikaneder."

His hands folded around Constanze's bony wrist. "I'm sure Wolfgang's music would've soothed our dear Gieseke."

I believed it unlikely the murdered actor would've been calmed by any reminder of my brother, whose death haunted his final days. No doubt Wolfgang's opera, sung in encores to the rapture of the audience, had been in Gieseke's ears when he was killed at the theater.

With another bow, Schikaneder went to take up his place in the choir.

Constanze crossed herself and followed him up the aisle.

I would've gone with her, but I was distracted by the sound of a heavy cough from the corner of the church. A woman knelt before a wooden crucifix in the side chapel dedicated to St. Nicholas. Her back was thin under her shawl. She shivered in the unheated church.

I assumed she was a pauper off the streets. Or a girl of the lower classes who had been shamed by Gieseke and now lamented that he'd never restore her honor through marriage. Yet, as she rose, I noticed that the material of her dress was expensive.

Stumbling, she reached out and grasped at the altar cloth. She dropped to her knees and, with her hand still tight around the embroidered silk, dragged the crucifix that stood upon it to the floor. She lay beside the cross trembling, her legs drawn up and her arms jerking in a spasm.

I hurried to help her.

Before I reached the step of the chapel a tiny, squat maid

lifted the fallen woman to her feet. She gave me a surly glance from under her thick eyebrows. I recognized her as the girl who worked for Mademoiselle von Paradies.

The haughty voice of the blind pianist came from behind me, too loud for the echoing church, too forceful for a funeral. "Do you like the chapel?"

I half turned, my attention still held by the shaking woman who rested against the altar. Paradies's eyes rotated like buttons in the sockets of a girl's doll. "The chapel?" I said. "It's quite beautiful."

"It was paid for by a royal chef over four hundred years ago."

"A fine gesture."

"It was to thank God for his acquittal."

"He'd been on trial?"

"For poisoning."

I would've sworn that the pianist's eyeballs ceased for a moment their oscillations and held on me like the most penetrating of stares by eyes that could see. Her hand hooked through the air until it caught on my elbow. She pulled me toward the chapel.

I crossed myself and dipped my knees. The woman who had fallen shivered now on a stool by the altar. Paradies reached out her free hand. With sudden gentleness she lifted the black veil from the woman's face.

Magdalena Hofdemel raised her chin. Her scars were raw against her pallid skin. Her eyelids fluttered, and she twitched her cheeks and brow.

"Why are you praying in this chapel, little one?" Paradies said to her. "Herr Gieseke's service will be at the main altar."

In clipped Italian, the pianist commanded her maid to bring a thicker wrap for her friend.

"I'm awaiting my fate," Magdalena said. She scratched hard at the back of her wrist, as though she itched deep beneath the skin. "My dreadful fate." Her voice broke. It could no more hide her wounds than the weeping scars shining on her cheeks.

She raised her eyes to the flat spandrels above the chapel's arch. A fresco of the Last Judgment blazed there in red and rich blue. I pitied the girl and worried she might have given up on the divine mercy that would see her redeemed on that Last Day. I knelt beside her and touched her cheek. She flinched, but her gaze remained on the fresco.

"What is it that afflicts you, my dear?" I said.

"Isn't that obvious?" Paradies said. "I haven't the capacity to *see* the scars on her face, but I *have* touched them."

"I meant that she fell into a fit."

Paradies hissed me silent.

The Italian maid draped a cloak of thick wool over Magdalena's shoulders. She rubbed the hairs on her dark upper lip.

Paradies snapped her fingers, and the maid was at her side. "Come and listen to Wolfgang's music, Magdalena." She spoke with a softness I hadn't heard from her before. Then her voice was hard again: "That man could even entertain the dead."

Magdalena covered her eyes with her hand. She made to draw down her veil, but I held her wrist and came close to her.

"Listen to me," I whispered. "Since I visited you at your home, I've learned some of the circumstances surrounding Wolfgang's death."

Tears ran through her fingers. She refused to look at me.

My hand was wet with her crying. "Wolfgang's death was something to do with—with things of which I can't tell," I said. "Secret, dangerous things. But your husband didn't kill him."

Her head shook. Tiny uncomprehending movements. Her eyes were reddened and brown and fearful.

"He died as the result of a bigger conspiracy," I said. "It wasn't your husband."

"My Franz," she murmured.

"You came to my inn. You told my maid you wished to repent. You have nothing to repent of, do you understand?" I kissed her cold hands and tasted her tears on my mouth. I made out the words "thank you" on her lips, though they were too soft for me to hear.

I left Magdalena in the pew beside Paradies and went toward the front of the church. In the aisle I stepped across a speckled flagstone. A bronze crest marked it as the entrance to the Pergen family crypt below the floor of the church. *No doubt the police minister even has spies inside the graves of the Viennese*, I thought.

Slipping into the front row, I looked about for Baron van Swieten. I couldn't find him. I sat at Constanze's side.

Her sister Josefa hurried up the aisle. She kissed Constanze, bowed to me, and entered the choir, where she was to sing the soprano part in the Requiem. The chorus of Schikaneder's theater formed up on the altar, jostling the rough wooden box where Gieseke's body lay. The soloists stepped into line with Josefa.

As the woodwinds opened the Introitus, Baron van Swieten took the seat beside me. He was flushed and his mouth was tense. "Forgive my late arrival," he said.

I inclined my head.

"There are developments at the palace. I was engaged until the last moment."

"I thought it impossible you'd fail to attend the funeral Mass for an actor you applauded with such enthusiasm. You're not that kind of man." I laid my fingers on the back of his wrist in reassurance.

He blinked in surprise. He was restrained by the mood of the funeral, but his joy was so intense that I felt it smolder through my gloves where I touched him.

Only one thing could've made us break the gaze between us. We turned to the choir, to Wolfgang's music.

God was in every note of my brother's Requiem. He carved through the pretense with which we guard our souls. He revealed us in all our sin. I imagined poor Wolfgang laboring over this last great commission, a Mass for the departed, even as he felt himself crossing into the realms of the dead.

I trembled at the baleful Confutatis Maledictis, when the choir sang of the souls of sinners consigned to hellfire and begged to be among the blessed. I closed my eyes and prayed—for Wolfgang's spirit, for my little lost daughter, for my mother and father, and for myself. But there was torment rather than salvation in the music. The singers sounded more like the desperate damned than those who were to be saved. My prayers were overpowered.

I glanced toward Magdalena. She bent forward, her hands clasped before her veil. I hoped I had convinced her that her husband might not be condemned after all. He was innocent of

Wolfgang's murder. Then I understood why she had wept for him beneath the fresco of the Last Judgment. Even if he was no murderer, he had been a suicide, an unpardonable sinner. I crossed myself.

At Magdalena's side, Paradies moved her lips with the Latin of the choir. Her hand ran over the pew in front of her, as if improvising on a keyboard.

I thought of Wolfgang's riddle, scribbled at the end of his sonata. Did it refer to Paradies? He had written of sightlessness and of Paradise. But he also wrote that "She repents her blindness as she is always penitent." I had yet to see Paradies repent of anything.

If he had intended admittance to his new Masonic lodge to be based on talent, Maria Theresia von Paradies was a musician second only perhaps to Wolfgang himself. No doubt he also sought a woman of determination. If the Princess in *The Magic Flute* had doubted herself, she'd never have made it. She won her place among the priests at the end of the opera because of her absolute firmness. That was a quality Paradies possessed to a degree no less prodigious than her talent at the keyboard.

When her sister sang of the eternal light shining on the saints, Constanze sobbed. I laid my arm across her meager back. The choir brought the Requiem to a close.

Four porters in rough coats hoisted Gieseke's coffin onto their shoulders. The body's bony parts, perhaps the head, the elbows, the ankles, rattled against the unpolished wood. Like all peasants, the porters still suffered the old terror of being buried alive. They hesitated, wanting to be sure that Gieseke hadn't revived. Even if he were living I was sure he'd have been quiet in his casket until the earth closed over him. Fear had seeped like sweat through his pores. Death would've seemed the only safety and rest for him.

I helped Constanze to the door of the church. Swieten took her other arm. The hearse rolled past the entrance, south toward St. Marx Cemetery a few leagues outside the city. Gieseke would rest near Wolfgang.

Constanze wept against Schikaneder's chest. Singers from the theater surrounded my sister-in-law. Though the service had been for Gieseke, Wolfgang's music had drawn Constanze's grief once more to their attention. Now that the body was on its way to the grave, everyone came to the little woman in black with a consoling hug, as though she were the widow of all the corpses in Vienna.

The music had finished, but I continued to hear it. I turned back into the church to catch its last echoes.

The pews were empty. Most of the candles had been snuffed. I passed once more over the Pergen family tomb. The slab moved with a gentle tilt beneath my foot. I hurried onto the firmer flagstones around it.

The chatter of the opera singers receded in the square outside. They'd take Constanze home, or perhaps to an inn. I had no wish to go with them. Within the silence of the church, I detected the beautiful strains of Wolfgang's Requiem. It was as if the angels behind the altar chanted it in a register audible only to me.

A voice came through the church. I listened until it separated from the angels. It was a woman singing. I tracked it toward the north transept. She sang a melody from Wolfgang's Requiem.

I came to a worn stone staircase. From below, the woman

sang the Domine Jesu Christe: "Lord Jesus Christ, King of Glory, deliver the souls of all the faithful departed from the pains of hell and the deep pit."

From a niche beside the stairs I took a candle and lit it on the flame of an oil lamp. I followed the voice down into the dark.

30.

*L*et them not fall into darkness."

The voice wasn't quite a soprano and the singer made no attempt at polish. She was all expression, as though her emotion and faith gave birth to the music that had, in fact, come from the pen of my dying brother.

"The holy standard-bearer, Michael, brings them back into the holy light," she sang.

My candle flickered in a draft at the bottom of the stairs. I cupped my hand about it and stepped into a long, vaulted crypt.

The air was chilly and dusty dry. Low, narrow containers crowded the floor. I thought to call a greeting, but I didn't wish to interrupt the music.

"We offer sacrifice and prayers of praise to thee, O Lord."

I touched the nearest of the containers. Dust and metal, a hinge.

I put down my candle to lift the lid of the box. Reaching

inside, my palm rested on something dry and stiff. I took the candle in my other hand and held it close.

A face. Empty eyes and a lipless grin.

I stumbled backward, my palm upright before me as though to fend off the corpse should it rise from its casket.

But the body lay still. The remnants of a woman's wig encased the head, stiff and russet like autumn leaves. Her hands were crossed on her chest in lace gloves.

I tripped over an uneven flagstone and reached out to steady myself. The wall spread its cold along my arm. Beside my hand in the shape of a cross were two long thigh bones.

I spun away. My shin struck the nearest coffin. It rocked on the timber blocks that elevated it from the floor in case of a flood. Then it tipped against the next one. The caskets tumbled along the row. As they fell, the bones within snapped with a sound like running feet in summer undergrowth.

The singing sounded farther from me now. "Let them pass, O Master, from death to the life you promised to Abraham and his offspring."

I hurried down the row of coffins, trying to halt their fall. My head struck a low span in the stone vault and I dropped back into a niche in the wall. Pain ringed my brain and bore down on it.

I opened my eyes. The niche was stacked high with pelvic bones. The first dead of the crypt, moved aside to make room for new corpses. I screamed with all my terror of death.

My shriek subsided into short breaths.

Silence beneath the church.

The coffins had come to rest. Only the dust that choked the air showed they had been disturbed.

The singing, too, had ended.

I held my candle before me, my arm locked as if I might extend it far into the darkness to light up the whole crypt. I turned to my right and left, staring and blind.

A footstep sounded, not close by. I spun toward it, but heard nothing more.

"Who's there?" I called.

Another step echoed through the vault. In my panic, I thought that a corpse, liberated from its coffin, had risen. I imagined it stumbling through the dark with limbs unaccustomed to walking, like a tottering baby.

The steps came closer.

I put the corpses out of my mind. I had been attacked only two days before. I had living, murderous men to fear, before I faced the spirits of the vengeful dead.

My arm weakened. I lowered the candle.

Measured and slow, the steps seemed still some way off.

Then she was before me.

"You'd do better without that pathetic little light," she said.

I started, and lifted the candle once more. Paradies licked her thick lips and let her mouth hang open.

I glanced at the candle and frowned.

"I can smell the burning tallow," she said, "if that's what you're wondering."

I stammered, "I heard you singing. I couldn't see—"

"Down here you're as blind as I am." She swept past me and extinguished the flame of my candle with her thumb and forefinger.

I cried out. She grabbed my wrist and twisted it so that the useless stub of the candle dropped to the floor. She wrenched at my arm.

"Come with me, damn it," she said.

I blundered along behind her. My knees struck the sharp corners of the coffins. I tripped over unseen tools, left against the wall by workmen. She hauled me deeper into the crypt.

"Before they built the graveyards outside the walls of the city, the wealthy were buried right beneath the churches," she said. "That's who you see around you. Hundreds of nobles and leading citizens, dried out and preserved by the air down here."

"It was as if the woman inside the coffin was screaming at me."

Paradies clicked her tongue. "The burial workers tie up the jaws of the dead before they put them in the coffins. If you thought you saw one screaming, it was only that the string around her head had slipped and her mouth had dropped open."

She thrust my hand downward. She ran it along a leathery surface. Even in the dark I knew it was the skin of one of the corpses. I struggled, but she was stronger. "Feel that? There?" she said. She rubbed my palm over the long bone of the thigh.

"It curves. It isn't straight," I said.

"Broken, but badly set. This one must've been thin and malnourished, even though she surely would've been rich to be buried down here."

My fingers explored the brittle leg, until I realized that Paradies no longer held me there. I pulled away.

"Now everyone but the emperor's family goes to a common grave. The new burial laws. You can have as many Masses said for you as you're prepared to pay for, but you'll still be interred next to a poor man."

My breath shivered through my teeth.

"Don't be squeamish. Poor old Gieseke would be pleased to be buried in a cemetery where no distinction is made by rank. Wolfgang, too," she said. "That's what the Masons want, isn't it? Equality. A pity they have to die to get it."

She took me by the shoulder and led me in a new direction. "They stopped putting bodies down here a decade ago, but I still come. I know them all from the inscriptions on the metal plates of their coffins. From the touch of their fingers, the bones of their cheeks and foreheads."

We moved fast. The wall was on our right. I thought I was beginning to see things, dark against darker. I wondered if that was how the world appeared to the blind woman who rushed me through the crypt.

She halted. I stubbed my foot against a step.

"You'll find a lantern down to your left," she said.

I lifted a small glowing oil lamp and flipped back the guard. It cast a long shaft of yellow light. The room, which had become somehow clear to me in the dark, receded. I saw only the single coffin before us.

"Metastasio," Paradies said.

I directed the lamp toward her. Perspiration stood out on her upper lip. She must have detected something of the lamp's glow, because she gestured impatiently for me to turn it back on the coffin.

It was a tall pine casket painted with lutes and skulls garlanded with olive branches. At its side, there stood a copper urn. "The Imperial Poet?" I thought of the expensive edition of the Italian's poetry presented to Wolfgang by the Milanese count.

"Fifty years as court poet. Wrote the texts of a few dozen operas, which were set to music by countless composers, including your brother. And now there he is—a gutted corpse."

"Gutted?"

"In the urn beside his casket, you'd find the heart that was the source of his poetry and the tongue that declaimed it. A few other organs, too."

"A great genius," I said.

"Now his guts are in a fancy bucket."

I gave her a sharp look. She flicked her wrist in dismissal, as though she had seen me.

"What've you been doing since you came to Vienna?" she said.

"I've had some business to conduct."

She sneered. "Ridiculous woman."

"I want to know who killed my brother," I said.

My words came back at me off the vaulted ceilings. I had spoken louder than I expected.

Paradies sucked in her cheeks. "Do you want *your* innards in a pot, too?"

"Are you threatening me?"

"Dear, I became blind when I was three. For a while I was bitter about it. Then I understood. In that time I'd seen enough of this dreadful world for it to live before my eyes forever. Without the distraction of sight, I see things as they truly are." She spoke through tight, emphatic lips. "I cared too much about your brother to let you go the way of the corpses down here. You know what you should do? Live with Wolfgang. Don't die with him."

Her stare was ferocious. I wondered how close Paradies had been to Wolfgang.

"Why am I in danger?" I said. "Is it the Grotto?"

"The what?"

"The Grotto. The Masonic lodge he was founding. It was you he intended to make its first woman member. I'm sure of it. But perhaps you don't want anyone to find out about it. Because of the emperor's restrictions on the order."

Paradies laughed. "If that was Wolfgang's intention, I'd have turned him down."

"I don't understand."

"I've made my own way in the world. In spite of my blindness. In spite of being a woman. I've supported myself by working as a musician. I've toured London and Paris, earned big commissions. If I seem scornful of you, it's because you had a talent at least equal to mine but you never broke free."

"I had to look after my father."

"True, I was never encumbered by anyone as domineering as that old bastard."

"Madame." I stamped my foot.

"I'm not genteel enough for you? You'd prefer me to say it in French, perhaps? Your father tried to limit even Wolfgang's career, because he wanted to be taken care of in his old age. Your brother barely made his escape. You didn't stand a chance."

I leaned against the wall. It was cold on my neck.

"Men destroy women. They refuse to acknowledge our talents. They ruin our bodies and our health with their midnight attentions and the constant pregnancies they bring. I avoided such misery. That's why I've been able to have a successful career. I never sought the aid of any man in my success, because such support comes at the price almost of one's life," Paradies said. "No man ever held me back, either. Masonry? I need no Brotherhood."

"What of friendship?"

She waved her hand. "I'm blind. I'm accustomed to being alone, even when I'm surrounded by a crowd. That's why I come to this crypt. In the church up there, death is a show. A Requiem by Maestro Mozart, a fine send-off. Down here I see better than anyone else. *This* is the reality of our lives—each shut up in our coffins, brittle and powerless. Music fills me with beauty, and I don't care if people recoil from my spinning eyeballs. The dead don't judge me the way living people do."

She dropped her chin. I sensed the isolation that led her to prefer such terrifying company.

"I have to go. I'm leaving for Berlin." Paradies seemed to debate whether to say something more.

I held my breath and waited.

"The Prussian ambassador hired me to perform some pieces by Wolfgang. One of them, he says, is previously unknown. He has acquired it from the widow Mozart," she said.

Her powdered face twitched with indecision. Then she seemed to relax. "I was at the ambassador's residence today. He gave me the commission and ordered me to depart for Berlin as soon as possible."

"I know the new piece. I played it myself this lunchtime."

"While I was there, someone else came into the room. He blurted out the words, 'Pergen knows.'"

I would've spoken, but Paradies raised her hand for silence.

"The ambassador and the newcomer became still, as though perhaps by a gesture or a look the Prussian had signaled that he wasn't alone. There was something nervous and secretive in their quiet. I knew it was my presence that halted them. Then they remembered that I couldn't see them, and I sensed their tension release. The ambassador rose and went to the door. The visitor whispered a few words to him. He said, 'I can't go on.' The ambassador told him to wait in another room. He didn't ask him; he ordered him rather forcefully. Then he dismissed me, with payment in advance for my journey."

I frowned. "'Pergen knows'? 'Can't go on'? What does it mean?"

"People behave as if I'm deaf as well as blind," she said. "They think that if they whisper I won't know who they are. But I recognized the voice quite clearly. I teach piano to his wife and I've played at his mother-in-law's salon many times."

"Who was it?"

"Prince Lichnowsky."

At the home of the man who had told me the prince was a scoundrel? What was Lichnowsky's connection to the Prussian ambassador? And what did he believe Pergen knew?

Paradies reached out her hand. I caught it in my own. "You have to be careful, Nannerl. Wolfgang cherished you to the very end. For his sake, take care."

Paradies touched my cheek. My tears fell on her hand. She led me to the steps of the crypt and pushed me up ahead of her.

In the transept of the church, the gray evening light struggled through the windows.

"Wolfgang wrote a riddle," I said. "If it wasn't about you—?"

"I'm no good with riddles. I'm blind. I detest anything that makes it harder to see the truth."

In the first pew of the church, the Italian maid stood up. She faced the altar, crossed herself, and came to take the blind woman's arm.

When the door creaked shut behind them, I felt a draft against my back. It seemed to rise from the entrance to the crypt. I hurried down the aisle and out into the growing darkness.

31

*A*ll Vienna seemed as lifeless as the crypt beneath St.
Michael's Church, as I went through the covered way
before the Spanish Riding School. The Lipizzaners craned out
of their stalls, their long heads gray and ghostly in the twilight.
Market women stumbled home, catatonic with fatigue at the
day's end. The air was still and freezing.

The fire blazed in the tall hearth at the porters' station of
the Imperial Library. I hurried to the head of the stairs and
crossed the hall to Baron van Swieten's chambers.

The baron rose from his dining table. He pulled a napkin
from his neck and tightened the belt of his green silk chamber
robe over his breeches. He took both my hands and brushed
my knuckles with his lips. Only then did I realize that he might
misinterpret my returning alone to him, the day after he had
hinted at love.

He gestured toward the table. "Will you join me? I'm so
happy you came. I lost you in the crowd after the funeral Mass.
I'm having *uccellini*. It was one of—"

He hesitated, staring at the platter beside his candlestick. A sage leaf protruded from a roll of veal. Twisted within it, a spiral of prosciutto was like a wound in the pale meat.

"One of Wolfgang's favorites," I said.

He touched his thumb to his lip.

I glanced at the door. A page stood beside it with his eyes averted.

"That'll be all," the baron said.

The page clicked his heels and left the room.

"My dear baron," I said, "fear has brought me to you."

Not love? I saw the question run across his eyes as though it had been inscribed there. I couldn't be sure if my answer was written as clearly, but I read in his face the response he found. The light that had illuminated him when I entered his chambers faded. *No, not love.*

I told him what I had learned of the Prussian connection to Wolfgang's Grotto, and that the king in Berlin tried to use my brother to infiltrate Viennese society.

"I fear someone may've taken Wolfgang for a spy," I said.

"It's possible."

"But if such activities *were* discovered, who would've— who would've punished him? Count Pergen, whose job is to eliminate foreign agents? Or the king of Prussia, covering his tracks?"

He led me to his couch. When he sat beside me, he brought the scent of jasmine. I remembered the perfume on his handkerchief when I had dried my tears of joy at the conclusion of *The Magic Flute*. A log dropped in the fire, and I started.

"This information is very important, madame," he said.

"Your Grace, it seems to me that it's also very dangerous."

He grinned. "Nothing at the imperial court is important unless it's dangerous, too. That's the nature of palaces."

"Then I ought to change my negative opinion of the obscurity in which I've lived these last years at St. Gilgen. At least there's no danger there."

"One risks avalanches in your mountain village, and an unnoticed death. But, in a palace, when one takes a chance, it's like a daring throw at dice for the richest pot in the casino."

He stood and paced the floor, slow ruminative footsteps, each making two clear connections on the floorboards, toe following heel. "And the pot, madame, is Austria. The future of its freedoms. If we cast a winning throw, we may save the emperor's subjects from the oppression of Count Pergen. We may grant them the liberty to think and speak as they wish. To inquire into the deep truths of new sciences."

I sensed it might be I who would rattle in the baron's hands and tumble across the gaming table at the mercy of chance. "How?"

"Our Emperor Leopold trusts Pergen only so far."

Swieten tapped his forefinger on the medal adorning his jacket, the red and gold Knight Commander's Cross of the Order of St. Stephen. "In my capacity as imperial librarian and head of censorship, I allow limited freedoms to publishers of books and pamphlets. I adjust those limits all the time."

"On what basis?"

"My latest discussions with the emperor. I carry out his politics as much as my own beliefs will permit. The same is true of Pergen. He's allowed to run his network of spies, to arrest dissenters and to punish them. But he mustn't overstep the bounds of what Emperor Leopold considers civilized."

"Has he ever done so?"

The baron sat on the arm of the couch. "The emperor reprimanded Pergen earlier this year. A publisher had distributed some pamphlets critical of the government. Pergen engineered the absolute ruin of the poor man's business. But he had gone too far. The emperor forced him to rehabilitate the bankrupt fellow. What if he was proven to have done something that couldn't be withdrawn?"

The dice were in the baron's hands. The throw was coming. "Murder," I murmured.

"Exactly. If the emperor could be presented with proof that Pergen's agents murdered a prominent figure like Wolfgang, it'd force the emperor to dispose of his police minister."

Make your throw, I thought. *I'm ready.*

"Your Grace, I'm at your disposal. Whatever you wish me to do, I shall carry it out immediately and willingly. If you'd have me write a letter to the emperor detailing what I've learned—"

"A letter?" Swieten waved his hand and shook his head. "Put nothing in writing. Speak to no one of this."

I curtsied. "I'll await your advice at my inn."

He reached for my wrist. "No, you're right that this is dangerous. I can't allow you to sit alone in a public inn. You'd be too exposed."

"But I must—"

"You'll stay here. I assure you, I'll devise a way to reach the emperor with this information. To prove what Pergen has done. You shan't be detained here for long."

I trusted him to take my part in this risky affair. But I also wondered if he didn't have another reason for keeping me at the palace. I knew him for a gentleman, but thoughts that are not absolutely guilty may not necessarily be without fault. The longer I spent with him, the more I feared that my own pleasure in his company might develop beyond the power of my shame to restrain me.

He led me through a high gilt door to his salon. The room was lit only by the fire and the evening moonlight. He left me in the shadows by the window and walked through the orange beam of the hearth.

Shoving aside a pile of papers on his desk, he slid open a small drawer. Then for a long time he was motionless.

When he turned, the fire flared and caught his eyes. He approached me soundlessly. The blaze was behind him then, and his stare was filled with the moon.

He lifted a cross on a delicate chain. "When my father brought her to Vienna from the Netherlands," he said, "he gave this to my mother, rest her soul."

The baron dangled the cross above my hand, so that it tickled at my palm. It was half the length of my smallest finger, gold inset with squares of amber. He let go of the chain. I caught it between my knuckles before it slid to the floor.

"I want you to have it," he said.

I followed the moonlight into his eyes. I unclasped the chain and fastened it at my neck. The cross lay over my collarbone. I knew I had its protection.

The crackling of the fire died down. I heard the baron's breath, then mine, short and urgent.

A song sounded in my head. The aria of love my brother wrote in *Così fan tutte* for Ferrando. *A loving breath from our treasured one brings the heart sweet solace.* My respirations joined the slow saraband rhythm of the aria. *The heart that's nourished by hope and love needs no better enticement.*

The cross glinted in the glow of the fire, quivering with each of my inhalations to the song's triple meter. The baron watched his gift, enraptured, as though he, too, heard the music.

He lifted his hand toward the cross. I took his fingers in mine. I thought to hold them back, but instead I placed them over the jewel he had given me. I went onto my toes. His other hand circled my waist.

When I kissed him the tiny hairs of his beard seemed so rough and sharp that I felt they might draw blood. I pushed my cheek harder against him.

32.

I reclined on the divan in the baron's chamber. The fire warmed my legs. My head lay on his chest, lifting with the soft motion of his breathing. His fingers moved through the heaviness of my hair and found my scalp. I let him massage me there.

With his toes, he stroked at my foot until I laughed. I rolled onto him for a slow kiss. His shirt was loose and I moved my hand inside it. "Are you cold?" I rubbed his firm shoulder.

"You're getting all the warmth of the fire." He smiled. "Move over."

"Is my body not sufficient to warm you?"

He pushed his face against my neck and breathed in. Then his head dropped back against the divan and he frowned at the dark ceiling.

I tickled at his chin with my nose. "What is it?"

"To see us together would've made Wolfgang very happy," he said.

Since the moment he had placed the cross around my neck, I had felt no guilt. I had sensed that I might've rushed to the palace not out of fear, after all, but out of lust, yet I hadn't reproved myself. When he touched me, I had thought of no one but the baron. I had experienced the same absolute absorption that came over me when I sat at the keyboard. With the mention of my brother's name I was overwhelmed by all the complications from which music—and now love—had been my refuge.

It was as if my father, my husband, and my confessor from the Church of Mariaplain jostled through the door, shocked and enraged by the position in which they found me. I pulled the thin muslin of my shift around my neck to cover myself from their disapproving glares. I watched the logs consumed by the fire.

"Forgive me." The baron touched my cheek. His hand left a trace of cologne in the air before my face like a screen. "I shouldn't have mentioned his name."

My sight blurred with tears, but not because of the baron's indelicacy. I had recalled where I had smelled the scent Swieten wore. It was the delicate blossom fragrance Constanze had savored when she unstoppered the bottle on Wolfgang's desk.

I had grown so far from my brother that I hadn't known his perfume. I wondered with what accuracy I remembered anything about him, his voice or his laughter. Would he be erased from my memory entirely in a decade, or even a year?

"He was the only one who wanted me to be fulfilled," I said. "When he came to Vienna, he wrote to tell me I should follow him. He was sure I could make a living here as a performer and a teacher."

"You were still unmarried?" The baron's face was stilled by what might have been, had we met then.

"My father was alone. I couldn't leave him in Salzburg."

Swieten's voice was impatient, as though I were denying him, rather than denied to him. "For heaven's sake, that's what servants are for."

I whispered, "And daughters, it seems."

He took a long breath. "So it seems."

"Wolfgang always understood me. He wasn't encumbered by my duties, so he saw what was best for me more clearly than I did."

The baron grasped my hip as though he feared I might slip away from him and leave the room.

"I didn't realize how much I missed him, until I came to Vienna," I said. "In the mountains, without any letters for three years, I consoled myself for his absence by playing his music. It was all I could know of him, and so it seemed to be enough. But in this city he wasn't just a name on a composition. He was a performer, a man who ate dinner and played billiards and loved his wife, and died. Everyone was his friend—or his enemy."

"Do you regret coming?"

I heard a plea in the baron's question. I smiled to reassure him. "All my memories of Wolfgang have been reawakened by Vienna. The magic kingdom we invented to pass the time on our first coach journeys when I was twelve. The room we shared in our house on Getreide Lane—my bed had a curtain for privacy, which he little respected. The time I became sick with typhoid in Holland and was so ill I received the last rites. Wolfgang joked that I might've remained a prodigy forever if only I hadn't recovered."

"God forbid."

I laid Swieten's hand in my lap. "I recall, too, how he looked at me when Papa left with him for a tour of Italy, his excitement edged with just a little guilt that I was to be left behind. I hated him desperately and went to bed in tears for a week."

"Yet he wanted you to come to Vienna."

"It was our father who created this antagonism between us." I had to pause, to hold back a sob and to understand what I had at last said, though I had known it for so long. "Wolfgang only wished to compose and perform. But when he broke away from Papa, he wanted me with him. He wanted me to fulfill my musical potential, too. To be at his side when he wore his fine red suit and sat at the piano before an audience."

"Our loss when Wolfgang died would've been much harder to bear had we not discovered you."

An image came to me—I was beside Wolfgang on the piano stool, playing his Sonata in D for four hands. He wrote it for us to perform together at a single keyboard. His red sleeve crossed my left hand to play a higher note.

"I'm a poor replacement, Gottfried," I murmured, distracted.

Swieten dropped his eyes when I spoke his first name.

The four-hands sonata came to a close in my head. Wolfgang and I played the final chord and lifted our arms in unison.

As sharply as the chord brought the piece to an end, I snapped upright on the divan. "But I'm not," I cried out. "Not inferior at all. In fact, exactly alike."

I grabbed Swieten's face and kissed it. In spite of his usual formality, he laughed. "What's this?" he said.

I threw my arms wide. "Tomorrow Mozart shall perform for the emperor."

"Indeed?"

"You shall arrange it."

"As you wish, maestro. What'll you play?"

"I don't know yet. But I do know exactly what I'll wear."

33.

*F*rom the window of the baron's carriage, I peered out at the maidservants walking to their work in gray shawls and white bonnets. Their faces were luminous and beautiful in the dawn. The clouds that had obscured the sky since my arrival in Vienna lifted. The morning sun lit the façades of the palaces, picking out all their elaborate detail.

The carriage crossed the Staff-in-Iron Square, rounding the stump at the center of the plaza where the apprentice had once chained an impregnable padlock. Satan claimed the young craftsman's soul in payment for this secret art. I reclined on the padded bench, shuddering across the cobbles, and smiled.

I knew then what I would play for the emperor.

Lenerl was on her knees preparing the fire in my room. She raised an eyebrow at my late arrival. I laughed with a freedom that, I believe, surprised her even more than the hour of my return.

Throwing my cloak on the bed, I dropped against the bolster. "Leave the fire for now, girl. Go to Baron van

Swieten's chambers. He'll have a package for you to bring to me."

Lenerl dusted off the knees of her skirt.

"Hurry, girl, hurry," I said, with a laugh.

She smiled at my good humor, took her shawl, and left the room. I listened to her clogs clipping over the cobbles in the square.

The scent of jasmine lay on my clothes from Swieten's embrace. Wolfgang's perfume. I went to the mirror on the dressing table.

I untied my hair and combed it down over my shoulder. It dropped almost to my waist. I twisted it into a single braid and gripped it in one hand. I picked up a pair of scissors.

Long and blond, always tied with colorful ribbons, this hair had been my pride. It had consumed so much of my attention that perhaps I had sometimes failed to consider what went on inside the head from which it hung. I lifted the scissors and cut with slow strokes.

As I laid the braid on the dressing table, my head felt light.

I pulled my remaining hair back to my neck and tied it with a single black ribbon. I was *him* again, as I had been when I stood before the mirror in St. Gilgen with the letter in my hand informing me of his passing. This wasn't the death mask reflecting his final sufferings back at me. In the glass, I saw all the creativity and joy I shared with Wolfgang. One stroke of the scissors freed me of the weight of womanhood. No one would've commanded this face to renounce such talent as I had, to tend an aging father and marry a bureaucrat in a tiny village. This face might enter the palace. This face might walk beside Baron van Swieten and greet the emperor.

I smiled at the mirror. "Maestro," I said.

Lenerl returned with the package, opened it, and laid out the contents on the bed. She gasped when she noticed the length of hair on the dressing table.

I ran my hand across Wolfgang's red frock coat. One of his hairs adhered to the shoulder. I left it there. I turned over his hat and saw the traces of his sweat where it had stained the band. The inseam of his scarlet pants was worn from the motion of his legs. The suit was alive with my brother.

"Undress me, Lenerl."

34.

*I*n the barroom, the innkeeper whistled a tune from Wolfgang's *Figaro*.

Lenerl crept to the foot of the stairs. She held up her hand for me to wait. "Joachim," she called, "let me have a bottle of your delicious Steinfeder."

"An early lunch, Lenerl?" he said. "I'll bring it up from the cellar for you right away, my dear." He descended the steps to his basement, singing. "*If you want to dance, Little Count, I'll play the guitar for you.*"

Lenerl gestured for me to hurry. I trotted past her, out to the baron's carriage.

I climbed inside. "How do I look?" I removed my hat and set it on the seat beside me.

Swieten rested his chin on the silver knob of his cane, shaking his head. "You look like—like Wolfgang." He reached over and touched the blond hair knotted at the nape of my neck.

I opened my hand. In my palm, tied with a thin ribbon, lay a lock of the hair I had cut away. "Wolfgang used to wear his hair long for a man, but I still had to hack off quite a lot. It seems a shame that it should be used only to stuff a pillow."

The baron put the lock to his lips and slipped it into the pocket of his vest.

I rubbed at my red breeches and slapped my thighs. "I don't know how you gentlemen wear such trousers. They chafe terribly."

"We're excused whale-bone corsets and stays designed to lift our breasts. We don't suffer as much as women, despite the restriction imposed by our leg wear. How does the hat fit?"

I pushed the three-cornered black hat with its gold trim onto my head.

Swieten adjusted it. "Wear it like this, a little to the side. Otherwise it sits too low on your brow." He sat back to take me in. "It's remarkable, remarkable."

"Did my sister-in-law suspect anything?"

He shook his head. "I insisted that I wished to buy Wolfgang's suit for my own use. Constanze knew this to be ridiculous. I'm more than a head taller than he was. The suit would never fit me. She took my purchase for a donation to my friend's widow which I disguised to preserve her dignity."

"And the emperor?"

"We'll await his pleasure shortly. He was reluctant at first."

"How did you convince him?"

"I told him that if he went along with our plan he'd discover something that'd truly astound him. He agreed. But he warned me that—" He halted and grimaced.

"What?"

"That if things don't work out as I told him they would, my position at court shall be forfeit."

"No, Gottfried." I reached for his hand.

"Don't fret about it. The emperor has given his agreement. He wishes to see evidence of the crime about which I spoke to him. It's up to us to provide it."

"And our most important invitee?"

"The emperor has commanded his attendance. He'll be there."

The coach went under the archway of the imperial ballrooms and pulled up in the Swiss Courtyard at the steps to the oldest part of the Hofburg. When the footman opened the door to the carriage, Swieten descended and held out his hand to me. I shook my head. "No need to be chivalrous now," I said.

He pulled his mouth tight at his error.

Schikaneder came through the ornate Swiss Gate and bowed to the baron. I reached up to slap his shoulder.

"Emanuel, old fellow, thank you for coming," I said.

If he flinched, it was only a flicker deep in his eyes. After his lifetime of dissembling, I could count on the actor not to give me away. He inclined his head. "Lead on, my dear sirs," he said.

We entered a staircase of white marble. A scarlet carpet covered the steps. The three of us went side by side up the long flight, each doubtless carrying a private dread. No matter how much of the spirit of my brother I had absorbed with his clothing, I waited for the palace guards to step forward and unmask me.

The chamberlain led us through the palace. Its corridors seemed measureless. The massive building represented sovereignty, as though no smaller palace could house the immense prestige of the emperor. But authority is never infinite. If it were, Pergen and his secret agents would be of no use. The greater a power, the more it advertises its tiny weaknesses.

I listened to the reverent murmur of our feet on the carpet. The whisper of distant doors. Clocks ticking in closed rooms as if they were the very pulse of the palace. Underlying it all, a silence like waiting itself, so that I wanted to stop at every keyhole to see who crouched behind it.

Wolfgang's clothes were comfortable now that I was accustomed to them. I followed the baron's step, matching my breathing to his steady rhythm. He caught my glance and winked.

The chamberlain showed us into a small concert salon. Its wall panels were carved with shells and clusters of leaves. A piano stood before a semicircle of chairs. Mute and still, it beckoned to me.

The piano was a Stein, like the one in Wolfgang's study. I laid my hat on top of it, and played an arpeggio. As the notes trailed into silence, I heard people approaching. The chamberlain bowed in readiness. Swieten stiffened.

The emperor swept into the chamber with a group of courtiers behind him. Tall and pouchy-eyed, he wore a short wig and an autumnal velvet suit that matched the rosewood on the walls. Across his chest he had a red sash.

Swieten bowed low, his arm stretching gracefully to his side. "Your Majesty," he said.

Schikaneder threw himself into a hurried bow.

I would've curtsied had Swieten not caught my eye in time. My bow was all the more formal because it was the first time I had practiced one.

"Herr Mozart," the emperor said.

I flushed, nervous now the deception was under way. Leopold ran his tongue over his teeth, watching me.

I hoped Swieten had briefed the emperor correctly. I coughed to disguise my voice. "Your Majesty." I prayed that I'd be required to speak no further—it would surely reveal me to be a woman.

The emperor took one of the chairs before the piano. The men who accompanied him went to their seats, too.

Except for one.

Count Pergen stood at the center of the room, staring at me. I saw the shock and indecision in his pale eyes. Usually so shrewd, they were gleaming and wide.

Swieten took the police minister's elbow. He shoved him to a chair tapestried with peasants dancing at a spring festival. Pergen dropped into it, his mouth falling open.

The emperor blinked slowly so that we knew it was his pleasure for us to begin.

Gathering myself, I played the melodious Allegro of Wolfgang's most difficult sonata, the F major. He had composed it during his visit to Salzburg with his new bride. I recalled the coldness I had shown Constanze then. I knew it had hurt my brother. I sensed his suffering in the music.

The second, slow movement in B-flat major seemed to carry all the proud melancholy I remembered in Wolfgang during his honeymoon visit. This music had protected him from my father's disapproval, though it also measured out the sadness of that rejection.

I glanced at the emperor when I completed the Adagio. He scratched at his pale jowls. Beside him, Pergen quivered like the disturbed surface of a pool, his hands tight together in his lap and his staring eyes never rising above the gold buckles of my shoes.

Through the first rapid scales of the Allegro assai, I kept my eye on Pergen. His neck jerked, as though the tumbling notes were blows that fell on him. *Like the poor prisoners he has condemned to a public beating*, I thought.

I struck a false note and sensed a fluctuation in my tempo. I understood that my vindictiveness interfered with my concentration and my joy in the music. I turned my eyes from the police minister. The keyboard came to life in the fast finale.

I played the concluding chord. The emperor rose and led his courtiers in applause. He lifted a hand to silence them.

"No one could've given us such a performance of this divine music," he said, "except the immortal Mozart."

Pergen swayed, ashen and trembling, as the emperor resumed his place.

"What'll you give us now, Maestro Mozart?" Leopold said.

I coughed and looked to Swieten in alarm, but he had already stepped forward to speak. "We had intended to perform a scene from the maestro's opera *Don Giovanni*," he said.

"Excellent. *Don Giovanni, or The Dissolute Punished*, its full title, I believe. A moral tale of which I approve with all my heart." The emperor clapped his hands.

"The maestro was to have played his own piano transcription," Swieten said, "while I was to take the role of the Stone Guest and Herr Schikaneder would sing Leporello, the manservant."

I noticed Schikaneder push out his chest. Once a performance was broached, he was full of assurance. I was less confident.

"Our Don Giovanni was to have been another member of Herr Schikaneder's company. To our distress, the fellow is ill. He was unable to accompany us to the palace," Swieten said, "so we may not perform the scene, after all."

"Can't Maestro Mozart sing the role himself?"

"He's no baritone, your Majesty. He won't do for the Don. We must abandon our performance." Swieten waited a moment. "Unless, of course, Count Pergen—"

"Absolutely." The emperor grabbed Pergen's shoulder and shook it. "Come along, Pergen. You have a fine voice, and a baritone at that. Perfect for the Don. Step up, fellow. I know you're more of a church singer, but we won't judge you harshly."

The mention of judgment from his sovereign's mouth jarred Pergen. He fixed Leopold with eyes that seemed to shake in their sockets.

Swieten thrust a score into Pergen's hands and maneuvered him across the floor. He kept a grip on the minister's elbow as they stood beside the piano.

Pergen's features were as transfigured as they had been when he spoke of wandering ghosts at early Mass in the cathedral. A sinner encounters supernatural revenge, he had said then. It must have seemed to him such vengeance was now undertaken. The ghost of his victim returned from the grave, forcing him into an ordeal before a man whose power was absolute and lethal.

Pergen pulled at his cravat to loosen it. But the tightness was within his throat. Nothing he could do would relieve it.

Schikaneder leaned close and whispered, "There's not much in this scene for me, you know. May I do Leporello's aria about the list of ladies the Don has seduced?"

"Perhaps that's not quite appropriate for the emperor," I said.

"You're right. Something else then? How about 'Night and Day I Toil Away'?"

"By all means, but only after we do this scene."

I struck the dramatic opening chords, announcing the arrival of the Stone Guest, the spirit of a man murdered by Don Giovanni, come to take his killer to Hell.

Schikaneder cowered, acting the part of Giovanni's fearful servant. Pergen shuddered with each chord. In a strong baritone, Swieten sang the Stone Guest's invitation for the reprobate Don to accompany him to the underworld.

Giovanni's first lines came. Swieten's fingers tightened around Pergen's upper arm. Pergen fumbled with his score and sang, bidding his servant set a place at the table for his terrifying visitor.

The audience seemed not to notice Pergen's nerves and weak singing. Their attention was consumed by Schikaneder's unrestrained mugging, as he urged his master to turn away from the disquieting spirit. The emperor, however, watched only his police minister.

Schikaneder's animation appeared to lend some backbone to Pergen. When the Stone Guest told Giovanni that he had come to claim his soul, it was time for the Don to respond: "None shall accuse me of fear. I shall succumb to no one." Pergen's chin lifted and, for the first time, he extended his jaw to let the notes resonate.

I worried that Pergen's self-righteousness might carry him through this ordeal.

The Stone Guest called on Giovanni to accept his invitation. Pergen replied that he was fearless and would accept. Swieten held out his hand.

Pergen hesitated. Swieten reached for him.

There was no acting in the cry that came from Pergen's lips when the baron squeezed his hand. He caught his breath and stuttered through the line about a deadly chill in his body. He pulled away, but Swieten held on.

"There's no repentance for me," Pergen sang. His eyes swiveled toward me. "Vanish from my sight."

I heard the fear of God in Pergen's voice, and I wished mercy for him. I thought of my prayers for Our Lord to show clemency toward my brother. I hated to think that there might be anyone from whom redemption would be withheld. I glanced at the baron, wishing that he might find some way to offer compassion. He didn't waver.

Still gripping the count's hand, Swieten forced his wrist down so that the poor man bent before him. With all the volume he could manage, Swieten sang: "Then dread the eternal wrath."

I had loved this scene onstage. But when I saw it unfold in the palpitations and sobs of a terrified wretch, I confess that my desire to unmask Pergen weakened. I whispered to Swieten, "Your Grace. I—"

Pergen squinted over the piano toward me, gasping. "No," he said. "No, no."

Swieten released him.

Pergen leaned against the piano, his shoulders heaving.

The emperor snapped his fingers at his distraught minister. "Come on, man."

Pergen swallowed hard, and sang: "Unknown terrors chill me. Demons of doom grasp at me. Is Hell let loose to torture me?"

The baron had read my reluctance to push this stricken man too far. He raised his hand as a conductor might, commanding and firm. I was as powerless to resist him as I had been when we kissed. I grew confident in the force of Wolfgang's music and Swieten's guidance.

He brought down his hand. I drove my fingers hard onto the keyboard to make the chords as loud as I might. In the deepest register I could manage, I sang the chorus: "Eternal torment awaits you. You'll burn in endless night."

Pergen bleated his final lines, though his distress was somewhat disguised by Schikaneder. The actor grasped for Don Giovanni, trying to haul him back as he fell into the flames. "The fire of doom surrounds him," he called.

Schikaneder would no doubt have dropped to the floor had he been playing the Don. Pergen had no need to mime a descent into Hell—he was already there. His eyes darted between the emperor and me. His palm dropped a pool of sweat onto the lid of the piano. His skin was as white as his periwig.

The emperor's companions lifted their hands, waiting for his signal to applaud. But when Leopold rose from his chair, he hooked his thumbs into the pockets of his frock coat.

Schikaneder leaned into a practiced bow. He looked about, perplexed by the silence. Swieten beckoned me to rise from the piano.

I reached out my hand to Pergen, as the baron had told

me I must. The room was empty of all sound, except Pergen's shivering breath.

"Take it," the emperor said. "Take his hand."

Pergen shook his head.

"I command you." Leopold's eyes, which had been hidden by sagging skin, grew wide and powerful. "It is the will of your emperor."

Pergen dropped toward my hand. I thought he might kiss it, but then I saw that he was collapsing. He fell at my feet.

"Forgive me, Mozart," he cried. "Forgive me, oh God, forgive me. Please."

His words seemed not to be generated by a voice, but rather by the tearing of a voice, as if his soul were ripped from his throat. He grabbed my ankles and wept over my shoes. Wolfgang's shoes.

"Do you confess to the murder of Maestro Mozart?" the emperor said.

"I confess it, and I beg forgiveness before his dreadful ghost. Go to your rest Mozart, and let me have mine." Pergen's fingernails drove into my legs. I stepped back, but he followed me on his knees. "I beg forgiveness of my God."

"You'd better implore that of *me*," the emperor said. "Take him away."

The chamberlain swung back the door. Two white-uniformed guards entered at a jog. They took hold of Pergen under his arms, hoisted him to his knees, and, without turning their backs on their sovereign, dragged the weeping man from the room. So limp was he that one of his shoes slipped off. The emperor picked it up and tossed it to his chamberlain.

He turned to Swieten with regret and disgust around his

tight mouth. "It gives me no pleasure to see my loyal servant dragged from the room," he said, "nor that he should be driven to madness."

The baron dropped his head. "Nonetheless, your Majesty—"

"Nonetheless, Pergen made a grave error in ordering the death of Maestro Mozart."

"It wasn't his only error, your Majesty," I said.

My clothing gave me a shield, like a mask at a ball or a costume at Carnival time. If my words displeased the emperor, they were uttered from a mouth not my own, because I wore the suit of a dead man. "Count Pergen saw revolution in my brother's innocent membership of the Masonic Brotherhood. And in the message of equality at the heart of the beautiful opera Wolfgang wrote with Herr Schikaneder."

The emperor's eyes flashed toward the actor, who bowed with a discomfited grin.

"If you persecute these good Masonic brethren, your Majesty, you'll drive them into cooperation with your enemies," I said.

Leopold raised a thin eyebrow. Even in my disguise I found it hard to endure his penetrating stare. I was almost compelled to confess Wolfgang's mission to Berlin, as though I had made the journey myself.

"Count Pergen has displeased me of late," the emperor said. "He urged me to undo many of the reforms of my dear brother Joseph's reign. Without enthusiasm, I did roll back certain important measures. But no more. That's at an end."

Swieten smiled and would've spoken. The emperor's frown halted him.

"Let no one make further demands of me. You'd do well to remember . . ." He hesitated. " . . . Madame de Mozart, that I must be on guard against threats to my crown."

"Of course, your Majesty. But they don't come from my brother's opera."

"Count Pergen's policies shall, indeed, be reversed."

I thought of the Grotto. "Might it be possible to grant permission for a new Masonic lodge? To honor my departed brother. A lodge in which women are allowed entry to the Brotherhood?"

He narrowed his eyes. "Madame, you exceed the bounds of propriety. You'd do best to retire from the room and put on appropriate clothing. You're not really Mozart, after all."

"Oh, but I am." I took my three-cornered hat from the lid of the piano and set it on my head as Swieten had shown me. "I certainly am."

With a bow, I went toward the exit. I shared a glance with Swieten. His eyes posed a question. Now that I had resolved the mystery that had brought me to Vienna, would I remain? With him? It was the life I had always wanted. Yet I had married Berchtold in the Lord's house, and hadn't Pergen's collapse shown me the consequences of betraying God's law? I caught my lower lip between my teeth. The chamberlain hurried to make way for me.

The door closed behind me. Pergen's other shoe lay on its side on the carpet, a memorial to the man who once strode with such confidence along this hall.

As I walked down the stairs and into the courtyard, I was pleased that this should be the last performance at the Imperial Palace by a Mozart.

35

*G*od is my light. But when I entered the cemetery of St. Marx, I felt He was also a shadow cast over the world. He draws us all toward eternal darkness.

Clouds blew across the sky, streaked silver by the obscured sun. The lace bonnet I wore on my newly shorn hair thrashed against my brow in the wind. Fallen leaves skittered over the path, tapping like rain against a windowpane. Crows flew in low loops.

Everything in the graveyard was in motion. No one could've convinced me that even the dead lay indifferent and still in the earth. I sensed they were barging each other for a plot closer to Wolfgang, so they might hear his music.

Now that the mystery of his death was settled, I wished to pray over my brother's body. Within ten years, the tombs of St. Marx would be plowed over, the ground reused for new corpses. It would be as if Wolfgang had been interred in a mass grave, his bones intermingled with hundreds of strangers. I wanted to touch the earth directly above him while I still might.

I left Lenerl at the foot of the hill. The walk was steeper than it appeared. My breathing seemed as heavy as the wind bending the birches. The graves were arranged twenty ranks deep on the hilltop, the newer burials at the back, farthest from the path. Someone moved at the rear of the rectangle of tombs.

A woman rose from her knees, her head bowed under a veil. She pulled her black cape around her thin shoulders and crossed herself.

I went along the muddy path. The wind dropped. The hilltop was silent. The woman heard my boots in the puddles. She turned.

The breeze started once more and caught her veil. Magdalena's scars shone with tears in the stark light.

"Do you weep for my brother?" I asked her, when I reached the grave. "You should know that he rests more easily than he did yesterday."

She looked down at a low mound of earth. A square of parchment nailed to the simple wooden cross bore his name. It rattled like the leaves in the wind. "He rests," she said. "That much I envy him."

I stepped toward her, but she lifted her hand to stop me.

"I repent every moment I was with him," she said. "I took such pleasure in it, but what did it bring? Only the madness of my husband. He took Wolfgang's life and his own, and he left me disfigured."

"But I already told you at Gieseke's funeral, it wasn't your husband who killed Wolfgang."

"Yes, it was. It was Franz."

"Let me explain. I know the whole truth now."

"You can't know." She reached under her veil to wipe her

tears, careful not to rub at her scars. But she flinched anyway. "Franz tolerated the closeness of my relationship with the maestro, because of the—the benefit to my health."

"I don't understand."

"You saw me suffer a fit at Gieseke's funeral. The falling sickness. It was a frequent affliction, until I learned to play Wolfgang's music."

"His compositions are very calming to me, too."

"More than calming. They're better than any physician's medicine. Without them it's as though I'm a madwoman."

She trembled. I wondered if she was about to succumb to another fit, but it was only the wind shivering her.

"To protect you against this sickness," I said, "your husband paid for the expensive services of a famous composer as your music teacher?"

"The maestro respected my talent," Magdalena said. "He invited me into his company more and more, because he valued my musical ability. It didn't matter to him that I was a woman. But Franz became jealous. He believed I was having an affair with Wolfgang."

"I've heard that rumor. But please let me speak. I've come from the palace where—"

"That's why Franz agreed to work for Count Pergen."

I stared through the veil at the gashes on her desperate face.

"My husband was an agent for the police minister. He poisoned Wolfgang during a meeting of their Masonic Brotherhood." She plucked a leaf from a lilac bush behind the grave, rubbed it with her thumb, and let it drop. "For this treachery he received payment from Pergen."

The lavish apartment where I first met her, I thought, paid for with secret bribes.

"How do you know this?" I said. "How can you be sure?"

"After Wolfgang died, Franz gloated. He told me he had taken revenge for my infidelity. He felt he had triumphed."

"Then he attacked you?"

"No. I told him that he was mistaken. I had been the maestro's pupil and nothing more. He didn't want to hear it, but I insisted. He saw what he had done. He cried out that he had been duped. That he had murdered a genius."

"Duped? By whom?"

"He asked me to forgive him." She sobbed. "That's all he asked."

"But you refused?"

"How could I excuse such a terrible thing? He destroyed the greatest gift God ever gave to mankind. He obliterated all the unwritten music Wolfgang would've created."

"So he decided to kill you and to end his own life."

"He went wild. He slashed me. Then he cut his own throat. I watched him die." She pointed along the row of graves. "He's buried over there, but I haven't stood before his tomb as I stand here now. I must do penance for the part I played in the maestro's death."

I wondered if Franz Hofdemel had given signs of his jealousy. Perhaps she might've persuaded him earlier of her innocence. She must've been so drawn to Wolfgang's astonishing gifts that they blinded her to the simple needs of her husband. Now she repented.

Blindness, penitence.

I stepped closer to her. "It was you."

She frowned.

"Of course," I said. "The riddle Wolfgang wrote at the end of one of his last sonatas. 'She repents her blindness as she is always penitent. At the keyboard her notes run riot like demons cast out. I will be with her as a brother in the halls of Paradise, at her side as always I've been, though not as my father intended.'"

Magdalena shook her head. "Me?"

"Penitent, as Maria Magdalena is always portrayed. You shared her name. In the Holy Bible she was possessed, but Jesus cast the demons out of her. Wolfgang did the same thing for you, soothing your fits with music. He chose you to be at his side as Jesus chose Maria Magdalena. He did it despite the disapproval of his apostles—his brothers."

"A riddle?"

"Scribbled on a manuscript. Listen, 'At her side as always I've been, though not as my father intended.' Not as the wife our father would've wanted for him, but as an equal companion in his new Masonic lodge."

"A Mason? Me?"

"Wolfgang intended to start a new lodge that would admit women, on the basis of special character and talent. You said he valued your talent as a pianist. You were to be the one who would join him in his new venture."

Magdalena laid a hand over her breast and stared at the heavy, damp earth on Wolfgang's grave.

"Your husband couldn't grant himself absolution," I said. "Perhaps now that you know how Wolfgang felt about you, you can at least forgive yourself."

She turned to me. Her scars were black beneath the veil. "Madame, I don't agree. About the riddle."

"But you *must* see?"

"I do," she said. "Surely it refers to you."

She went along the line of graves, past the spot where her husband was buried.

I watched her descend the path to the graveyard gate. The muscles of my face hung as if stricken with some wasting disease. The wind rustled the lilac bush. I turned my back against the cold gust and gazed at Wolfgang's grave. He had written the riddle at the end of a sonata dedicated to me, to "my Nannerl."

" 'I will be with her as a brother in the halls of Paradise,' " I whispered, " 'at her side as always I've been, though not as my father intended.' "

What had my father intended? For me to marry a provincial official who provided a comfortable home. But not for me to display my accomplishment as a pianist, to earn a living by my music. That was what Wolfgang had wanted. He had seen how it grieved me that I was ignored while he took all the accolades. He had wanted me to have what he had.

We had been apart so long, it seemed impossible that he had been so concerned with me at the end. Yet now it struck me that Constanze, Fräulein von Paradies, and Magdalena Hofdemel had told me Wolfgang often spoke of my talents, up until his final days. I recalled how I had walked home from early Mass in the snow, before I learned of his death. I had wondered whether the same snow fell on him so far away. All that time we had thought ourselves estranged, yet we were bonded to each other as if we shared the same soul.

I wiped away a tear. It seemed to freeze on my fingertip.

Wolfgang's new lodge had been for me. A magic kingdom of music and love and equality, like the ones we invented for each other on those long, playful coach rides when we were children. My brother and me, our talents complementing each other but not competing. Together in our Grotto.

The wind caught the parchment on Wolfgang's cross. Its edges stuttered against the wood. I kissed my finger, and laid it over his name.

36.

*A*t early Mass I feared my spirit would burst from my body and run howling out of the cathedral. For once my fervor wasn't for my dead brother. My supplications for *his* soul were at an end.

When I left St. Stephen's, the Danube fog muffled the wheels of my carriage and dampened my skin like a loveless kiss. At the Imperial Library, the footman told me Baron van Swieten was at the Estates House on Herren Lane, where the government ministries had their offices. I ordered my driver to take me there.

A workman balanced on the top rung of his stepladder, polishing a lantern in the entrance. He came down from the steps and touched his brow in deference to me. The light swung above him like a hanged man. I told my coachman to wait in the courtyard with Lenerl, and I went to the stairs.

A slim, tall man sauntered onto the landing above me. He paused before a statue of a classical Greek maiden stretching out of an alcove. He tipped his wide-brimmed English hat to her like a gallant strolling in the Augarten, and laughed at his jest. When he descended the stairs, his shoes tapped on the marble as though he were dancing.

He looked like Prince Lichnowsky. But his bearing was so carefree that I couldn't believe this was the stiff, nervous man I knew. He had passed by me before I realized that it was, indeed, he.

"*Guten Morgen*, my prince," I said.

Lichnowsky's mouth, usually so constrained, widened in an uninhibited smile. I was reminded of the relief and triumph on the faces of my stepsons when they expected a beating for some misdemeanor but escaped with a scolding. He touched the head of his cane to his hat in greeting. The ring on his little finger bore a cameo of the emperor's profile.

"Heavens, I'd never have known it was you, Madame de Mozart. What've you done to your hair?" he said. "I've not seen you in a bonnet before. You've had rather a severe trim, haven't you?"

"This style accords better with my true personality. As I hope does the smile I'm seeing on your face for the first time."

He laughed, raising his arms wide. A joyous welcome for the whole world.

"What business brings you here, my prince?"

He leaned against the white marble wall. "I came to see a friend. To congratulate him on his elevation. There's a new police minister, as I believe you know." He winked.

I thought of Pergen whimpering at my feet. What had Lichnowsky to do with the Police Ministry?

His exuberant mood made me curious. He was transformed from the wretch Fräulein von Paradies overheard cowering before the Prussian ambassador less than two days before. *I can't go on*, she had heard him say. *Pergen knows*. I pictured his expression when he had told me about the murderer broken on the wheel in the city square: furious and impotent, like someone finding himself trapped. It occurred to me that he had been under a threat of some sort—a threat which had been lifted when Pergen lost his post.

"I know of Count Pergen's dismissal," I said. "I was unaware he had been replaced."

What could've endangered Lichnowsky while Pergen was in power?

The prince smirked. The easy grin of a practiced liar rewarded for his deception.

Deception. Reward. The substance of his lie was as evident to me as the teeth in his broad smile. "The mission to Berlin with Wolfgang wasn't on behalf of your Masonic lodge," I said. "You went as a secret agent."

"An agent?" he snickered. "For whom?"

"Not Austria, because the mission caused you to fear Pergen."

"Why on earth would you think I fear—?"

"You worked for the Prussians. But Pergen found out." Why else would Lichnowsky have needed to tell the Prussian ambassador that *Pergen knows*? Paradies had overheard a visit from a spy to his master.

The prince leered. "You should limit your improvisations to the piano, madame. I've nothing to worry about, in any case."

"The new police minister may be your friend. But no matter who fills that position, a Prussian agent will be his enemy."

"Do I look like a man afraid?"

I hesitated. Could I be wrong about him?

"Well, do I?" he said.

I shook my head, puzzled. "You worked for the Prussians. Yet you don't fear the Austrians."

He rubbed his thumb along his lip. "Which can only mean—? Madame?"

With a shock, I understood how he had escaped danger. "You must be in the pay of our imperial secret police, too. A double agent."

His smile broadened.

"Where does your loyalty truly lie?" I said. "With Prussia? Or Austria?"

"Who commanded Wolfgang's loyalty?"

"My brother was no spy."

"That's not what I meant. He refused to be a musical servant to the Archbishop of Salzburg all those years ago. He came to Vienna to be independent. He'd spin out a tune for anyone who paid him."

I saw his meaning. Lichnowsky maneuvered between Prussia and Austria to his own advantage. He served no master. But I resisted his comparison. "Wolfgang's loyalty was to music."

"Tell that to poor Franz Hofdemel."

Magdalena. As he died, her husband realized he'd been duped into believing in her infidelity with Wolfgang. "That wicked rumor was of your making," I said.

"Hofdemel was quick-tempered, easy to provoke. He trusted Wolfgang as a brother. Anyone could see he'd turn violent if that bond was violated."

The same lodge. Hofdemel and Gieseke, Wolfgang and Lichnowsky. All the dead, and this one living man connecting them to Pergen, who had confessed before me to Wolfgang's murder.

The prince's eyes didn't belong to the prisoner broken on the wheel after all. They were blank and sadistic, like the executioner smashing the bones of the condemned man.

"You made Hofdemel believe that my brother carried on an affair with Magdalena," I said. "So the jealous fool poisoned Wolfgang."

Pergen had given the order for Wolfgang to die. But Lichnowsky had carried it out.

I stumbled on the steps and reached out to steady myself. I was in the presence of the man who truly had devised my brother's death.

Lichnowsky came toward me, his cane clicking against the marble steps. "Madame Berchtold, you're faint," he said.

My married name was like a taunt on his lips. He spoke it with heavy emphasis, as though he wished to tell me that the death of Mozart was no concern of mine, for whom years ago the maestro had ceased to be family.

He was wrong. Lichnowsky hadn't seen me in the red frock coat at the palace.

I was Mozart.

My stomach stung as though the poison that killed my brother burned through my innards. I pushed away the hand the prince offered in support.

The handwritten page in my pocket seemed to pulse against my hip. My brother's idea for a new Masonic lodge. "The Grotto."

Lichnowsky's lip twitched. "It really isn't your place to involve yourself in such things, madame."

"The Grotto disturbed your arrangement with Pergen somehow," I said. "What did Wolfgang's new lodge mean to you?"

"It was the idle fancy of a man who ought to have restricted himself to music." The voice of a judge, pronouncing sentence on Wolfgang. The executioner's eyes again.

"You told me Wolfgang tried to interest the Prussians in the Grotto. How did the Grotto endanger my brother?" I looked into Lichnowsky's face and found the absolute ruthlessness of a man accustomed to living in fear. In fear of Pergen. *Pergen knows.* "Wolfgang returned from Berlin and started work on *The Magic Flute*, filling it with Masonic symbols. To Pergen, it looked like the Prussians were backing the opera, funding its subversive Masonic ideas. Isn't that right?"

Lichnowsky clicked his tongue. "So what?"

"A popular opera about a secret society. Funded by the emperor's enemy, the king of Prussia, who's also a Mason. Organized when you and Wolfgang were together in Berlin. Maybe the police minister decided his double agent's loyalty was really to the Prussians."

"Pergen is hardly the point now, my dear lady," he said.

"Perhaps Pergen never was the point. But what was?"

He prodded the wall with the tip of his cane. "By all the saints in Heaven."

"When I came to Vienna, I wondered if my brother's killing was the result of Hofdemel's demented love. But that man's jealous rage was of your making. What then? Did Wolfgang die because of international espionage and Pergen's secret plots? Or was it a dispute between Masons over admitting women to the Brotherhood? I will have the truth from you, sir." My voice grew loud. It echoed around the enclosed staircase.

"Madame—"

"Why? Tell me, why did my brother die?" I shouted.

"Money." Lichnowsky's face was red with fury. He leaned over me from the step above. "Pergen's bribes. The Prussian bribes. That's all. Money killed Wolfgang."

I whispered, "You feared Pergen would halt your payments, even more than you dreaded disgrace."

The ferocity dwindled on his face. A cold contempt replaced it.

It had all been for money, then, that Lichnowsky arranged Wolfgang's death. To keep Pergen's bribes coming by proving his loyalty. To maintain the payments from the Prussian ambassador, who didn't know that he was also working for Pergen.

Lichnowsky glared at the lanterns across the courtyard, hanging on the fog. I wondered if the intensity in his face was murder itself.

Would I recognize it? Surely it had been in the eyes of the two men who entered the baron's box at *The Magic Flute*. I realized now that they had been sent by Lichnowsky. They must've waited outside until Gieseke came to speak to Swieten. Then they dragged him backstage and killed him. While I sat entranced by my brother's music.

Who had been singing their encore when those thugs returned to commit murder? The astonishing high F coloratura of the Queen of the Night's aria sounded in my head as if she stood beside me on the steps. *Hell's vengeance boils in my heart*, she sang. The last words Gieseke would've heard. The force of the Queen's anguish overcame me.

"You took the life of a great genius." My hands tightened into fists. "You'll be punished for it."

He smiled. "Yet here I am, walking free."

"Not for long," I said. "I'll tell the new police minister about your double game."

"Do you think a prince is to be punished for his secret work on the emperor's behalf? Simply because a scribbling musician met an unfortunate end?"

"How dare you."

"If you don't like it, go to the minister and tell him what you know."

"I shall."

"I encourage you to do so. Really, I do." He gestured up the stairs with his cane. "The big doors below the gold crest of a two-headed eagle. That's his office."

I looked up the steps, then back to the prince.

"Run along, madame," he said. "The sword of justice ought to fall on me swiftly, don't you think?"

His laughter was soft, as I rushed up the stairs.

I crossed the broad white corridor toward the police minister's office. The eagle crest was topped by the emperor's crown.

The minister's door opened and a man slipped out. He carried a stack of ledgers in his arms. When he saw me, he gave a little bow. It was the baron's assistant, Strafinger.

Lichnowsky's footsteps descended the stairs behind me. My pulse ran fast. It couldn't be as I feared.

Strafinger stood aside and held the door open for me.

Behind a standing desk, Baron van Swieten was reading a document. He looked up and smiled.

I shook my head, disbelieving. I felt a pressure within my chest, as though my heart would shatter. He laid down the paper and dropped his guilty eyes.

37

*E*verything within the police minister's office sank into black, as though the light of the sun had never once penetrated the room. The baron's assistant left and shut the door. I opened my eyes wide, though I wished most of all to pretend I didn't see the man I loved before me.

The room was paneled with light chestnut wood, carved in the ornate style of the Renaissance. On one wall a tapestry depicted in dull blue and green a hunt in the Vienna woods. The floor was of polished ceramic, the tiles arranged in dark chevrons. Fog clung to the window.

Swieten crossed the room and took my hands in his. He was unshaven. The skin beneath his eyes was gray and puffy.

"Nannerl," he whispered, kissing my fingers. "My dear."

His face bore the same hopeful, querying expression as it had when Pergen was dragged from the emperor's room. It asked if I was free to stay with him. I still could give no sure response.

Don't let him lie, I thought. *If he does, I know I'll have to leave Vienna.* "Gottfried," I murmured.

He closed his eyes and stroked my face.

I looked at the papers on the desk. "Pergen's office?"

"I've been here all night. The emperor commanded me to review the files, so that we might know in what other ways Pergen overstepped his authority."

"A great opportunity," I said.

"I'm so glad you see that. I really can change things throughout the Empire. To improve the lives of millions of people. The emperor gave me this chance. But I owe it to the bravery you showed yesterday when you performed at the palace."

A brown ledger lay open on the lectern. I touched the edge of the page. "What've you found?"

"The scope of Pergen's secret operation is enormous. But I must confess I've spent most of the night on a single case." He flipped the ledger shut to show me the label pasted to the center of the cover: "Mozart, Johann Chrysostom Wolfgang Amadeus."

I ran my finger beneath my brother's name and thought of the paper fluttering in the wind on his grave. I longed to tell Swieten what I knew of Lichnowsky's treachery, but I needed him to volunteer the truth. "Show me."

"Come." He took me to a divan of scarlet velvet. He riffled the pages of the ledger, stiff as winter leaves with the ink that covered them. "In here, the truth about Wolfgang's death."

"Was it—?"

"Poison, as we thought."

"How was it done?"

"At a meeting of the Masonic lodge. Hofdemel administered *acqua toffana* to Wolfgang in a cup of punch."

"He murdered Wolfgang because he thought he had been cuckolded? But at the palace Pergen confessed. Did he mislead Hofdemel into killing my brother?" I knew this was only half the story. Was I trying to trap the baron into covering up for Lichnowsky? A lie that would send me back to my village?

Swieten tapped his fingernail against his teeth.

Gottfried, don't hide from me, I thought. "Is that how it was?" I said.

He laid his palm flat on the ledger. "That's how it was."

If I had thought my heart had broken when I entered the office—when I had seen that it was my own lover who had allowed Lichnowsky to go free—now it was shattered for certain. It ruptured with the force of my guilt, my betrayal of my good husband and my children and my God. I put my hand to my mouth and sobbed.

He made to comfort me, but I shook my head, and he knew that I didn't weep for my brother's death.

I pointed toward the door. His eyes narrowed in pain, as though he saw across the hall to the traitor on the steps. "Lichnowsky," he whispered.

He reached for me, but I moved away along the divan.

The baron pressed his hands against his eyes. "I wish to explain to you," he said.

Those words. The aria I had sung to him in the Imperial Library just before I had seen that he loved me. *I wish to explain to you, O God, what my grief is.* I heard the song in my head, but even Wolfgang's music seemed discordant now. The aria faltered, and fell silent.

"This is my chance to bring Wolfgang's ideas to the attention of the entire Empire." He turned his dark eyes to me. They were tearful. "If I could give up this life here in the palace and travel Europe with my violin, playing his music in every village square, you know I'd do it. But I'm a mediocre musician. I can't transmit his message that way. I'm a politician. Wolfgang's values—freedom, equality, brotherhood—it's within my power now to make them law."

His fingers knitted together, strong as they had been when he held my body.

"But you loved Wolfgang," I said. "How can you forget your devotion to him?"

"Wolfgang and I talked so often of these enlightened ideas, of how they'd transform the Empire. I do this for him."

I clicked my tongue. He flinched, as though I had spat on him.

"Don't you think I wish Lichnowsky all the torments of the innermost circle of Hell?" He slapped his hands together. "But if I try to punish him, the emperor will get rid of me. Treachery by a prince? No, that'd make the emperor himself look threatened. If he couldn't count on the loyalty of a prince, then he must really be in a vulnerable position. Don't you see?"

The agitation in my breast subsided. It was replaced by something as heavy and still as lead.

"My choice is clear," he said. "An ineffective action leading to my dismissal. Or the possibility of reforms which would be a true memorial to Wolfgang's wonderful soul."

A horse stamped on the cobbles of the courtyard below. My carriage. I couldn't quite believe that I'd have to ride that coach all the way back to my village—that I'd be without my baron.

"I understand why you chose as you did." My voice was broken and shaky. "What'll happen to Prince Lichnowsky?"

Swieten hesitated. "Well, he's *my* agent now."

He bowed his head in shame.

"I see." I knew what I must do. As for Wolfgang's case, only the details remained.

"How much money?" I said. "How much did Lichnowsky receive? What was the price of my brother's life?"

"Hofdemel got ten thousand gulden a year to work as an agent for Pergen. Lichnowsky received much, much more, and from the Prussians, too. He was able to recover his family estates, even though they'd been under Prussian control since King Friedrich captured Silesia forty years ago. The return of his lands—that's how the Prussians first persuaded Lichnowsky to work for them."

I thought again of the richness of Magdalena's apartment. The piano Wolfgang had played there, bought with the money that would purchase his murder.

"Wolfgang had to be silenced—to keep the money coming," Swieten whispered.

"Because of *The Magic Flute*?"

He shook his head. "The Prussians ordered Lichnowsky to set up a new lodge. He was supposed to recruit powerful Austrians who'd think they were working to promote their Masonic beliefs. In fact they'd be enlisted as Prussian spies."

"And Wolfgang knew about this."

"He was with Lichnowsky in Berlin when the orders were issued. So, yes, Wolfgang knew." Swieten glanced at the ledger with all its details of my brother's case. "He threatened to make the pro-Prussian lodge public, unless Lichnowsky helped him launch his Grotto."

"But Lichnowsky—" I sensed the odor of the prince's Spanish cigars on the air in the office, lingering from his meeting with Swieten.

"Lichnowsky couldn't allow the Grotto to go ahead. He was recruiting men for his Prussian lodge and passing the names to Pergen. Helping Wolfgang's new lodge would've made Pergen think he was engaging other Prussian spies without the police minister's knowledge."

"Yet Pergen confessed. He said he ordered Wolfgang's death."

"Lichnowsky told Pergen about the Grotto. So that Pergen wouldn't suspect him. He identified Wolfgang as a Prussian agent and the secret founder of an illegal Masonic lodge. For that, Pergen decreed Wolfgang's murder. But Lichnowsky engineered it, to protect himself."

Swieten reached along the divan and squeezed my fingers. His face was hopeful and tentative.

I withdrew my hand and went to the window. I laid my palm on the pane. The skin seemed to stick to the freezing glass. "The intrigue of the capital wasn't for my poor, naïve brother," I said. "It's not for me, either."

Swieten stood behind me. I sensed his hesitation before he spoke. "Is there nothing in the imperial city for you?"

Had the fog cleared from the courtyard of the Estates House, I'd still have seen nothing through the tears that obscured my sight. "Gottfried, I must return to my children."

His hand was on the bare skin of my shoulder, edging into

the hair at the nape of my neck. I froze. I awaited his command, as I had waited all my life for instruction. He held his fingers there a long time.

"I understand," he said.

Precisely because he accepted my decision, it was hard to maintain my determination. "Even when you and I are apart, we'll both play his music," I said.

"For me, the music is at an end." His sad eyes rested on my neck, the cross of ambers he had given me. "Anyway, I always believed he composed only for you."

I thought of what Magdalena had said at the graveyard, her solution to Wolfgang's riddle. I understood that Swieten was right. There was passion for me in Vienna with the baron. But the world would lay its corrupting touch upon us and make our affair seem tawdry. The love that was left to me was in Wolfgang's music.

I hurried down the stone stairs and into the courtyard. The fog froze my tears.

Lenerl averted her eyes as I climbed into the carriage. If she told tales on me when we returned to the village, my sobs would be the least of the strange things she might relate. I let them come.

The driver circled back to the entrance. The horses' hooves clattered toward the vaulted gateway.

Swieten came down the steps three at a time. He caught the coach at the gate as the traffic on Herren Lane forced it to pause.

He laid his hands on the side of the carriage. I heard again the music of the aria I had sung for him in his library. This time the strings and the soprano were in harmony. I saw that he heard them, too. He smiled at me, though his jaw trembled.

The carriage pulled into the street. With a snap of the whip, the horses took me away from the baron. I leaned out of the window. The mist and the traffic closed about him. He became as invisible as if he had been consigned to the cells with Pergen's victims.

Within a half hour, my carriage was in the countryside, adrift on a fog that smothered Vienna in its enclosing silence forever.

EPILOGUE.

I read throughout the night. By the morning I was feverish with excitement. I rushed down the mountainside to Aunt Nannerl's home. I carried the journal she had given me, recording the events of that week in 1791. Its secrets, revealed for the first time after almost forty years, were so strange that I needed to feel their weight in my hand. Otherwise I might have believed that I had dreamed them.

I headed through the narrow streets at the foot of the mountain. I crossed the cathedral square and hurried up the steps to Aunt Nannerl's apartment.

Her maid opened the door. She held a handkerchief to her eyes. "Master Wolfgang, I'm so glad you're here. Dear God has sent you." Franziska wiped at her tears and only then noticed my own agitation. She hesitated.

"What is it, girl?"

"She's had a terrible night, sir. She's very weak." She sobbed. "I don't think she has long. She won't let me call for a doctor. But she's been asking for you."

I went through to the bedroom. Aunt Nannerl lay as I had left her. Under her bonnet, her face was so pale it seemed to have been dusted in flour. A thin hand lay across her shawl.

I sat beside her, and touched her shoulder gently.

She snapped her head toward me. "Wolfgang," she whispered.

"I'm here, Auntie."

Her blind eyes were milkier than ever. "You read it? You know now?"

"I can't believe it, Auntie."

She snorted. "Do you think such things could be made up?"

"Why did you never tell?"

She pursed her lips—the pause of one who must concentrate hard to accomplish the mere act of breathing. Her maid might be right, I thought: Aunt Nannerl seemed close to the end.

I touched her wrist. The flesh was cold. "Did you want to protect my mother? Was that why you told no one?" I said. "You didn't want Mamma to suffer, to know the truth of how her husband was taken from her?"

Her pale eyebrows descended, a grimace.

"Don't tax your strength, Auntie. I understand. Mamma will never know."

She nodded toward the piano.

"You wish for me to play for you?" I raised my voice as though I spoke to a child or a foreigner.

She beckoned with a slight motion of her hand. I leaned close. Her breath was bitter and metallic, like a coffeepot that has lain unwashed for a day.

"I wish to explain to you," she murmured.

"That's why you gave me the diary?"

Her head shook. "Sing it for me."

The aria was for a soprano, but it was hardly the time to quibble with my aunt about musical technicalities.

I laid the journal on the edge of her bed and sat at the old Stein. In my head, I formulated the letter I must send that day to Innsbruck, to her sole surviving child, Leopold, urging him to come bid her farewell. Under my breath I found the right pitch for my voice. I played through the introduction, transposing the orchestral part directly for the piano, and sang:

> *I wish to explain to you, O God,*
> *what my grief is.*
> *But fate condemns me*
> *To weep and remain silent.*

My aunt's head lay to the side. She stared toward the window. I wondered if, in her blindness, she detected traces of the strong morning sun off the cathedral towers, perhaps as an undefined glow before her eyes. Her lips moved, but I couldn't tell if she was singing with me or struggling for breath.

> *My heart may not crave*
> *for the one I wish to love.*

At the dramatic conclusion of the aria I confess the music took hold of me. I no longer was aware of Aunt Nannerl, small in her bed. I brought out the highest C-sharp I could manage and, as often happened when I played my father's music, I felt his hand guiding mine across the keyboard.

Part from me, run from me.
Of love, do not speak.

With the aria at an end, I closed my eyes and listened to the final chord resonate in the body of the piano. Something brushed the back of my wrist and I started in fright.

I turned to ask Aunt Nannerl if she had enjoyed the aria. She lay so still I decided, instead, to tuck her hand beneath the blanket for warmth and tiptoe to the sitting room.

I lifted her arm. It was heavy, like a sleeping child. I bent close to her and whispered her name. Her head remained on its side, facing the window, eyes closed. I raised my hand before her lips and nose, but felt no breath. Her chest was still.

While I had been singing, she had gone.

I took her hand between both of mine, as though my warmth might revive her. She held something there. I turned her wrist to see what it was.

A thin gold chain looped around her middle finger. In the center of her palm, at the end of the necklace, lay a cross embedded with ambers.

FRANZ XAVER WOLFGANG MOZART
Salzburg, October 10, 1829

This novel is based on real historical events. Mozart's anticipation of his own death, his risky plan for a new Masonic lodge of some kind, and his mission to Berlin are matters of historical research. Pergen's secret police persecution of the Masons, Hofdemel's suicide, and his mutilation of Magdalena are also well documented, as are many of the other details of the characters, their relationships, and their membership of secret Masonic Brotherhoods. That women would have been members of Wolfgang's new lodge is drawn from the text of *The Magic Flute*, which I interpret as a forceful argument for women's inclusion in the Masons.

I altered the histories of several characters, allowing myself fictional license of varying degrees. In fact, Nannerl never visited Vienna after Wolfgang's death. Gieseke fled the imperial capital, only to turn up in Greenland and later Dublin, where he died in 1833, a respected professor of mineralogy. Count Pergen really was fired by Leopold II. But he was reinstated soon after the emperor's sudden death, which came only three months after Wolfgang's passing. It was suspected Leopold had been poisoned by Freemasons.

Before he died, Leopold dismissed Swieten, whose membership of the Masonic Illuminati had become known. The baron never returned to public life. He died in 1803.

Magdalena Hofdemel went back to her family's home in Moravia. The capacity of Wolfgang's music to soothe various disorders is the subject of many recent scientific studies. A paper published in the *Journal of the Royal Society of Medicine* in 2001 found Mozart's piano sonatas reduced epileptic activity in sufferers like Magdalena.

As for Wolfgang, no one can be sure exactly how he came to his end. But he might really have died this way.

The Music.

Mozart's work was catalogued for the first time by Ludwig Ritter von Köchel, an Austrian music historian, in 1862. The music is identified these days by his so-called Köchel, or "K," numbers. Mozart's contemporaries, of course, wouldn't have used K numbers, so I didn't refer to the music that way in this novel. But if you want to look up and listen to the music featured in this book, here's a list of the K numbers:

PROLOGUE

"Vedrai carino" ("You will see, my dear"), aria from the opera *Don Giovanni*, K 527

Sonata for Piano in A, K 331

CHAPTER I

Piano variations "Ah, vous dirai-je," K 265

"Per pietà, ben mio, perdona" ("For pity's sake, my darling, forgive"), aria from the opera *Così fan tutte* (*Thus Do All Women*), K 588

Sonata for Piano in A Minor, K 310

CHAPTER 32

Sonata for Keyboard for Four Hands in D, K 381

CHAPTER 34

"Se vuol ballare, Signor Contino" ("If you want to dance, Little Count"), aria from *Le nozze di Figaro* (*The Marriage of Figaro*), K 492

Sonata for Piano in F, K 332

Finale from *Don Giovanni*

About the author

About the book

Read on

Insights,
Interviews
& More...

Meet Matt Rees

I'VE ALWAYS BEEN A WRITER. It's the only thing about myself of which I've never been the least uncertain. I've known it since I was seven (a poem about a tree, on the classroom wall with the teacher's gold star beside it). The years between that poem and my first novel (which also won a kind of gold star in the form of a Dagger Award from the Crime Writers Association in London) were taken up with refining my writing skills and finding the wisdom within myself about which I might write.

I was born in 1967 in Newport, which was a steel town in Wales until Margaret Thatcher closed the steelworks. My family there was big and close. My maternal grandmother had three of her many sisters living on the same street. My cousins used to invade the park across the road each weekend. My father's from Maesteg, which was a Llynfi valley mining town until Thatcher had a look at the mines and . . . well, never mind. I loved the landscape of the valley, the treeless hills carpeted in ferns of russet and green, and the rain, always the rain. At eighteen, I took my bleached blond hair to Wadham College, Oxford University. I received a degree in English language and literature, focusing on post-structuralism, deconstruction, and Marxist literary criticism. For a would-be writer, it was like becoming a mechanical engineer when I really just wanted to drive the car. I did an MA at the University of Maryland and partied my way around New York for five years before I made the move that changed my life.

I found the sense of inner tranquility that, I think, is a worthy version of wisdom in an unlikely spot: Jerusalem. I came here in 1996. For love. Then we divorced. But the place took hold. Not for the violence and the excitement that sometimes surrounds it, but because I saw people in extreme situations. Through the emotions they experienced, I came to understand myself. Writing for *Newsweek* and *Time* magazine, I built up a stock of knowledge ▶

about these deep emotions that I knew I'd never fit into my journalism. So I wrote my Palestinian crime novels, which have been translated into twenty-one languages.

I'm still in Jerusalem, where you may be surprised at how convivial the lifestyle is. I'm blessed to have traveled far enough through the world to have a met a wife I'd never have bumped into had I stayed in Wales (she's a New Yorker). I go to bed very happy, knowing that, unlike during my days as a journalist, no one will shoot at me when I go to work in the morning and no distant boss will pretend to be worried for my safety. I'm at my desk by 8 a.m., though I usually don't bother getting dressed until the afternoon. I write standing up, doing yoga stretches, and listening to Mozart. My three-year-old son bursts through the front door at about 1:30 p.m., yelling "Daaaaaddyyyy." At which point, my writing day is most definitely over. ∼

The Story Behind
Mozart's Last Aria

IN 2003 I WAS COVERING the violence of the Palestinian intifada as a foreign correspondent. I had seen terrible things and lived through dangerous moments in the previous three years, working every day in the West Bank or Gaza. I was fairly sure the trouble wasn't over. I needed a break—to get out of the desert for some calm in the mountains of Europe, to see some beautiful cities where the people weren't killing each other, to be transported by music. I traveled to Austria and the Czech Republic with my wife, Devorah, and I found all those things. But the main pleasure of relaxation for me is that it brings me to life creatively. So the journey also gave me an idea that bubbled in my head for years, until it became *Mozart's Last Aria*.

Despite all the other attractions of Vienna, Salzburg, and Prague, our trip drew us again and again into contact with the Mozart family. On a sunny spring day, Devorah ▶

and I visited the Salzburg apartment where Wolfgang was born. There we found a small exhibit about Nannerl. In her portrait she looked almost identical to Wolfgang. On our way to the village we had chosen as a mountain retreat, we happened to pass through the lakeside village in the Salzkammergut range where Nannerl lived as the wife of a boring local functionary (and where, coincidentally, her mother had been born). I became curious about the largely unacknowledged talent of this child prodigy.

We took a train to Prague. In the eighteenth-century Estates Theater, where Wolfgang premiered *Don Giovanni*, we saw a production of that great opera. Somewhat neglected under communism, the opera house had been left untouched by the architecturally philistine sixties and seventies. It's just as it was in Mozart's day. Sitting in my box on an old bentwood chair, watching this great opera, I was transported back over

two hundred years, imagining
the man behind this great artistic
creation and those who had known
him. The figure who reached out to
me from that time most insistently
was Nannerl. She was the one whose
life posed the most unanswered
questions.

A couple of years later, I was
having dinner with Maestro
Zubin Mehta, formerly the
musical director of the New York
Philharmonic and now holder of
many top positions in the world of
classical music. I asked him which
of all the great composers he valued
most highly. "I'd find it hard to live
without Mozart," he said. That gave
me a new kind of focus for my
thinking about those people who
had lived with Mozart, and Nannerl
in particular. After his death at only
thirty-five, what had it been like
to live *without* him? To have lost
one of the greatest geniuses in the
history of the world? Maria Anna
Mozart (Nannerl means "Little
Nanna" in German; it's ▶

pronounced "NAN-erl") had been almost as talented as Wolfgang, yet she was cooped up in the mountains while her little brother became famous in Vienna. Close as children, their relationship was strained by separation. I started to think about her response to his death. Did she imagine all the music he might've written that she'd never have a chance to play? Were there things she might've wanted to say to him, after he was gone?

I came up with the idea of posing Maestro Mehta's question through Nannerl. A musical prodigy who's been forgotten by history except as a footnote in stories about her famous brother, she knew him better and longer than anyone. What was her response to losing him?

Well, that's how I decided to write the novel. Then came the research. In some ways, it may not be exactly what you might expect.

Of course, I read many books and documents about Mozart and also *by* Mozart—Wolfgang, Nannerl, and their father Leopold were all big correspondents and many of their letters survive, so it's possible to have a sense of how they might have spoken to one another and expressed their thoughts. Music historians have also researched even the tiniest elements of Wolfgang's life and work. For example, I was able to draw on lengthy studies of the layout and contents of Wolfgang's final apartment on Rauhenstein Lane. Despite all this minutiae, many questions remain about Wolfgang, and about his death in particular. Constant new discoveries about Wolfgang's music and life gave me a great deal of material to weave into a cohesive (fictional) theory of how he might have died.

But beyond traveling to Vienna, reading up on my subject, and listening to Mozart's music wherever and whenever I could, I also tried to enter into the life of Nannerl and Wolfgang. I did this with meditation and ▸

concentration techniques. The essence of these techniques, as I've adapted them, is to still my judgment and to open up my heart, so that I find myself in the presence of the energy of, say, Nannerl Mozart. Our world being a fairly cynical place, I don't tell many people about this technique because some people think it sounds like I believe in ghosts—yet here I am, writing about it for you. But you've read the book, so I hope you'll understand why it's important. I've discussed these techniques with many creative artists, and they all use them to some extent. The emotion you're trying to portray is "out there," and you have to find it, focus on it, and open up to it. How else does a dancer identify the emotion her body needs to portray? How can an actor inhabit the feelings his character is supposed to experience? It won't just come to you; you have to go out and find it. Well, I found Nannerl. Or perhaps she found me . . .

This technique helped greatly in my portrayal of Nannerl. But it didn't help my piano playing. I learned piano as a kid, but I gave it up out of laziness and a healthy spirit of rebellion. I kept on playing music, featuring in several bar bands on guitar and bass. But for this book I decided to relearn piano. It certainly taught me that I'm no Mozart. Still, it was important: to revive my understanding of written music, to see inside the structure of Wolfgang's pieces, to be able to communicate with talented musicians who helped me understand how they perform the great sonatas and symphonies.

Often I found myself talking to musicians about the structure of Wolfgang's music, not just the surface details of melody and rhythm. The organization of his work, which of course lies beneath the surface, was one of the things I found most attractive. In the classical period, music was almost rigidly precise. Mozart took this ▶

The Story Behind *Mozart's Last Aria*
(continued)

sense of order and undermined it, creating musical tension almost without our hearing it. He resolves the tension at the end of each section or of each piece, so that listeners are left deeply satisfied by the restoration of order. Sounds a bit like a crime novel, I thought: a murder disturbs the protagonist's life; at the end, some kind of order is restored. This made me think about using Wolfgang's music to structure my novel.

I laid out the novel in terms of one of Wolfgang's piano sonatas. Intimate and rhapsodic, these are my favorite pieces by the maestro. I chose one of his most disturbing sonatas, the A minor (known by its number designation K 310). Many people think of Mozart as a purveyor of happy little tunes, compared to the sweeping emotionalism of Beethoven. But this sonata demonstrates the ardent depth of Wolfgang's music. He wrote it in Paris, alone and distraught, after his mother died there. (She became sick while accompanying him on a concert tour when he was twenty-two.)

How does this sonata fit the form of a crime novel? It begins with an Allegro maestoso that is disturbing and almost discordant. Listen and you'll see what I mean. In *Mozart's Last Aria*, I have Nannerl play this movement after she hears of Wolfgang's death. I thought of this as the introductory theme of Act I of my novel, in which the calm world around Nannerl collapses with news of her brother's death and she resolves to find out what happened to him.

The thoughtful second movement (Andante cantabile con espressione) is Act II of the book, the central section in which Nannerl explores the Vienna that Wolfgang left behind. She finds out about his delicate relationship with his wife, the fears of his friends, and the dangers that may have hounded him.

Act III is the final Presto ▸

movement, in which the disturbing themes of the first movement are resolved in a series of climactic scenes, just as Nannerl uncovers the truth over the last couple of chapters of the book.

This idea gave me an emotional framework for the plot. Given that the A minor sonata was written in response to a death—that of Wolfgang's mother—and that I wanted to explore Nannerl's feelings about her dead brother, it seemed natural to use this sonata.

So here you have it: my crime novel in A minor. ～

Recommended Reading and Listening

Books

Mozart: A Life
by Maynard Solomon
A thorough historical record that also gives many insights into Mozart's music.

The Mozart Family: Four Lives in a Social Context
by Ruth Halliwell
Given the intense nature of Wolfgang's relationships with Nannerl and his parents on their long tours of Europe, a focus on the family is revealing.

Vienna: A Cultural and Literary History
by Nicholas T. Parsons
History as if told by a knowledgeable raconteur over a meal of Wiener schnitzel and tafelspitz.

Recordings

Mozart: Favorite Works for Piano
by Alfred Brendel
The greatest interpreter of Mozart performs his most exquisite works. ▶

15

Recommended Reading and Listening
(continued)

Mozart: Die Zauberflöte
by Otto Klemperer
A classic recording of
The Magic Flute from 1964.

Mozart: Symphonien Nos. 35–41
by Karl Böhm
Sometimes controversial, but an
inspiring rendering of the last and
greatest of Wolfgang's symphonies.

On the web

http://www.mozarthausvienna.at/
Recently renovated, the Vienna
house where Mozart lived while
writing *The Marriage of Figaro* is
an extensive museum. However, the
location of his final apartment on
Rauhenstein Lane is now a modern
department store. ∾